BEYOND THE KALEIDOSCOPE

A Trilogy of Arcane Tales

Jayson Walker

iUniverse, Inc.
Bloomington

BEYOND THE KALEIDOSCOPE
A TRILOGY OF ARCANE TALES

iUniverse books may be ordered through booksellers or by contacting:

iUniverse
1663 Liberty Drive
Bloomington, IN 47403
www.iuniverse.com
1-800-Authors (1-800-288-4677)

ISBN: 978-1-4620-6476-2 (sc)
ISBN: 978-1-4620-6477-9 (ebk)

Printed in the United States of America

iUniverse rev. date: 11/28/2011

BEYOND THE
KALEIDOSCOPE

TABLE OF CONTENTS

In memory of my beloved mother,

Ann, who will never see her son's crowning

achievement. How I wish you had lived to read this

book, Mom—and to share in my joy.

After my life's brief struggle is done, I shall see

you in Heaven, dear Lady . . .

EPIGRAPH

"What hath God wrought?" Samuel Morse's message on the first telegraph communication in 1844.

PREFACE

People frequently ask me two questions: "Where do you come *up* with this stuff?," and "Why aren't you published?" I'll answer the second question first and with another question: "Published? *Me?* This is just fun for me—the stuff just comes into my head, and I write about it. I don't think a *publisher* would have any interest . . . ."

So there, (admittedly) you get only partial answers to questions one and two. But it's more complicated than that, I think, and more intertwined . . . .

So let's start again. It's not really too hard to nail this down, I guess. I'll just do what I always do—sit down at the computer, let my fingers do the walking, and let my mind do the talking.

Usually, I get ideas from conversations, unusual expressions like *Maundy Thursday*, or (ironically) from statements that I misunderstand. These nuggets all have one thing in common, though—a hook that begs exploitation! An example of the latter might be something like a friend's recent comment that "broken-down appliances seem to rule my life." *Whoops . . . hold up, pardner!* How about a story about a man who discovers that he must keep his antique washing machine running to stay alive . . . something akin to *The Picture of Dorian Gray?* (The story's already in the works—thanks for the idea, Joe Northropian!)

OK, enough said about all that. Most of the rest comes from my reading in popular science periodicals and books on physics, cosmology, and mathematics . . . or just my fevered mind trying to make sense of the pain and chaos surrounding us. But always . . . . ALWAYS . . . the ideas seem to come in light of the Grand Concepts like relativity, space-time, higher dimensions . . . and, naturally, the metaphysical: the spiritual, *the emotional.*

In fact, anything at—or just beyond—the bounds of normal waking human consciousness is grist for the mill . . . .

I truly hope you'll enjoy this little book. I poured my heart and soul into it. I *can* guarantee that it will twist your mind in interesting new ways, make you think, and, hopefully, make you feel at least a *little* uncomfortable!

If not, I hope you'll give me a second chance when my next literary effort hits the stands!

So long for now, my new friend—and happy reading!

Jayson "Jay" Walker

August, 2011

A STROLL
IN THE PARK

CHAPTER I

Opening Game

The entrance to Anishinaabe Recreational Area was barely visible from Highway CR-31, a secondary highway maintained by the county in a time when there still were counties. A dense tangle of underbrush rendered the park access road nearly impassable. This came as no surprise to Martin Brush. There was little demand for public recreation these days, of course. Government funding for parks—and most everything else, for that matter—had dwindled to nothing twenty years ago.

Martin clambered painfully down from the Penitate hay wagon, which, coincidentally, had been parked in front of the little general store across the street from Martin's "rabbit hole." Luckily for Martin, the Penitates, a religious sect somewhere between the Mennonites and the Amish on the doctrinal continuum, still used mostly horse-drawn transportation. The Penitates rejected the secular world's man-centered view of morality but very little else about it. Their chief mode of transportation had been retained solely on the basis of their "man's oneness with his environment" philosophy, which had gradually expanded to encompass their rejection of heathen (Muslim states') control of the oil supply. Now, with most of that oil dangerously radioactive, the Penitates maintained business as usual while the rest of the world essentially ground to a halt.

The friendly man unloading burlap bags had happily offered him a ride. "The old state park? Out on CR-31? Sure, I go right by

3

there on my way home. Might take a coupl'a hours, though. I got a few stops to make along the way. Gotta drop off some ammo. Will that be OK?" Martin allowed as to how that'd be just fine. "My name's Yoder Weaks," the man said, extending his hand.

"I'm Martin," the old man responded, shaking Yoder's hand.

"So, what takes you out to the old park, sir? If ya don't mind my askin' . . ."

"Just a stroll, son, a stroll in the park."

"How will you get back home, sir?" Yoder asked, a look of puzzlement crossing his broad features. "Ain't many passersby out there . . . ."

"I know. Don't worry. I've made arrangements, son."

"Well, OK," Yoder replied uncertainly.

"I'll be *fine*, boy. Don't worry about *this* ol' man," Martin cajoled.

Martin's arthritis was particularly bad today, probably due to the weather. The old man gazed longingly at the park entrance. Yoder smiled and waved aside Martin's offer of a small pouch of gold shavings. "Please accept my thanks, then, Yoder," Martin said, extending his hand.

Yoder shook it enthusiastically. "I have everything I need and more, my brother. Here, take this with ya," Yoder said, rummaging a plump little sack out from under his driver's seat. "Sarah makes the world's best bear jerky—tender, not stringy, ya know? I snack on it sometimes while I drive. You take this. I got plenty more back at the shack."

Martin gladly accepted the gift, examining it with a stupefied expression on his face. "You—you actually hunt *bear,* Yoder?"

"Well, not usually, but last winter we had to, and rabbit, possum, muskrat, squirrel—whatever we could get. We really don't have big enough caliber rifles for the he-bears, though, so we had to take mostly cubs and make a lotta precision head shots to the mommas. Usually we hunt deer, but somethin' killed off most'a the herd last year. We just thank God and accept whatever He provides, you see?"

"But—you shot *cubs?* Were they in season?"

Yoder laughed heartily and honestly. "In season? Surely you jest, my friend! The artifice that man calls society has ceased to exist! Its extravagant promises of wealth and well-being lie rotting like filthy rags at our feet. And we, God's people, stand *vindicated!* Yet still the artifice reaches out from the grave to smother us with its regulations! Hunting seasons? What truly *is,* my friend, is God's plan, God's law, and God's providence! God's *seasons,* if you will! Man's 'seasons' hold no sway with Him—nor with us. We are *His* people, Martin! In God's Season of Trouble, we gratefully accept His gift of whatever game animals He sees fit to provide! Do you understand, my brother?"

Something echoed in the back of Martin's mind: " . . . a lot of things are way more important than just being safe, following rules . . ." He shook his head as if to clear it. "Yes, of course, I do see, Yoder. God means for His people to survive, and He provides the way." He raised his eyes to the smiling Penitate. "Thanks, my brother."

"It's His gift, not mine, Brother Martin. I'm just happy to pass it along. May God go with ya."

"And also with you," Martin replied, borrowing a phrase from the Catholic services of his distant youth—*how many years ago?* There was a sharp whistle and a snap of the reins, and Yoder's swayback mare, Jezebel, lurched reluctantly forward, resuming her long walk home.

Martin stood at the park entrance for a few minutes, catching his breath as he watched the wagon recede into the foggy half-drizzle. It always seemed cold and dreary these days, probably due to the airborne particles from all the volcanoes—and the nukes, he mused. Even on the few relatively clear days, the sun was dim and blood-red, and it seemed to set earlier every day; it was always pitch-black by six in the afternoon. Far off in the distance, he heard the *chuff-chuff* of a coal-gas steam truck laboring up a long grade, probably back out on the crumbling interstate. *Don't hear that sound much anymore,* the old man mused. These days, coal was almost impossible to come by, and most peasant farmers and artisans traded only in local markets when they traded at all. Most of the Arab oil reserves were still too radioactive to use following the spate of "retaliatory tactical actions" by the United States of Judea (formerly Israel, which had recently swelled to encompass the former Palestine, Jordan, and a large slice of western Syria):

> *Historical note:* " . . . hostile Arab entities had mounted a concerted attack on the now-USJ, and unlike Operation Desert Shield of the early 1990s, the U.S. released its IFF (Identify Friend or Foe) codes to the Israelis. The way was cleared for unfettered retaliation without threat of American intervention. The USJ launched their entire fleet of shiny new XF/B-15JU aircraft—fast, agile fighter-bombers, embellished with conformal fuel tanks and new, superlight screamjet (supersonic combustion ram-enhanced auxiliary multimodal jet) engines on each wingtip. It was a new century and a new war, and this time around, the Judeans plied the enemy ground forces liberally with daisy cutters and MOABs—and when a wave of logy Saudi F-15s and tanks was spotted approaching from the south, the incredible XF/B-15JUs shrieked out of the sun, annihilating the Arab forces in a trice and launching their low-yield tactical nukes directly into the midst of the fertile Saudi oil fields.

> "Within the hour, the show was over, and within a month, hordes of Palestinian and Jordanian refugees were being relocated at gunpoint to miserable refugee camps in what remained of Syria. Naturally, much of the world's oil supply had just been rendered unusable, but USJ was having a field

day. For better or for worse, Palestinian, Jordanian, and Syrian territory was finally under Judean control . . . ."

Kevin P. Bloch, *An Illustrated Encyclopedia of Tactical Conquests* (New York: Apocalypse Publishing Company, 2071), p. 192.

Martin Brush sighed deeply as he again faced the inevitable conclusion: commercial distance hauling was essentially a thing of the past. Critical shipments like weapons and other military cargo now monopolized the designated carriers: aircraft, coal-gas tractor-trailers, steam wagons, and hybrid ethanol vehicles. All else accrued to horse or goat carts, rickshaws, or the backs of pack animals—*or men*. A chill wind soughed through the mostly barren treetops; the forest beckoned.

Then: It seemed like only yesterday, but it had been nearly twenty years since Martin Brush lost his second paper fortune in the worldwide financial collapse known as Black November, aka "The Big One." He'd been a rich man before the first meltdown in 2014, lost everything then and regained most of his former wealth by the time the Big One hit. This time, though, he'd secretly hedged his bets with precious metals, which were subsequently legislated into illegality on the heels of Black November.

One fateful night in Black January (it seemed everything carried the prefix *black* in those days), Martin was working late in his underground bunker, when suddenly the home intruder alert sounded. *Someone had just broken into his house—and Amelia was there alone, with their daughters, Meghan and Kayleigh!* Martin immediately called 911666, the special emergency access number known only by the privileged few *illuminati* like himself. A synthesized female voice responded: "Hi. You have reached the offices of Universal Security Services, a wholly owned subsidiary of TeraBank International (a Five-Star Global Investments company). This call may be monitored for training and quality purposes. Please listen carefully as our menu has changed. *Para español, presione quatro; pour le français, appuyez trois; für Deutsch, drücken Sie zwei;* to continue in English, please press 1. For all others . . ." Martin punched 1.

"Thank you. Your response indicates that you wish to continue in . . . *English*. If that is correct, please press 1 and then star. Otherwise, press . . ." Martin pressed 1*.

"Thank you for selecting . . . *English* . . . as your language of preference. Your customer profile has been updated to reflect your language preference . . . *English* . . . and you will not be prompted to repeat this information again the next time you call. If at any time you need to update your personal information or if you need to make a change to your profile, please contact us at www . . ."

Martin smashed his cell phone on the floor, sobbing as he ground the device to powder under the heel of his Gucci loafer. It was too late, *too late! Fuck and double-fuck!* His home intercom had broadcast the horrible reality as Civilian Security Forces, LLC (another proud member of the TeraBank International family), bullets tore through the sacks of hamburger that had once been his wife and daughters.

Somehow they'd found out about Martin's little canvas bags of gold—*his financial safety net for his family!* Martin could see the now-meaningless bags from where he sat, and he vomited copiously.

Martin had again become a very rich man, albeit a multi-millionaire with assets that were negotiable only on the black market. World currencies were being devalued hourly; the Dominion was now literally worth less than the high-tech, counterfeit-proof paper it was printed on. The presses cranked out new denominations of currency weekly to follow the Dominion's slide. A crisp, new three-hundred-dominion note might just buy you a loaf of day-old bread if you could find an open thrift store before the next devaluation. Gold was now the only real game in town, and the Money Men meant to have it *all!*

Ironically, Martin was only two miles from home and ten feet underground when his family was butchered. His vision had proven oracular; construction workers had put the finishing touches on his secret hideaway scarcely two months before the Big One rocked the world. The bunker was designed to house four people in nominal comfort for ninety to a hundred days—hopefully long enough for Martin and his family to formulate an escape plan after the financial tsunami he'd predicted. But he'd just listened to his family's real-time dying screams in the very shelter he'd designed and built to save them!

There was absolutely nothing he could have done that night. They were already dead before Martin could have climbed to the surface. Of all fate's deft agents, Irony seems to be the most singularly insidious, uniquely equipped to chew up a man's soul and spit it squarely back in his face. In Martin's case, Irony had "sweetened" the pot even further—it had kept him alive to wonder why he hadn't died with his family.

The extravagant hole in the ground had served as Martin's home for more than twenty years now. Barring a catastrophic failure, the little steam-driven generator would provide electricity well into the next century. The tiny hot-spring reservoir a half-mile or so beneath the surface would ensure that. But the shelter's food supply eventually ran out, and Martin was forced to surface, weak and malnourished, to barter and scavenge—and when that failed, to trap and eat the occasional small animal.

The Present—Rewind to earlier that morning: Seven-thousand-plus nights of fitful sleep surrounded by perpetually cold concrete had gradually taken their toll. Martin was nearly immobilized by arthritis most days, and even on the best days, the ten-foot climb up to the surface was well beyond excruciating.

Today was not a best day. He hadn't slept well at all. Last night, he'd dreamed about the bear again. He'd awoken bone-weary and deeply exhausted, and this morning his joints were singing the Hallelujah Chorus. *It must be damp outside today, and cold,* he guessed correctly.

For some reason, Anishinaabe State Park came to mind: the long walks he took there as a child when he needed some time to think, and where the bear had—or had he only dreamt that? He didn't know for sure. What he did know was that he wanted the solace of the park more than anything. He donned his filthy trench coat, stuffed his tattered Bible into the pocket, and mounted the ladder with no forethought as to how he'd make the ten-mile trip to Anishinaabe. At the moment, though, he didn't particularly care; if he died trying, that would suit him fine. He'd joined the ranks of the living dead twenty years ago, in a constant state of mourning for his family—and the Book of Revelation promised infinitely worse times to come. The old man's joints screamed in protest as he pulled himself up to the ladder's first rung, just as a Penitate farm wagon lurched to a stop in front of Joe Carmi's crumbling general store. The old Bible felt heavy in his pocket . . . .

Martin had never figured out where it had come from. He'd discovered it one night in his bottom desk drawer, buried under a sheaf of papers. Strange . . . Though not a religious man, he'd taken to reading the dog-eared book after cracking open Revelation one evening in search of an inscription, a note, anything that would tell him something of the book's previous owner. He continued reading, and the passages would haunt him for the rest of his days.

CHAPTER 2

Middle Game: Down the Road

As he limped painfully around another deadfall, the old man's hand strayed unconsciously to the Bible. He thought again of the Apocalypse, of the Tribulation. One of the Dominion's biomachines, a flying scorpion, buzzed past his right ear, its tail pregnant with neurotoxin; apparently it had a target other than Martin in mind. He thought of the scorpion locusts of Revelation, whose tails stung with a venom so painful that victims would "desire to die, but death (would) flee from them." Overhead, fighter jets rumbled above the ground fog—"like the roar of a thousand lions."

Martin decided to head off into the relatively sparse forest. There appeared to be a trail there, and the access road looked hopelessly blocked. He squinted, trying to see if it eventually cleared, but after a hundred feet or so, the pavement disappeared in the mist. Martin squinted harder; the light was starting to fail. It looked like there was a sign or something lying in the road, about fifty feet ahead . . . .

Then—Curiosity: Although Martin wasn't a cat, curiosity had nearly killed him several times. Well, technically, it *had* killed him once, when his heart stopped briefly during the glue-sniffing incident. Martin was sixteen at the time and old enough to know better. He and three classmates had purloined a quart bottle of PVC cement from the janitor's closet, and with the aid of a few sandwich bags, they got high one day out behind the crumbling monstrosity known as Stafford High School.

Fortunately, Mr. MacPherson, the janitor, noticed the glue missing and ran out to the loading dock, only to find Martin lying blue and not breathing as his classmates stood around him, flapping their arms helplessly. "Big Mac" applied a quick thump to the chest, and Marty immediately regained consciousness, coughing violently as the color rushed back into his cheeks.

MacPherson paced to and fro, stroking his chin. He had the boys' rapt attention. "Gather 'round, boys. Listen up, now. School regulations says I gotta report this to Principal Slotter. But Marty will get into a lot o' trouble, and you three, too—prob'ly the juvie hall, or at least summer school." Big Mac paused, still stroking his chin contemplatively.

"Now listen up, boys." All eyes were on the janitor; their young lives hung in the balance, and all four were sweating profusely, even in the chill April breeze. "I'm thinkin' two things. First thing is, you broke the rules. Marty here almost died. Second thing is, school's for learnin'—learnin' *lessons*. An' there's a lesson to be learned here, boys, a big one. Anyone wanna tell me what it is?" Big Mac looked from side to side, his stern glare meeting only blank faces . . . until little Marty looked the janitor straight in the eye and raised his hand. Big Mac laughed with obvious pleasure. "Yes, Marty, speak your piece, son. What is it?"

"W-well, Mr. MacPherson, I think, uh . . . I . . ."

Marty felt absolutely no remorse for his actions, and he had no compunctions whatsoever about feeding Mr. Mac his smoothest line of bullshit. Martin Brush was <u>good</u>, and he intended to lay it squarely on the old man, thick and stinky.

Big Mac smiled warmly. "Take your time, son. We ain't in no hurry here."

Marty blanched and looked away, appearing to gather his thoughts. Finally, his answer came. "Well, Mr. Mac . . . the rules are there to keep us from getting hurt. If we break the rules, we can get hurt, like I did today."

"Good, Marty. *Very good.*" MacPherson stopped midstride in his pacing and resumed stroking his chin. "One more thing, Marty."

"Yessir, Mr. Mac? What is it?"

"Well, we all know rules is put there to keep us safe. So why do you think people break the rules, Marty?"

At the critical moment, Marty slipped up, suddenly reverting to type. Smirking, he rolled his eyes and started to laugh. MacPherson's face flushed bright red. "What's so damn funny, boy? You best speak up *right now*, y'hear?"

"Ahh, c'mon, Mr. Mac. Don't you get it? I guess some people just think that life's way more important than being 'safe'—kissing ass and following other people's rules." The group of boys broke into giggles and outright guffaws, and an infuriated Big Mac grabbed Marty by the scruff of the neck and marched him off to the principal's office.

That was all it took. Martin Brush and his cohorts spent the following year in the Maxwell Nixie School for Boys. Having learned his lesson well, Martin kept his mouth (figuratively) glued shut and graduated with highest honors, garnering straight A's and the coveted Nixie Achievement Award for Most Improved Student.

Nixie had been a cakewalk for Martin, who'd already taken college prep math courses and Advanced Composition at Stafford High. The vocational classes at Nixie were a breeze, and actually kind of fun, especially machine shop. He'd always written well, and his 1,000-word final essay for English Comp, titled "Life, Liberty, and the Pursuit of Common Sense," was published verbatim in the school paper, *Maxwell's Megaphone Monthly*.

The other boys fared less well. Tyrone Washington finally earned his GED and wound up peddling used cars at Sloppy

Seconds Affordable Auto down in Plumbersville. Jeremy Cart got an associate's degree in electronics and landed an under-the-table job with the local cable company. Only one boy failed truly miserably. Lugar "Greenie" Hawking succumbed to chronic inhalant abuse, flunking every class at Nixie. Greenie dropped out the day he turned seventeen and graduated to the back alleys of East LA, where he fed his solvent addiction by eating loogies off tenement walls for spare change.

Now: First Caress: Martin thought he felt something clammy brush the back of his neck. An icy chill rushed up his spine, and his knees suddenly felt wobbly. *He had to sit down!* He lost his balance and crashed, butt-first, onto the deadfall lying across the road behind him. *Shit, I haven't eaten today,* he thought. Suddenly ravenous, Martin rummaged through his pockets for the packet of jerky Yoder had left him. *He couldn't find it! The meat was gone!* Icy fingers of dread plucked at his entrails as if they were harp strings.

Sometime during the course of the day, Martin had more or less resolved that this stroll in the park was to be his last. He would simply wander off into the woods, walk until he collapsed, and die peacefully beneath the pines. But now, having just felt the Reaper's first frigid caress, Martin was suddenly far less certain that he wanted to dance with Death just yet. The old man wearily buried his face in his hands. Unbidden, four simple words flashed through his mind: *You're sitting on it.*

Aha! Yes, that's it! Martin remembered and reached frantically for his hip pocket. *There it was—Yoder's bag of jerky!* He staggered to his feet, struggling to pull the sack free, but it was wedged tight. Martin shook his head. The bag had slid easily into his hip pocket that morning. *If he didn't know better, he'd swear the damn thing had gotten bigger . . . .*

Finally managing to work the packet free, the old man tore into its contents, immediately gulping down two or three strips of barely chewed jerky. Not surprisingly, his stomach recoiled, and Martin barely managed to keep the meat down. After a couple more (thoroughly masticated) strips, he felt refreshed. Martin looked ahead, surveying the roadway once again. There on the pavement lay a Forest Service sign of some sort, apparently torn free of its rotting post by a gust of wind.

Martin rose painfully and stumped up the road, his legs now stiff from their brief period of inactivity. He picked up the sign. It was badly faded and difficult to read in the deepening twilight, but he could make it out.

Above the hideous visage of a leering bear wearing a campaign hat, its snarling canines stringy with saliva, was the inscription "Toothy Says Don't Feed the Bears!" Beneath the image was a line of smaller text: "My Next Snack Could Be Your . . ." The text was badly scuffed and Martin couldn't quite make it out, but underneath was an even smaller line, barely visible: "See you in the woods, unless you see me first! Signed, *Toothy*."

Martin shuddered, dropping the metal sign, which clanged alarmingly on the roadway. The old man felt an overwhelming sense of foreboding, as if the shadow of unrequited destiny had just fallen across his grave. *Long gone are the days of Smokey the Congenial Caniform, admonishing us with a gentle wag of its forefinger to snuff our butts,* he thought. "My Next Snack Could Be Your . . . *what?*" *Shit, these forest rangers really quit pulling their punches since I was here last.*

Indeed they had. In these final days, the wildlife had become markedly more aggressive, especially the carnivores. Martin, having cut his Internet cable to avoid detection after his family had been slaughtered, had remained oblivious to the relentless progression of events. The world had changed radically since the Big One, and not for the better by any conceivable human standard. The wanton increase in the carnivores' ferocity was but one tiny piece of the bleak jigsaw puzzle confronting mankind . . . .

Historical note: " . . . the slaughter of Pope Cornelius I by Muslim extremists; the nuclear retaliation by the Zion-Christian Coalition; the reconstruction of Solomon's Temple in Jerusalem following the ritual demolition of the Mosque of the Dome by conventional weapons; the unlikely and precipitous rise to power of the popular rapper who calls himself 666, or Seizer Six-Pack, and his establishment of the so-called Dominion . . .

"The United States had struggled to maintain its sovereignty, and for the most part it had succeeded, even after the secession of three rebel states: Utah, Louisiana, and Texas. But suddenly, Alaska, Cuba, and Alabama were also threatening secession. Alaskan oil was now essentially the world's only major source of nonirradiated conventional fuel, save for the newly discovered Cuban deep reserves in the Gulf of Mexico and the vast natural-gas shale fields of Alabama . . . . A Constitutional Convention was convened, and the Thirtieth Amendment was ratified by a narrow margin of state legislatures. The Dominion as we know it was officially born on June 6, 2066, and Seizer Six-Pack was appointed by Dominion national fiat as Prime Minister for Life . . . .

"The Dominion immediately negotiated treaties permitting it to overfly U.S. sovereign territory to link its disparate and noncontiguous states. A cargo plane could, for example, fly from New Orleans to Juneau, Alaska, without fear of retaliation from the United States. In return, the U.S. dollar would be linked to the new dominion currency, but only on the upswing; any weakening of the dominion would have no effect on the value of the dollar.

"Just as it seemed that an uneasy peace had been struck, the Dominion released tens of thousands of biomachines from a purported cargo jet flying over Minneapolis, Minnesota . . . ."

Ries Auld, PhD, EdD, *A Contemporary History of the North American States, United and Confederate* (New Orleans: Apteryx Books, 2112, pp. 331–343).

Martin had watched it all happen, not with his senses but vicariously through his Bible readings. In those arcane passages, the old man had grasped at some deep, visceral level the essence of what had transpired outside his rabbit hole. His brief forays outside had imparted some knowledge: as an Alabamian, he was now an unwilling part of Seizer Six Pack's Dominion of Confederate States. Biomachines were everywhere, "keeping the peace." The groundwater was an evil merlot color due to a pernicious red algae infestation that had started in the Great Lakes, and it stank of dead fish. The days were a third shorter, and the sun was the color of blood—just as the Book of Revelation had predicted. *The end was near, and it wasn't going to be pretty.*

Martin sat reading his Bible for a while. It was getting too dark to read. Suddenly, his resolve returned. *Martin Brush was done, and he knew it.* The old man cut to the right and trudged off into the blackening forest. Maybe he'd find ol' Toothy out there; he remembered the wave of foreboding that had swept over him earlier, and he remembered dreaming about a bear. *"I'll see you in the woods if you don't see me first."*

It was almost totally dark now. Martin was exhausted, bruised and lacerated from his numerous scrapes with low-hanging branches and the constant undertow of shin-busting deadfalls and ground flora. Literally unable to walk another step, he gratefully flopped full force onto his back in a small, grassy clearing. Martin closed his eyes, moaning with pleasure as his nemesis, gravity, released its agonizing grip on his legs and spine, its relentless pull gradually diffusing through his supine frame . . . .

Martin drifted off into a tormented sleep, his dreams commencing almost immediately as he closed his eyes. *They were walking along a sunlit path. Dappled sunlight bathed them in golden light as it broke past the soughing boughs fifty feet above them. Momma cradled Baby Shawn in her arms, cooing and singing little songs to the snoozing infant. His brother, Jake, ran ahead and returned with "walking sticks" for everyone. "Let's rest a minute," Papa said, opening the Igloo cooler they always took on their family outings. In a moment, the kids were gulping peanut butter sandwiches and Kool-Aid. Papa smiled and lit his pipe; it smelled sweet, like cherries. It was a fine day . . . .*

A sharp branch or a rock poked Martin in the back, and he awoke briefly, cursing. He rolled onto his side . . . .

"Marty, you hold the baby for a minute, son. Momma's got something special in the cooler." BROWNIES! Marty just knew it! He grabbed his little sister and began rocking her back to sleep. "Shawn's my fav'rite baby; no, I don't mean maybe . . . ."

"Sshhh! Quiet, everybody. I heard something in the woods." Papa slung the rifle off his shoulder, checking the load. He racked the bolt, chambering a round. "Everybody be quiet, now. I think there might be a bear back there . . . ."

Martin groaned in his sleep. This time, though, he didn't wake up—and the dream continued.

"Oh, God. What can we do, Frank?" Momma whispered to Papa. "Don't move. Don't talk. Drop the food," Papa whispered back.

Out of nowhere, the bear charged. Papa's first shot caught it in the right ear, and for a moment, the animal recoiled, pawing at its wound. Papa racked another round into the chamber and fired, this time catching the bear squarely in the left shoulder. Martin panicked; he dropped his little sister and ran . . . .

The dream, and his recollection of the incident, always stopped there. Entire chapters of his life were missing. He could draw only one conclusion:

He knew for a fact that Shawn had died; ergo, the bear must have eaten her after he dropped her and ran away.

He had no evidence to support this conjecture. He could recall nothing after dropping Baby Shawn. Ma and Pa had ordered her cremation, and the bear incident—too painful for all—was never discussed. Somehow, Martin remembered the cremation taking place in the fall, two weeks after the bear attack. He'd never summoned the courage to ask his parents the hard questions, and they'd never volunteered the information. They bid farewell to little Shawn, and the chapter was closed.

Years later, Martin drew himself up and went to the county courthouse to search out Shawn's death certificate. It was a miserable Tuesday afternoon in November, and sleet coated his glasses as he slipped and slid up the hill to the records center. The clerk of records was leading Martin back into the archives when everything abruptly went black. Apparently, ice had just taken down a power line somewhere. The emergency lights kicked on, bathing the clerk's face in a stark bluish hue. "I'm sorry, sir," she said. "It looks like the main power's out. We have lights, but the microfiche readers are on the main 220 line. They're out of commission, Mr. Brush. Can you come back tomorrow?"

Martin felt a flush of relief. *You'll never see me again, lady!* Martin managed his best Cheshire smile and lied. "Of course, Ms. Taylor. No problem. I come down here almost every day anyway. I'm an investment banker, you know? I have clients in Corleigh Towers, just across . . ."

"OK, fine, then. Please be careful on your way out." Ms. Linda Taylor, clerk of records, spun on her heel, her shoes clacking imperiously on the tile floor. *My, aren't WE important?* Marty snickered to himself. He felt FREE—unjustifiably, probably—but for a moment at least, the weight lifted from his chest, and he drew his first deep breath in years. *Fate has intervened. Case closed. Goodbye, yellow brick road.*

Except, of course, in his dreams . . .

There in the light of his campfire stood a hulking she-bear, her head seeming to retreat into her massive shoulders. Martin squinted hard into the twilight. *Shit, she was one of the Dominion's damn hybrids! An abomination—white fur splattered with brown spots!* He'd often had palaver with itinerant farmers and woodsmen over the years as he bartered for food and other goods. Martin had learned that these man-made animals all shared two distinguishing characteristics: a prominent dromedary—like lump of flesh at the base of the neck *and a voracious appetite for human flesh.* Martin, transfixed by the bear's honey-brown eyes, dropped his remaining scraps of jerky on the ground.

The 1,200-pound predator smelled it. Sniffing the wind, she approached slowly, *slowly,* finally stopping to sniff at the scrap of meat as Martin shivered in his paralysis of terror. The huge bear looked straight into his eyes with what Martin correctly interpreted as a glare of accusation coupled with undistilled contempt that said, *You eat our babies! I SMELL them!* Martin heard something moving through the woods, far away. *More bears,* he wondered, *or something even worse? Oh, dear God, have mercy . . .*

Saturday Morning: It was already well past noon when Yoder finally found Martin. *That old fart really made some headway,* Yoder Weaks said to himself as he approached Martin's still-sleeping form stretched out in the tall grass. *I bet them ticks are suckin' the lifeblood outta him right now.*

Yoder mopped his brow. It had gotten warm last night, and the temperature might well hit 70 before sundown. "Hey, Martin!"

Yoder shouted, clapping his hands. "Wake up, brother! Time for breakfast! You like bacon and eggs?"

"Ahh-agghh, there's a bear, get away," Martin said, thrashing as he fought through the veil of sleep. The old man's head whipped from side to side, his glassy, unfocused eyes finally coming to rest on Yoder. "Run, brother, get away—the bear . . . ."

"Calm down, Martin. Ain't no bear here, old friend. Just me, your buddy Yoder. I stopped by to see how you're doin'. Man, you covered almost four miles yesterday. Quite a hike over broken trail. I never woulda found you if I didn't track animals for a livin'. You feelin' OK, Marty?"

"Yeah, I guess so. But the bear . . ."

"Hey, Marty, listen up—*ain't no bear here*, chief. Trust me. You musta dreamed about it, OK? It's all right now. The bear was just a dream, Marty, and it can't hurt you. You hungry? I got bacon and eggs. How 'bout we start a fire? We'll be eatin' in twenty minutes. Sound good?"

Martin briefly considered the content of his dream, concluding that Yoder indeed spoke the truth. Shaking off his apprehensions, Marty nodded. "Yeah, sounds good, brother. *Real* good!" He limped to the edge of the clearing and began gathering sticks for the fire. Within fifteen minutes, eggs and bacon were sizzling, and Yoder was whistling some old spiritual or hymn.

Both men ate voraciously. As Martin gobbled the last few bites of his meal, Yoder tossed another fistful of bacon into the frying pan. "Hope you're ready for a second helping, brother," Yoder grinned.

"Oh, yeah, you bet. Bring it on," Martin mumbled around a mouthful of food.

There was a heavy rustling in the woods. The men looked each other in the eye. Martin's facial expression said, "I told you so," and Yoder's simply registered alarm. Yoder rose from his squatting position. "You just sit tight, brother. Mind the food. I'm going to check it out," he said, racking a cartridge into the chamber of his deer rifle. With that, the big man strode toward the thicket.

As he watched Yoder disappear into the woods, Martin lost his breakfast. *Toothy the Devourer was on his way.*

CHAPTER 3

End Game

Twenty minutes later, Martin heard three sharp *cracks*, almost certainly from Yoder's rifle. He waited and waited as the fire dwindled to a bed of embers. By 3:30, his friend had not returned, and twilight was already starting to darken the umber sky. As Martin gathered up the cooked foodstuffs, he realized that he wasn't going anywhere today; his right knee had swollen to the size of a cantaloupe, and it hurt like hell. Only one option remained: he'd have to stay the night and wait for Toothy.

He'd need more firewood. *All wild animals feared fire.* He wondered if Yoder had brought a hatchet. Martin crawled on all fours to his friend's backpack. There it was—a razor-sharp little axe, hanging suspended in a loop on the side! *He was saved!*

Martin set about the task of survival. He crawled to the edge of the forest, where several deadfalls lay. He began chipping away bark, small chunks of dry wood, and branches. He gathered an armful of dry twigs for kindling, then leaves and pine needles. He carefully arranged the pile. Searching through Yoder's backpack, he found a little metal box containing three wooden kitchen matches.

"OK, here goes," Martin mumbled to himself as he struck the first match on a nearby rock. The matchstick snapped in the middle, and somehow Martin retrieved the business end, striking it again. This time, it flared to life. Martin touched the flame to the little pile of twigs and leaves, which caught fire immediately. He fed the fire carefully, watching with satisfaction as the little blaze blossomed into a bonfire before his eyes.

He was saved! And he was STARVING! Martin peeled several pieces of the cooked bacon and egg whites from their paper wrapper, gulping them down shamelessly. He licked what he could of the yolk from the wrapper, and within minutes he was stuffed. By then, though, the feeble red sun had nearly set. Deep in the forest, dusk came early. It was well past 4 p.m.—*he'd better gather some more wood before he lost the light.* Martin grabbed Yoder's hatchet and crawled back into the thicket.

Yoder Weaks wiped the blade of his formidable buck knife on the leg of his fatigue pants. Losing the light, he'd worked frantically to glean at least the best of the meat from the black bear's small carcass. In better days, prior to his sect's ban on the use of motor vehicles, his Ford pickup had proudly displayed two bumper stickers—"I eat my road kill" and "You kill it, you eat it." All six of his children were enrolled in the No Carcass Left Behind program at the Penitate Evening School, where they learned basic hunting, fishing, and dressing skills. During the daylight hours, of course, they, like all good Penitates, worked the fields alongside their parents.

Yoder wrapped the bloody booty in his shirt and strode, bare-chested, toward the clearing where he'd left Martin. He whistled a hymn to let the old man know he was coming. He preferred to avoid a tragic encounter with his own hatchet; after all, he'd just sharpened the cussed thing . . . .

Martin heard the whistling as he dragged a birch log out onto the roadway. "Over here! Over here, whoever you are. *Help me!*" he cried at the top of his lungs. At that precise moment, Yoder stepped into the clearing, covered in dried blood.

The old man dropped the log and began to sob. "Oh, thank You, dear Lord God, thank You! Thou hast delivered me from the very jaws of death!" Then he did an abrupt about-face. "Where the *fuck* you been, boy? I'd given you up for dead! I heard three rifle shots—and then *nothing!* For hours and hours!"

Yoder simply laughed his honest, ingenuous laugh. "Been out shootin' your bear for ya, Marty—and strippin' our supper off his bones. Ya gettin' hungry? Looks like you're makin' a fire."

Feeling a little chastened, Marty replied, "Yeah. Welcome back, my friend. You're a sight for sore eyes. I been workin' on this fire like my life depended on it."

Yoder regarded the old man sternly. "You were right to think that, Marty. It does. No fire, no supper—and them woods's fulla bear. They're a'scaird of fire, though."

"Guess I'd better get to choppin', then," Marty replied.

"Nah, you fix up the meat; I'll cut the wood. Been doin' it all my life. Here, take my dressing knife and grab that bag of marinade outta my backpack. The red powder. Sarah makes it; it's called dry rub. You rub it into the meat, and it seasons and tenderizes it. I found some wild peas and scallions back yonder, too. We'll be eatin' like kings tonight!"

A long string of drool issued from Marty's lips. "I'm all over it, chief!"

"Hey, Marty. Cut that meat kinda thin—about half an inch. Slice it across the grain, see? Like the muscle's a loaf of bread. Then rub in the red powder with your fingers and let 'er sit till I get a nice blaze goin'. Drizzle a little bit o' water from my canteen on it, too—*not too much*. Just enough to keep it moist and help the spices work in. Got it?"

"Got it, Yoder!"

The Penitate swung his hatchet expertly, and wood chips flew everywhere. Within fifteen minutes, as advertised, Yoder's bonfire roared. "I cut some sticks, Marty. That's the best way to cook 'em." He handed a sharp, ramrod-straight skewer to the old man. As the meat sizzled, the two talked. "Why exactly did you come out here,

Marty, to the woods?" Yoder asked. "You tryin' to kill yourself or what?"

Marty sat, turning the meat over and over in the flames, his chin buried in his chest. "Yup," he replied without further comment.

Yoder was incredulous, and he stared, uncomprehending, at the old man. "Marty, *why?* Why would you want to do that, man?"

Marty met Yoder's gaze firmly. "I lived in a hole for twenty years, boy. Dominion storm troopers gunned down my wife and kids right after the Big One. When I turned to the Bible for comfort, it only told me that things are going to get worse and worse from here on out. My body is all shot to hell. I can barely climb to the surface anymore. Yesterday morning, I just decided to take a long walk in the woods and keep going until I die. I only wish it was winter. They say freezing to death is just like falling asleep. Get the picture, son?"

"But, Marty," Yoder said, "our Lord promises to deliver His people . . . ."

Martin interrupted. "Yeah, well, fine then. I'm open to that. He can 'deliver' me before a bear eats my liver. Or I starve to death. I guess we'll find out, huh? It's all the same to me. I no longer really give a tinker's fuck either way, my friend."

Yoder sighed deeply, spinning his stick over the fire. "Better eat your dinner, Marty. Looks like it's done."

The two men ate in silence. Yoder swallowed his last bite. "Your mind is made up then, Marty? You really want to die alone here in the woods? You could come live with us, old buddy. Lotsa love, lotsa food, a warm hearth . . . a *family!* Good, God-fearin' folks all around. I mean it, Marty! Please, come home with me, OK? We can walk back to the wagon tonight. I'll carry you if I have to."

Martin shook his head, a lopsided grin twisting his face. Tears poured down his cheeks. "God bless you, son. I just don't know. I just don't! Can you gimme a day to think it over? My knee's feeling a lot better. You go home to your family tonight, Yoder. I'll work my way back toward the highway. Just meet me here on the park road tomorrow sometime. If you can. That's all I can ask of you for now, my friend—a little time to think."

Yoder pondered for a moment and then nodded curtly. "Fair enough, Marty. A little time to think. Yeah, a man needs time to think. You just sit here by the fire tonight, pal—and *read your Bible!* Promise me that, Marty. That's all I ask of *you* for now, brother."

"Of course, Yoder. I promise. Thank you, my friend."

"My morning services let out at 10. I'll be back at the park entrance about 11 and start walkin' in. Here, take my watch," he said, producing a gold pocket watch and handing it to the old man. "This was Great Grandpapa's, Marty. Must be a hundred years old, if it's a day—and it's never lost a second of time that I know of in all them years. Start lookin' for me early tomorrow afternoon. And look here—I'm leavin' you my revolver. It's a sweet single-action .45. And a box of rounds. Twelve hollow-points in there and six already in the cylinder. And my hatchet. Here, *take 'em, man.* There's plenty of firewood. And you'll need this flashlight, matches . . ." Yoder rummaged through his backpack and began stuffing the items into a small shoulder bag. "Here's the rest of the meat, too, and my canteen."

Yoder shouldered his backpack, preparing to leave. Martin touched the Penitate's shoulder. "Wait a second, Yoder. I have something to give you in case I don't—well—make it."

"Sure, Marty. What is it?"

"Yoder," Marty continued, "I told you I lived in a hole. Well, it's a bunker, about 300 yards south-southeast of the general store—off the southeast corner of the building, actually. There's about fifty pounds of gold down there, and it's all in little canvas bags. They're bright orange. You can't miss 'em. Here's the key and a map. Take your compass and head directly south-southeast until you see a big pile of busted-up concrete with rebar sticking out everywhere. Jink to your right about ten degrees, and walk about thirty paces. You'll see a boulder, and next to it something that looks like a manhole cover, but it's domed and gray; it's made of composite. I want you to have it, son."

Yoder gasped. "Fahh—fifty *pounds?* You mean *ounces?*"

Martin chuckled sadly, "No, son—*pounds*. It was worth close to two million U.S.A. dollars after the Crash, and who knows *what* it'd fetch today. And I have something else here for you." The old man produced a crinkled sheet of paper from one of his pockets, unfurled it, and handed it to the young man.

Yoder took it and began to read aloud. "*I, Martin Ioudas Brush, being of sound mind and body, do hereby bequeath all of my worldly possessions to Yoder Weaks . . . .* Martin, this is your *will . . . .*"

"Yes, it is."

"What would a simple sodbuster like me do with so much *fortune,* Marty?"

Marty chuckled again. "Read the last paragraph, Yoder."

"Hmmm . . . *to be dispersed for the express purpose of spreading the Gospel of our Lord to all the nations of the Earth.* Oh, Marty—I'm just a simple farmer! Please, don't put this on my head."

"You sound just like Moses right now, son. Surely you hear it!"

Yoder hung his head. "Yes, from my own rebellious lips. Very well, Marty—and I pray you live to be a thousand."

"Bet you do, my brother, bet you do."

Martin watched sadly as Yoder walked off into the darkness. Poor kid. *Well, it seems that God has called him.* Martin said a short prayer for the Lord's new point man. *May You, in Your infinite mercy, bless Yoder and keep him.*

After Yoder disappeared, Martin retrieved two more chunks of wood from the edge of the clearing and tossed them on the fire. Seating himself in its warmth, he worked the Bible free of his pocket and began reading from the Book of Daniel. *Again, there it was . . . the horror of the approaching Apocalypse.* He flipped ahead to the Book of John. *For God so loved the world that He gave his only begotten Son, that whosoever believeth in Him shall not perish, but shall have eternal life.*

Martin heard a shuffling sound in the woods. Reluctantly, he looked up and spied a pair of gold-tinted eyes glinting in the firelight. Then a second pair appeared. He dropped the Bible and worked Yoder's pistol free of its holster. He cocked the hammer and waited.

From behind him came a chuffing noise, accompanied by the sound of rustling trees. Martin turned to look; three more pairs of golden eyes regarded him from the darkness.

He was surrounded by bears.

Martin made a snap decision—and fired.

1:21 p.m. Sunday: Yoder recoiled in horror. What must be Martin's body (the head was mostly gone, leaving only a pool of dried blood and gore on the grass) languished beneath a cloud of flies near the ashes of his campfire.

The remains appeared mostly untouched. The forest's denizens had not yet begun their methodical dismantlement of what was now merely a lump of carrion rotting in the sun. Yoder noticed that his revolver, lying beside Martin's corpse, was oriented strangely. It suddenly dawned on him—*Marty had shot himself in the head!*

Yoder vomited copiously and then buried Martin under a mound of stones just off the clearing.

What to do now?, the Penitate wondered as he began his trek back to CR-31. *Will I be the Moses of the Apocalypse—or the new Solomon? Lord in heaven, help me . . . .*

Ninety minutes later, Yoder climbed aboard his waiting cart. With a sharp whistle and a snap of the reins, Jezebel the Swayback Mare rolled her cloudy eyes and began her weary trek to the southeast corner of Joe Carmi's crumbling general store.

THE TRUTH SOURCE

A NOVELLA

CHAPTER I

"In September of 1974, a disc-shaped object streaked out of the Russian sky, scorching its way deep into the frigid soil two-hundred kilometers southwest of Tobolsk. Following a frenzied paperwork shuffle and tens of strident phone calls, a Red Army detachment, accompanied by a KGB 'observer,' was dispatched to the crash site . . . ."

Sonny and Kat Mildauer, *Perchance to Ponder* (Kiev: Shimanov Publishing Company, 2017, 2021), p. 12.

KGB agent Sergei Kasparov's boots crunched on the snow as he and eight Regular Guard troops approached the object buried seven feet deep near a stand of scrawny pines. A film crew followed them, recording still and motion images of the event.

Kasparov huddled against the wind and lit a miserable, unfiltered Russian cigarette. How he longed for an American Marlboro! Sergei was spoiled, having spent three years working undercover in the opulence of his country's chief rival. And now here he was, in Siberia of all places! Four hours from the universally acknowledged end of the world, Tobolsk, investigating the crash of a so-called UFO, itself an American term. Best to just get on with it; they'd have to hustle all the way back to Tobolsk tonight, another four-hour ordeal. It was nearly 2 p.m, and the sun's meager rays were already waning, casting long shadows across the desolate landscape. The deep, frigid Siberian night would be upon them all too soon.

But, yes—*there it was!* And it was unlike anything Sergei had ever seen. It was clearly a huge disc. Amazingly, it appeared substantially intact, relatively untouched by the violent impact, and almost completely buried. Probably only the topmost third remained above ground.

Sergei sniffed. There was a strange odor in the frigid air. It smelled like ozone—hot electrical wiring – but there was something else, too, like meat roasting – pig, maybe? And did he smell burnt hair? He couldn't tell for sure.

The snow had melted in a ten-foot radius around the object. *This thing must have come in fast—and hot.* Sergei motioned the troops forward and ordered them to start digging. He noticed that the bare ground was uncharacteristically soft; great clumps of warm, pliant soil flew from the soldiers' shovels. *If this thing had thawed the ground when it hit twelve hours ago, it must have been glowing cherry red when it hit.*

Kasparov nosed around the site while the Regular Guard continued their excavation. The object was nondescript, really—silver-gray in color, a smooth, flat finish, like matte platinum. *Just a big, billion-ruble, platinum disc sticking out of the ground—nothing special,* Sergei mused, snickering to himself. But then he noticed an inscription on the disk: *U3&NzT7.* It looked vaguely Cyrillic, but it made no sense. He leaned forward for a closer look, and not thinking, he rested the palm of his hand on the structure . . .

. . . *and shrieked in agony.*

Sergei pulled his hand back, regarding it with a look of dumb shock and awe. His palm was badly blistered, and some of the flesh looked slightly charred as well. *Ahh, fuck me. Looks like a second-degree burn,* he thought. *Screw it, I'll survive.* He plunged his hand deep into a nearby clump of snow; it seemed to help, temporarily relieving the pain.

Curiously, Sergei thought, *there was no heat radiating from the disk, yet it was hot enough to sear flesh.*

Another whiff of roast pork or chicken wafted past his nose, and suddenly it dawned on him: *There's a crew cooking alive inside that thing! We must get them out—NOW!*

Agent Kasparov dispatched a team to open the vehicle immediately and enact emergency rescue and life-support protocols. He barked at the remaining crew to deploy the emergency shelters. Tonight they would shiver miserably in their frigid tents under the dispassionate Siberian stars.

Corporal Andrei Sokolovich fiddled with the field radio, but only static and a piercing whine issued from the set. He swept the tuning knob back and forth, but interference was all he heard across the entire frequency band. He glanced over at Sergei, who was squatting in the snow, writing something in a small notebook. "No luck, sir. The radio is out. All I get is noise."

"What else do we have?" Kasparov asked. Sokolovich shot the agent a quizzical look. "What do you mean, sir?"

"Another radio, Corporal. Don't we have some kind of backup communication with us?"

"No, sir. Just walkie-talkies. This mission was only intended to be a brief recon."

"Very well. Dispatch one of your Guard to drive back to Tobolsk, and get us some support. Have him take the light ground vehicle. *Right now,* Corporal. It's already getting dark!"

Sokolovich bristled but then saluted Kasparov. "Yes, sir. Right away." The soldier turned and strode briskly toward the circle of Jeep-like vehicles. Two minutes later, Kasparov watched as the small truck, driven by Private Samolyev, sped off into the sunset. Sergei noted the time: 3:15 p.m. Even with luck, they probably couldn't expect logistical support until late tomorrow morning. It was going to be a chilly night for the reconnaissance team; the temperature had already dropped to about nineteen degrees Fahrenheit, and it would get only colder when the sun set in an hour or so.

Sergei Kasparov had always been diligent in his logbook entries. Had he not, history would have no record of what was about to unfold, and the entire event would remain yet another blip on the screen of obscurity.

In the 'seventies, fueled by the Cold War, the Soviet army was still fairly well equipped. Even expeditionary squads like Kasparov's carried generous rations and ancient but adequate tents—but no can opener, mind you, and only one radio. A couple of the soldiers had already scrounged some deadfalls from the woods, and a bonfire roared near the excavation site. Private Margolovich was using a hatchet to hack open cans of beans and pickled herring. It would be a meager supper, but adequate.

Sergei felt oddly disoriented. Once again writing in his logbook, he found himself growing increasingly confused. *It's been a long day for all of us,* Sergei remarked to himself.

Sergei glanced over at the disc. It seemed to be getting bigger. *Whoa, get a grip, man.* Maybe a shot or two of Stoli would help. He strolled toward the bonfire. "Where's the vodka, Private?" he asked. "It's been a rough day. You have the rations, yes?"

"Yes, of course, sir," Margolovich said, a little uneasily. "How much do ya want?"

"How much have you got, Private?"

"Lemme check, sir." Margolovich pulled an ungainly key ring from his pocket and unlocked a metal box. "Mmm, three liters."

"Just gimme one, soldier."

"One *liter,* sir?" Margolovich asked incredulously. Agent Kasparov just nodded.

"Yessir, right away," the private said, pulling a bottle from the lockbox and handing it to the agent. "Will that be all, Officer Kasparov? Supper's almost ready. Will you join us?"

"No, got work to do. Thank you, Private." Sergei snatched the bottle and walked briskly toward his private tent.

Margolovich shook his head and turned back to the fire, where a small pot of beans had started to boil. "Have a good evening, sir." Kasparov offered no reply.

The soldiers dug all through the frigid night in three-hour shifts, returning periodically to the fire to thaw their hands and feet. Finally, at about 4 a.m, they unearthed what appeared to be a crew hatch and managed to pry it open. Agent Kasparov had been awake all night, and he bolted to the crash site when he heard the excited conversation of the excavators.

They had retrieved a body from the wreckage. The small cadaver lying on the snow was badly burned, its skin crisp and golden-brown, like that of a roasted turkey. It looked superficially human, but upon closer inspection, Sergei noticed that it had two opposing thumbs, one on each side of its hand. It was small, and it had no nose, only a trio of vertical slits. There was an orifice that looked something like a puckered anus where the mouth should have been. Its single intact eye was wide open, and the brown-gold iris resembled that of a cat.

One of the soldiers squeezed out of the hatch, carrying a gray object about the size of a brick.

Kasparov scribbled furiously in his notebook, which would survive as the sole extant official record of that night's strange encounter. The camera crew shivered in their tent, having long since expended their film. Sergei heard a scraping sound. He looked back at the disc. *The damn thing was moving, and there were still three soldiers in the hole!* "Get out of there, men," he cried. "Move, *move!*"

The disc broke free of the soil and righted itself about a hundred feet in the air. It wobbled perilously, but it remained aloft. Abruptly, the object disappeared in a brilliant flash of light.

All three soldiers died within a year, eaten alive by radiation poisoning. Sergei Kasparov lived on for three years after that and died at the ripe old age of forty-seven. His mind was gone, the result of early-onset dementia and brain cancer. Most of the remaining crew gradually succumbed to insanity and eventually went the way of Sergei Kasparov.

Even during his rapid decline, Sergei continued his logbook entries. He scribbled furiously, day and night, until he passed out from exhaustion. Sergei told the doctors he feared his head would explode. *There is too much in there,* he'd moaned, *and I have to get it out!*

The six extant volumes of Kasparov's log were seized by the KGB following his death, and they languished untouched in an obscure vault for years. But, miraculously, a double agent named Boris Markovich smuggled four of the little notebooks and some of the photo stills to Canada.

The authorities were intrigued. After reviewing the material, the Canadian Security Intelligence Service contacted its American counterpart, the CIA. Ironically, the CSIS's initial point of contact at the CIA turned out to be a chubby, myopic-looking man named Emerson "Sonny" Mildauer, who was, putting it mildly, enchanted by UFOs and paranormal phenomena. He also happened to be semi-fluent in Russian. Emerson started most days with a stack of TASS news releases and a mug of coffee—and, naturally, a cigarette. Right at his desk. *Right in his office!* It *was,* after all, the nineteen-seventies . . .

CHAPTER II

Sonny had started smoking at the tender age of fifteen, the very day his father (whom he describes to this day as "Momma's sperm donor") pulled up stakes and left his family to fend for themselves. Mom did all right by the kids, though. As it turned out, Celeste Belt-Mildauer possessed an undiscovered talent for writing science fiction and Gothic romance/horror. It hadn't taken long for Celeste's gift to *become* discovered.

On a whim—mostly to stave off her morbid ruminations following the abandonment—Celeste Belt signed up for a creative writing class. Six months later, her *The Twilight Staircase* was selling like hotcakes at major bookstores.

The following year, her first full-length novel, *Chokedamp Crossing*, skyrocketed to eighth place on the *New York Times* Best Seller list. The family survived, handsomely. Momma was never around much after that; but then, neither was Sonny.

Sonny's best bud at school actually had a small reflector telescope, and (so he claimed) he had seen a real flying saucer—*with his own eyes!* And *real space aliens!*

"Donny! When? Where?" Sonny gasped, his voice little more than a whisper.

"Down there by the marsh, Sonny. C'mon. I'll show you."

Donny: The heart of a true showman, a master of intrigue, beat within Donny Claxton's young chest. He came by it naturally; his mother, one Alyashai Claxton (née Tartakian), was descended from a long line of Gypsies, "carnies" one and all. Alya drew her first breath one sultry evening in August, just after the season's

39

final Budapest show, in a trailer surrounded by tall, undulating switchgrass.

Donny was Sonny's only real friend, the only other boy he'd met who wasn't in the total thrall of baseball, football, whatever-ball. Whether the product of nature or nurture (or both), Sonny's innate rebelliousness steered his course during the formative years, and it set him apart from the other boys, whose lives increasingly revolved around physical games involving spheres being kicked or tossed.

Sonny wasn't so much a loner as he was a misfit. Most kids his age preferred a quick game of scrimmage or stickball to a universe of reading, observing, and experimenting with incendiary materials.

By the age of nine, Sonny had already blown the back toolshed off the garage and rebuilt the gas engine in his father's lawnmower (not that The Sperm Donor gave a shit one way or the other. Screw the shed anyway. And the grass still never got cut unless Sonny cut it).

By age ten, Sonny had heard the first faint peals of the siren song that was to mold his life ever after . . . the allure of the paranormal, the beckoning call of universes unimaginable . . .

Now: These days, Sonny's outward bearing and demeanor could be best described as "prototypical middle-aged government bureaucrat." His coarse black hair, which he wore slicked back from his prominent forehead, had only recently started to thin. The agent radiated what others commonly mistook for apathy or lassitude, and he walked with the trademark "CS shuffle" that somehow managed to eventually overtake all career civil servants. Sonny wore long-sleeved white shirts and brown neckties every day of the year, and his thick, jet-black, government-issued spectacles and polyester slacks further cemented the stereotype.

A casual observer would probably guess that Sonny was a typical middle-aged government drone riding his desk to retirement at the local post office or DMV. Nothing could be further from the truth; Sonny was neither lethargic nor apathetic toward his job. *And today, Fate had dropped the answer to Mildauer's lifelong dream squarely into his lap.*

Sonny set the sheaf of papers aside for a moment and lit another cigarette, his thoughts drifting back to one sunny morning in a long-forgotten June . . . .

<u>The Site:</u> Sonny and Donny were together (as always), enjoying the first day of summer vacation by doing what they loved most: exploring. "Look, Sonny, right down there! Do you see it, man? That's where the saucer landed!"

Sonny replied skeptically. He knew Donny was a born sideshow barker, a carnie through and through. "C'mon, Donny. You're playin' with me, ain't you? I don't see a thing."

Donny retorted, "Shit, champ, not that much to see! I said I'd show you where the saucer *landed,* not the damn thing itself!"

Sonny replied, a tinge of regret in his voice. "Sorry, Donny. I didn't mean nothin' by it. Can we go on down? To where it was?"

Donny's handsome Mediterranean features brightened. "Sure, Sonny, but you're gonna get wet. It's all marshland down there—knee-deep water in some spots. You ready?"

"I guess so . . . ."

CHAPTER III

Dmitri Vasiliev came to America in 1977. He took English classes and acquired a rudimentary vocabulary, sufficient to ask directions to the nearest soup kitchen or homeless shelter, and adequate for wheedling pocket change and cigarettes from passersby.

Dmitri's career had advanced rapidly. Just last week, he'd quit his floor-sweeper's job at the school to assume the lofty position of Cab Driver. He loved his new job, which paid a staggering two dollars per hour plus tips. At the close of each twelve-hour shift, the dispatcher paid Dmitri twenty-four dollars in cold, hard cash. No questions asked and no taxes paid.

Vasiliev was one of the lucky few who had been patrolling the far outer perimeter, about a mile from the crash site, when the saucer rose and vanished into the Siberian sky. Having suffered only mild radiation sickness, he'd later had three suspicious moles hacked off his face by Red Army medics. He was discharged from the Guard two years after the saucer incident, armed with a pocketful of pills and a diagnosis of borderline schizophrenia.

I'm not crazy, Dmitri had whined, the gauze on his forehead still weeping blood. The Army doctor just shook his head. Vasiliev had dug a half-inch hole partway through his skull with an army knife. *My brain is too full. I have to let it OUT!*

With better meds, administered by a caring doctor at George Washington Charity Hospital, his condition improved dramatically. Most people now regarded him only as a bit odd, mostly due to his incessant *writing*; Dmitri scrawled constantly in a spiral binder. Unbeknownst to the outside world, the hermit's one-room walkup flat was stacked waist-deep with notebooks. Save for a few narrow pathways through the chaos, most of the floor space was occupied by precarious towers of his feverish scribbling. What's more, line after line of neatly printed Cyrillic text and arcane mathematical symbols covered every wall. Dmitri's brain was *too full*, and he had to let it out, *somehow*.

Agent Mildauer had done his homework. Tonight he would pay a visit to the youngest of the survivors. He trudged up the three flights of rickety stairs leading to Dmitri Vasiliev's flat.

Dmitri was, not surprisingly, writing in a new spiral notebook when he heard Sonny's knock. *Who can this be? I have no friends*, he thought. He walked to the door and opened it, just a crack. "Who is there, please?"

"A friend, Mr. Vasiliev. You don't know me yet. If you could spare me a few minutes, I'd like to talk to you. Would that be all right?"

Dmitri's throat constricted in terror. He peeked through the opening and spied a pudgy little man of about fifty sweating miserably in the midsummer's humidity. He appeared to be a friendly, harmless fellow, and Dmitri's new Haldol was kicking in; the paranoia had started to subside.

Vasiliev opened the door. "Please come in, sir. You must excuse my home. I am something of a writer. I have few visitors, and I will have to find something for you to sit on. My name is Dmitri Vasiliev. To whom do I owe the pleasure of this visit, sir?"

The agent smiled broadly, extending his hand. "Sonny Mildauer, my friend. May I smoke in your home, sir?"

"Of course, Mr. Sonny. May I have a cigarette also, please?" Mildauer shook out two Camels and lit Dmitri's first. "My pleasure, comrade."

"So, you know that I am Russian?"

"Of course, sir. I actually know you quite well, and I have wished to meet you all of my life."

Dmitri carried a milk crate to the foot of his recliner and plopped down a tattered pillow. "Please be seated, Mr. Sonny, and excuse me for a moment. I will bring for you a pleasant surprise." The Russian smiled over his shoulder, and soon Mildauer heard glass clinking in the kitchen. Dmitri reappeared, winding his way between the stacks of books. The Russian handed his guest a large tumbler of cherry-red liquid and took a sip of his own drink. "*Salut*, my new friend—*to knowledge!*"

Their glasses clinked together. "To knowledge," Sonny echoed.

While in the kitchen, Dmitri had downed a couple of Ativan tablets, and his anxiety was evaporating like the morning mist. He plopped down unceremoniously in his badly worn recliner, which was propped up on one corner by a stack of—you guessed it—spiral notebooks.

Agent Mildauer took a long drag on his cigarette and began. "So, may I call you Dmitri?" Dmitri nodded, smiling. "You appear to write a great deal, sir. What is it that you write about?"

"Most times I do not myself know, Mr. Sonny. My hand simply writes. Much of what I write appears like equations, and mostly I do not comprehend."

"Yes, I see it on the walls. Why did you do *that,* Dmitri?"

"Ohh," Dmitri laughed, "one night I ran out of paper. But my head is too full, and I need to get it out, so writing on the walls. Do you see?"

Sonny Mildauer nodded sagely, chuckling at the Russian's ingenuous response. "I think I do, Dmitri. KGB Agent Kasparov had the same problem, you know? But the poor fellow went insane and died."

"This I know—and almost every man there that day died or went mad. I must have been far enough away from that saucer to escape the worst of it. The medics cut a few moles off my face, but Kasparov was right there when it took off. To this day, I still have problems. *I cannot stop writing. My brain is full, and I must get it out!* Surely you see this, sir. The scar on my forehead? I tried to open my skull to let it out."

"Oh, you *poor man*! It must be *terrible* for you!"

Dmitri chuckled. "Well, yes and no, Mr. Sonny. Always I feel more than alive, like I have the electric charge inside. But it is very disturbing. It is much like an itch, but deep in the soul. All this is inside me, and I must to get it out. That is why I now write instead, and not boring holes in my skull. Can you see this, friend?"

"Ahhh, Dmitri. I'm so sorry, my friend. Perhaps I can offer some explanation of what you're going through, though. Do you think that might help?"

Dmitri finished his vodka and cranberry juice. "This would not be bad, Sonny. But first, I shall prepare for us another drink. It is hot, and we are both very thirsty. May I have another cigarette as we begin?"

Dmitri returned with two sweating tumblers. Agent Mildauer lit Dmitri's Camel and began. "I see it this way, Dmitri. That crashed saucer probably carried something called a 'truth source'—a box of some kind that radiated tons of information into your brain. Did any of your comrades' heads actually explode?"

"Well, no, I do not think so. But many of the Advance Guard died of brain hemorrhage."

"Mmm, that's telling, Dmitri. A truth source is something like a main memory bank that provides loads of information to coordinate the other parts of a system: time, position, stuff like that. But it's possible that this alien truth source also dumped its programming information into your brain—and into Kasparov's. You probably got a lighter dose, being farther away, so you didn't go mad like he did. Most people's brains would have probably just shut down from the overload. They would have gone insane, Dmitri, and most of them did."

Dmitri nodded solemnly. "Yes, this I know, Sonny."

"But *you* didn't go insane, Dmitri! That has to mean *something!* Somehow, you survived to produce your notes and memoirs. Do you feel that you need to keep all these books, my friend?"

Dmitri paused, sipping his drink. "I do not really know, Sonny. I must think about."

"Of course, Dmitri. But if I could just borrow your notebooks, I'd photocopy them. I promise to have them back to you in a week or so."

Dmitri pondered for a moment and then raised his glass. "Very well. The deal is done, Sonny. *Salut—to knowledge!*"

"To knowledge!" Mildauer broke out a pair of fresh Cuban cigars. His Russian host again topped off their drinks and proceeded to ply his new friend with vodka and his recollections of the saucer incident until the dawn's early light crept across the eastern sky.

Then Dmitri dropped a bombshell. "They found a body, Sonny—in the saucer."

Mildauer's jaw dropped. "A *body?* One of the aliens? What happened to it, Dmitri? Was it preserved somewhere?"

"I do not know. Agent Kasparov packed it in snow and drove it back to Tobolsk that night."

"Did you see it, Dmitri?"

"Only for one moment, I saw. It looked like a child, but the face was different—not a human face. It had no nose, just three slits. The skin looked white in the search lamps, and half of the face was burned away. And no hair."

"Can you sketch it for me, Dmitri?" Sonny asked.

"Yes, I think," Vasiliev replied and picked up his latest notebook. After a minute or two, the Russian handed Sonny the pad. "It was something like this." Dmitri asked for another cigarette as Sonny examined the sketch.

"Of course, my friend," Sonny said, handing him the pack. "You draw well, Dmitri. I feel like I could almost reach out and touch the face."

"Am drawing since I was a boy. To bring me peace."

Dmitri rummaged in his pocket for a moment and retrieved a key ring. He worked a worn brass key loose and handed it to the agent. "I will trust you, Sonny. I must work every day twelve hours, so I give you my spare key to pick up notebooks."

Sonny jammed the key in his pocket. "Thank you, Dmitri. I'll send a truck by later to get them."

Seating himself again in the recliner, Vasiliev regarded Mildauer sternly. "If you come to understan' all of this, Sonny, you mus' tell Dmitri. Yes?" His words were becoming slurred, his speech heavy. Dmitri tossed his head back, breathing deeply.

"Yes, Dmitri. Of course I will." Sonny shot the man a bittersweet smile and rose from his milk crate. "But now, I must go, my friend. I too must make a living." He extended a pudgy hand, but his host was already snoring sonorously in his recliner. Agent Mildauer walked quietly to the door and let himself out.

On the way back to his office, Sonny found his thoughts unexpectedly wandering to his childhood buddy Donny Claxton. Maybe this was like the closing of some celestial loop, one whose ends had remained untied for most of his life. The two boys' ultimate dream had been to one day meet the occupants of an actual UFO. But that dream was not to be, at least not for Donny. After graduating high school, Donny had signed up for the Air Force's top-secret Manned Orbital Vehicle, Earth-Recon (MOVER) project. Two years later, Captain Donhold Claxton III died when his single-stage-to-orbit rocket plane, a sleek masterpiece identified only by its tail number, XR Alpha-9, broke up on reentry.

In an unusual move for such a highly classified program, Donny's fiery death did receive a brief, perfunctory treatment in the media. *Channel 99 Nightly News* viewers watched in awe and dismay as an ever-lengthening streak of light traced across their screens, only to end in an abrupt plume of orange flame.

"An official Air Force spokesman, speaking on the condition of anonymity, reported today that a highly classified experimental vehicle apparently lost control and burned up as it reentered the Earth's upper atmosphere. When prompted for further details, the spokesman would say only that the craft was manned and that its unidentified crew was presumed lost. Back to you, Lisa."

"Tsk. Hmmm, tragic. Thank you, Scott Robeson, for your report from Vandenberg Air Force Base in California. Coming up right after this break, a soccer mom in River Mills gets a new lease on life after her . . ."

Sonny had uncovered the awful truth years later in the course of a totally unrelated investigation. *So long, Donny. See you in my dreams, buddy.*

CHAPTER IV

Boxes of Bones—1978

The old Quonset hut was slated for demolition, but according to Army regulations, the contents had to be catalogued first. Then all items were to be properly dispatched to rotting warehouses elsewhere. The skinny junior lieutenant in charge finally managed to coax open the stubborn padlock after soaking the tumblers with fish oil from a squeeze bottle. With a gentle shove, the door screeched open. As it did, a whoosh of dusty, stale air hit the lieutenant in the face.

Neither the lieutenant nor his men were adequately dressed for the biting wind whipping across the abandoned air base. He motioned for his twelve-man detail to follow him into the building.

Save for a sliver of light at the open door, the building's interior was blacker than night, and the darkness itself seemed heavy and vaguely threatening. It seemed even colder inside the hut than it was out in the wind.

The lieutenant checked the thermometer on his belt: minus one degree Celsius. *Warm for this time of year*, he thought. It was, after all, early September. Flashlight beams swept to and fro as the other soldiers made their way into the hut, Building A-51.

Even with the additional light, the darkness felt cloying, intractable, as if reluctant to give ground after so many years of unchallenged domination. The lieutenant ordered the floodlights deployed. Within ten minutes, the portable generator was roaring outside, and a dim, yellowish gloom filled the hut. Junior Lieutenant Aleksei Korsaskaya grabbed a second flashlight and made his way down the center corridor to the rear of the building. It was a disheartening stroll.

Building A-51 looked far larger inside than it did on the outside. There were so many crates in here; it seemed like *thousands* of them. They'd have to fudge some of their entries if they were to meet schedule. In the dim light, the lieutenant stumbled several times over debris and potholes in the eroded concrete floor. *Too many Siberian winters,* he thought. *That'll make it tough to move all this garbage out of here. Maybe we should just peel the skin off this bitch right now and be done with it. At least we'll have some decent light to work by.* As he approached the rear of the building, Junior Lieutenant Korsaskaya felt something watching him. He glanced to his left.

Something moved in the corner. Aleksei gasped, dropping his second flashlight. He grabbed a chunk of broken concrete off the floor and slung it toward the source. His projectile clanged against metal. Then he saw something running toward him.

An emaciated rat charged, full-speed, between his rubbery legs. Aleksei screamed.

The rodent continued its sprint down the center corridor toward the open door. Aleksei immediately heard a static-encrusted voice on his walkie-talkie. "You OK, Lieutenant?"

"That's a confirm. Just a rat, soldier. Startled me."

"Shit, a RAT? You never seen a *rat* before . . . Lieutenant?" Korsaskaya heard distant laughter and whoops from the front of the building. Aleksei laughed good-naturedly. *Strung too tight, I guess. It's just an old frigging Quonset hut.* "Yeah, one or two. But this one was bigger'n a dog, and he looked hungry. And he almost ran up my *skirt!*"

He'd played their game, and once again, he'd won. Lieutenant Korsaskaya smiled, satisfied by the hearty laughter now echoing through Building A-51. The lieutenant's guys loved him. He was one of them . . . kind of a pussy in some ways but a regular guy, deep down.

"We got 'im, Lieutenant." Anatoly stomped decisively on the rat's little head. "Gonna have him stuffed for ya—a *trophy*," his voice chided over the walkie-talkie. More laughter from the door.

"Awright, fellas, as you were. I gotta get to work back here—check it out, make sure it's safe for you *real men* to charge in!" Another chorus of hoots and jeers issued from the front. "Let's get moving boys. Anatoly, you get the men some rations, and *fix 'em the way you always do!* Don't cut corners. This job sucks, but we gotta get it done. It'll go a lot better on a full belly. Anatoly, make it double rations. We're gonna peel this bitch of a building tomorrow, but tonight, we celebrate. This is not combat duty. Get 'er goin', *double time!* Tonight we bivouac in Hotel 51."

The walkie-talkie crackled again. "The boys are all over it, First Lieutenant!"

"Lieutenant out." Aleksei turned toward the front of Hotel 51. As he did, something else caught his eye. Off to his right, he saw that one of the wooden crates had been pried open. The splintered cover lay askew beside the box. He decided to have a quick look. That quick look probably changed the course of human history forever. He walked over and peeked inside.

The lieutenant reeled at the sight and realized that nothing would ever be the same again. That knowledge was more than simple foot soldiers should have to bear for the rest of their lives. Aleksei hoisted the lid back onto the box and beat the nails back into place with the tube of his heavy flashlight.

Aleksei had studied human anatomy at Moscow University before he washed out of the program and joined the Army. His boys shouldn't have to see this . . . *the rat-eaten, badly decomposed remains of something not of this world.*

51

CHAPTER V

Three Years Ago

Agent Sonny arrived at work promptly at 8 a.m, just as he had for the past twenty years. Mildauer was one of a rare breed—excited about his work and genuinely thrilled to be there. In fact, this morning he could not wait to get back to the reports of an intriguing discovery at an abandoned Russian air base.

Sonny lit a Camel, and smiling, he opened the first binder . . .

Journal Entry 367.B—Siberia, 09/11/1978 (paraphrased): It was 9 a.m., and the aroma of frying bacon, powdered eggs, and rehydrated potatoes filled Hotel 51. Lieutenant Korsaskaya snapped awake, gasping as he looked at his wristwatch: 9:01:16! The frigging Russian Army piece of crap had failed to wake him at 6 a.m.! The wristwatch's programming was byzantine, yes, but he was *sure* he'd set it properly. He rechecked the settings; they were all correct. *Just another equipment failure*, he thought. *Pretty routine. You're in the Army now.*

But judging by the delicious aroma now filling the Quonset hut, Anatoly had things well in hand. He peeled away the sleeping bag and rose painfully from the concrete floor. Lieutenant Korsaskaya stumbled toward the crowd gathered near the front of the building.

A grinning Anatoly quipped, "Nice that you could join us, First Lieutenant! You are in for a feast—wheatcakes! Eggs with goat cheese! Bacon! Fried potatoes! Boiling hot coffee! And the

Commander always gets first portion—or have I breached protocol, Lieutenant?"

"No, you are, in fact, technically correct, Anatoly. Thank you. Paragraph seven, subsection 2.2.4.9 of the *Field Operations Manual* indeed states, in part, that the Commanding Officer shall receive first portion. But he may defer that option and assign first portion to a deserving soldier of his own choosing. Today that deserving soldier is you, Anatoly! Sit down, relax, and eat well, my friend, and then we shall serve the others together. I'll mind the cooking while you eat."

The other troops whooped and applauded. A comical loudmouth named Pavel Yeksigian shouted from the rear, "Looo-*tenant!* Rah!" Aleksei hurried out to the supply truck and reappeared carrying a canvas stool. "Sit, Anatoly. *Sit!* I shall serve you, my friend!

"Where is that in the field manual, sir?" the sergeant quipped.

"Ah, Sergeant. Perhaps I must assign you another cover-to-cover reading of the manual." The rapt and hungry audience responded with a chorus of "ooohs" and catcalls. "But perhaps that is not necessary. After all, the manual is silent on this very fine point. Your lieutenant may interpret the white spaces as he sees fit. Now, sit, my friend, and eat before the eggs burn in the pan." Whoops and cheers erupted from the crowd.

As Aleksei scooped scrambled eggs and cheese onto Anatoly's plate, he was again struck by the similarity of his little performance to that of a first-school teacher manipulating a group of nine-year-olds. Aleksei was a natural leader, and he was continually amazed at the parallels between his troops' behavior and that of young children. For him, command had always seemed no more and no less challenging than shepherding a flock of fourth-graders. Aleksei had not reached this conclusion in a vacuum; as a young officer candidate at the Red Army Academy in Moscow, he had taught fourth grade part-time at Moscow's People's Elementary School.

And, always, he'd found the carrot to be far more effective than the stick.

CHAPTER VI

Now

Sonny Mildauer frowned as he pondered the set of equations in Dmitri Vasiliev's notes. As a young college student, Sonny had completed his education in mathematics, save for three elective courses. But then, for reasons unknown even to him, he'd switched his major to criminal justice with dual minors in law and psychopathology studies.

Divine intervention?

His mother had been incensed. How *dare* he, after nearly completing his math degree?! *You're on your own now, young man! Better start looking for a new place to live tomorrow! I mean it, Sonny-boy.*

Sonny-boy was curiously unconcerned; somehow, he knew it would all work out—and so it had. Scarcely two years later, Sonny found himself sitting in a cubicle with two other new agents—at the CIA! *In Washington, D.C.!*

The text danced before Sonny's tired eyes. It was late, and it was becoming increasingly difficult to keep Vasiliev's fevered scribbling in clear focus. He remembered having seen all of the equations before, but one looked subtly different: one called Euler's Identity. He donned his strongest reading glasses and took a closer look. *The fabled equation matched his recollection almost exactly, but it contained an extra term composed of characters he'd never seen*. Beside it, a note was scribbled in the margin. Sonny thought it said "Svetlana grave." It was hard to tell for sure.

It was probably still early enough—only 7 p.m. He grabbed the phone and called Dr. Weggers . . .

Journal Entry 371.A—Siberia, 09/12/1978 (paraphrased): Lieutenant Korsaskaya groaned in frustration. Peeling back the skin of the old Quonset hut had proven far more difficult than expected. As always, the men were poorly equipped. They had only a single ladder to work with, and the wind had come up again. Thirty-mile-per-hour gusts rattled the skin of the building, and the lieutenant decided to halt the process for fear of losing a man should the wind catch the metal and toss him to the ground. The lieutenant had seen combat duty, and razing a stinking old warehouse was not worth the risk of human life.

"Come down from there, Petrov. Now!" the lieutenant shouted to the man on the ladder. He'd just checked the little anemometer they'd set up, and he saw the needle briefly jump to 41 mph. *This is too much. Nobody needs to die for the sake of a doomed building.*

Petrov's foot had no sooner hit the frozen dirt than a powerful gust ripped loose the panel he'd been working on. The torn sheet of corrugated steel tumbled frighteningly across the open field to the south. Both men gaped in awe. "Good call, Lieutenant. Thank you," Petrov gasped.

Aleksei, his face waxy and ashen, said nothing as he watched the deadly panel loft again and plaster itself against a tree. Then he turned to face Petrov. "Not soon enough, Corporal. Nobody needs to die for this piece of shit. Get the vodka. I think we deserve to celebrate right now. Meet me inside."

Petrov offered his best approximation of a salute. "Yes, *sir*, First Lieutenant. Right away . . ." But Aleksei was already striding toward the front door of the hut.

When Sergei returned with a litre of slushy vodka, he found the lieutenant standing outside, barking orders into a bullhorn. Within five minutes, the crew had secured most of the equipment, and Aleksei ordered his men inside.

A single untethered toolbox went airborne and crashed against the building as Aleksei wrestled the door shut. "Petrov, get me Tobolsk on the radio," the lieutenant barked when everyone was safely inside. Private Andrei Petrov furiously cranked the handle on his field radio. Then, "They're answering, sir. Captain Blegorovich on the line." Petrov passed the handset to the lieutenant.

The lieutenant groaned inwardly. He knew Blegorovich all too well—the lying, self-serving parasite! He grabbed the handset in disgust. "This is First Lieutenant Aleksei Korsaskaya of the First Property Detachment, Seventy-Third Demolition. Do you read, Captain? Over."

"Loud and clear, Aleksei. What is it?"

"Captain, we are experiencing inclement and hazardous weather conditions on-site. Efforts may be delayed. Request you postpone transport vehicle deployment until this storm blows over. Over." Aleksei fundamentally detested this military-speak. Blegorovich, on the other hand, reveled in it. The captain's silky reply came back over the static of the field radio. "Request denied, Aleksei. Your deployment will proceed according to schedule. That is all."

It was getting dark fast, and two of their five portable lights had mysteriously blown out during the skinning of Hotel 51. It was time for some team-building. "Anatoly, come with me. We need to feed the boys. It'll be a bonfire tonight—indoors. We now have a nice gaping hole in the roof. All the smoke will drift right out of it. Please help me gather some wood. Petrov, grab two others and join us at the tree line. Yeksigian, you're the bartender; don't let our friends' drinks run dry while we're gone. Hop to it!"

The Present: Dr. Weggers' health was delicate. He'd survived two major heart attacks since Sonny Mildauer's college days, and he'd aged badly. The old man groped for the phone and finally managed to croak a reedy "hello" into the handset.

It was Sonny! The old man's spirits soared. He'd forgotten most of his students' names, but he would *never* forget Sonny Mildauer! "How are ya, son? Long time no talk. It's *so good* to hear your voice right now, Emerson."

"Same here, Doc, same here. How have you been, sir? The years been treating you well, I hope?"

"Nah, I'm a sick old man now, Sonny. Just waiting for the final blow, you know?"

The line was silent for a moment as Sonny collected his thoughts. "Well," he sighed, "you still sound as alert and brilliant as you ever did, Doc. You must keep your beautiful mind active, huh?"

"Ahh, yeah, I guess, Sonny, when I'm not flat on my back or at the doctor's. You know . . ." Weggers's voice trailed off. A tear sped down Sonny's cheek. Suddenly the old man spoke again, fresh with enthusiasm. "But, Sonny, do you still remember Euler's Identity? Ahh, you *must*, if I do!"

"That's really *weird*, Doc. *I just called you to ask a question about Euler's Identity!* Can you *believe* it?"

"Hang on, Sonny." There was a lengthy pause and then a loud THUMP! *Oh no, the Doc must have just hit the floor. I'd better call an ambu . . .*

Suddenly, Doc was back on the line. "Sorry, Sonny," he said, "but what you said—I just felt it ripple through me. I jumped up and got the book. It's a thick one. I just dropped it on the table here. Sorry."

Sonny sighed with relief. "It's OK, Doc, it's all right. But I have something really intriguing to discuss with you. I think you'll enjoy this. I found some old writings that show an additional term to

Euler's Identity, but it's in arcane symbols I can't understand. Not Arabic numerals, for sure. Are you interested, Doc?"

"Mmmm—yes—hang on a minute, Sonny. I'm trying to find it here . . . aha! There it is, Mr. Mildauer! A contemporary of Euler posited a second term to the famous equation. The man's name was Korsakoff—Russian—and he wrote to Euler after first publication of the Identity. Korsakoff's reasoning was totally valid, so far as I can see. That added term evidently does nothing other than project the fourth-dimensional component of the original equation! Does that make sense?"

"Whew. OK, Doc, please stay with me for a minute here. I have an equation here that looks for all the world like Euler's Identity, but after it is a plus sign . . . and then something that looks like a lambda, and another character I don't recognize at all. What do you make of it?"

Again, there was a long silence on the line—and then Doc's voice reappeared. "Does the second character look like an E on steroids, Sonny?"

"Yeah—yessir, something like that, Doc. What is it?"

"That symbol is the Hebrew character *he*, and it represents the entirety of Korsakoff's Postulate. It's little known. Euler was jealous of his own work, and he ruthlessly quashed any and all contenders, including Korsakoff. In intellectual exile, Korsakoff sought to disguise his work by using obscure symbols. This huge book I have before me may be the only extant copy of Korsakoff's 'lost' treatise. I purchased it years ago from a street vendor in Ankara. It's a weighty tome—you heard it hit my side table a couple of minutes ago. This damn thing must weigh twenty or thirty pounds, Sonny."

"Yeah, Doc, I heard that. I thought you might have dropped dead! Sorry."

"Don't give it a second thought, son. You were, in fact, very close to the truth. The doctors can't fathom how I'm still drawing breath after my heart attacks—still smoking my Camel straights and still eating bacon cheeseburgers and pizza to my *heart's content*, no pun intended".

"None taken, Doc," Sonny quipped.

Doc chuckled. "Hey, Sonny. I believe the universe possesses an inherent synchronicity. Events conspire—*apparently* causally unrelated events. Call it God, if you will . . . *I* do. The Father will call us home in His own time, not in ours. All the cholesterol and cigarettes won't make a whit of difference in the end. You know what I mean, Sonny?"

The old man was still sharp as a tack, and, to Sonny's mind, he was one-hundred percent on point. "Yeah, I'm with ya, Doc."

"God bless ya, boy. Write down this formula. It's Korsakoff's Identity." Sonny complied, scribbling furiously. "And on the other side of the equal sign is—*guess what, Sonny? C'mon, humor me.*"

"Well, you could view it three ways, I guess, Doc. It *does* equal zero, but there's a couple other ways you can rearrange the entire equation . . . ."

"Yes, *yes*, Sonny! You hit the nail on the head. Play around with rearranging that equation; use substitution! I guarantee that you'll be intrigued by the implications! I won't spoil the surprise ending, though. *I scribbled a lot of my own conclusions and derivations in the back of this fifty-pound textbook here. Don't peek until you think this over for a while. Draw your own conclusions, Sonny.* I'll send you that book in tomorrow's mail. I won't be needing it much longer anyway."

"Sure, Doc. I see a lot of implications already. I'd love to take a look at your notes."

"God bless you, son."

Sonny choked back a sob. "God bless you too, Doc. Let's have a toast together, OK? Do you have any liquor on hand?"

"Sonny, you'd be hard-pressed to name a spirit the Doc *doesn't* have. What have *you* got, son?"

"I'm still at the office, Doc. All I have is a half-pint of Hennessy that I rescued from the Christmas party. You game?"

"Then cognac it is, son. I hope your math skills are still there. You were my prize pupil—you know that, don't you?"

"Wha—but Doc, my *grades* . . ."

"You were better than the rest, Sonny. You made stupid arithmetic mistakes—please forgive me, son. I was tough on you because I wanted to force you to think—*really think*—and to come back to me with questions. But you never did, lad . . . *God*, I'm sorry, boy . . ." Sonny heard the old man sniffle, and it broke his heart.

"Rest easy, Doc. I, too, believe in a Universal Plan—just what you said. We see only darkly, but through, I think, a kaleidoscope rather than a looking-glass. There's a Master Watchmaker in charge, and He's not blind. He has a plan for us all—and back then, He let me be a rebellious kid. But destiny always reasserts itself, I think. And evidently I was destined to be a CIA agent at this point in my life. A CIA agent pursuing his lifelong dream—investigating extraterrestrials visiting our planet."

The line was dead silent for a moment; then Doc choked, "You said *what*, Sonny?"

Sonny spoke softly. "Yeah, Doc. Little green men, except they're not exactly *green*—they're kinda gray. But they *are* little—under five feet tall. And they have six fingers and toes. They're real. I've heard and read literally thousands of accounts from credible witnesses. This information is hidden deep in obscure vaults that will never see the light of day. How's that grab ya, Doc?"

It grabbed him. No answer came. Doc bolted to his feet, and he was dead before he hit the floor. The tiny aneurism that had throbbed away in his brain for over fifty years finally gave way. The old man convulsed briefly as his brainpan filled with blood.

"Doc! Doc, are you there?" Sonny spoke, slightly perplexed. Then Sonny heard a thrashing sound and retching. He pushed the big red 911 button on his DumFone.

<u>Side Note: Electronics for the Technologically Challenged</u>: Sonny loved his DumFone, designed for the growing client base of baby boomers, people who simply rejected the "phone of the day" concept and all its intrinsic complexities: the microscopic keypads, the bells and whistles, menus that changed with every new iteration. The little DumFone sported an iridescent, green-yellow case—*yeah, you could pretty much always find the damn thing just by looking around!* DumFone, LLC, had made billions by marketing their product to baby boomers and others who simply rejected the extraneous *crap* that the Brave New Digital World increasingly heaped onto their plates . . . *change for the sake of "change," if that's all you have on you, but we also accept all major credit cards.* Contrary to popular opinion, "different" did not always equate to "better."

There was always a *person* to talk to when you called DumFone's RealHelp Line. Even if the agent was in India, Botswana, or Bangladesh, he or she was always exquisitely proficient in the English language. The company had evidently sniffed the winds of change and had caught the prevailing drift. DumFone, LLC, realized early on that American English was, for better or for worse, still the universal language, and so far their foresight had paid off. Their hiring policy was simple and concise: Can't speak fruent Engrish? No soup for you. Take some correge crasses and get back to us in a year or two. If you can tok Engrish good by den. *U sabby?*

Within four minutes, an ambulance had collected Doc's contorted body off the floor of his stylish townhouse. Nine minutes later, Sonny Mildauer pulled his car into Doc's driveway. All the townhouse's windows were dark; the front door was locked tight. Sonny saw that Doc used a deadbolt for security. The agent always carried a set of (unauthorized) lock-picking tools in the trunk of his car. He retrieved his little black bag, clicked on his flashlight, and started to work. Thirty seconds later, the door swung open. *Piece of cake.*

Personal Diary Excerpt (Lieutenant Korsaskaya's notes, undated), Siberia, circa 1978 (paraphrased): The wind whooped and wailed around Hotel 51, rattling the building's skin and threatening to tear more bits of metal loose. As the feeble September sun waned, the crew continued with food preparation and the setup of two-man "cocoon shelters" inside the building. The temperature would likely dip well below freezing tonight. The remaining structure would provide modest shelter from the gale-force winds, but the crew needed more thermal protection than the ruined building could provide. Hence the cocoons.

The two-man habitats represented a spark of brilliance in Soviet engineering, if not in actual implementation. The tentlike structures were little more than double-walled balloons; once inflated with expanding chemical foam, the soft-walled tubing surrounding the crew cavity became rigid, defining the interior shape of the cocoon. A second can of more porous pressure foam was then shot into the space between the inner and outer walls to provide an effective thermal barrier. Unfortunately, the foam canisters did not work well in temperatures around zero Celsius.

First Lieutenant (Junior Grade) Aleksei Korsaskaya recognized the problem immediately. "Anatoly!" he snapped. "Cease food prep! Save that pot of water! We need it to heat these canisters! Send two men to gather more snow."

"Yes, sir," came Anatoly's immediate reply.

In short order, the cocoons—ten of them, anyway—were open for business. Small Sterno heaters burned within, warming the fireproof interiors of the habitats. The evening's meal was done, and vodka and conversation flowed freely. Private Yeksegian came stumping back from the far end of the building. "Lieutenant! First Lieutenant, come here *right away!* You need to see this right *now,* sir!"

Aleksei blanched. *Shit, Yeksegian's found my box of bones.* And so he had, plus several more boxes containing more than just body parts. "On my way, Private," Korsakaya barked and hurried down the aisle.

The Present—Dmitri: Vasiliev greeted his doctor's pronouncement with mixed emotions. On the one hand, his emotional suffering could all be over in perhaps a year or less. Alternatively, he could elect to fight his liver cancer and survive in misery for years.

"It's up to you, Dmitri. Think it over; discuss it with family and friends. If you should decide against active treatment, I can assure you of effective hospice care and adequate palliation. You won't suffer, Dmitri. I promise."

Dmitri liked Dr. Domenici personally, and he nominally trusted his physician. "Well, Doctor," Dmitri replied, "I have no family and one new friend only. My life has been a living hell for too long already, do you see? How long can I expect to live in hospice?"

The physician sighed, placing his hand on his patient's shoulder. "Maybe a year, Dmitri, at most. And I *swear* to you, my friend—you *will* be pain-free. *I will see to that personally.* In fact, your final year may well be the best year of your life. It's a goal of mine, in a way. Do you understand?"

Dmitri nodded, smiling. "Yes, Doctor. I am ready to go. I just want to live long enough to talk to my new friend, Sonny. It could take awhile. I have much to tell."

"I oversee the hospice personally, Dmitri, and you are my patient. We will do our best to give you all the time we can to talk to Mr . . . . Sonny? And to keep you from suffering. We intend to help you leave this world a happy man." Dr. Domenici stifled a sniffle as he gazed intently into his patient's bright blue eyes.

Hotel 51, Siberia, 1978:. A wave of dread swept over Lieutenant Korsaskaya as they approached the distant, tenebrous end of

Hotel 51. Stepping into the shadows, Private Yeksigian wrestled the top from a large, ancient-looking crate. "Take a look in here, Lieutenant."

Korsaskaya played his flashlight beam back and forth across the interior of the pinewood container. The big box seemed to contain nothing more than ruined clothes, but upon closer inspection, the lieutenant noticed the *size* of the garments. *And he noticed the smell.*

They were tiny, appearing suited only for nine—or ten-year-old children. They looked like one-piece jumpsuits, and they bore a strange inscription across the chest: *U3&NzT7.*

What in hell did this mean?

"What is this, Yeksigian?" Aleksei Korsaskaya barked, his voice betraying his bewilderment. "Are these children's clothes? Are there other crates back here like this?"

Yeksigian chuckled disturbingly. "Follow *me*, Lieutenant." The swarthy private walked about thirty steps to yet another open container. Shining his flashlight inside the box, he motioned to Korsaskaya. "What do you make of *this,* sir?"

Korsaskaya reluctantly peered inside. The crate contained rack upon rack of what looked vaguely like laboratory test tubes, but they were about forty millimeters in diameter. The lieutenant slid a tube out of one of the racks and held it in his flashlight beam, examining it.

The tube had a label of some sort pasted on the outside. He tried to read the inscription, but it appeared to be printed in a foreign language: **r{K: v}**<*U3&NzT7.* He squinted, peering through the yellowish fluid filling the tube. He gasped; there was something floating inside, something that resembled a shrimp, or a crayfish, or . . .

A human embryo? Korsaskaya ran a quick mental calculation. Based on the size of the crate, it probably contained a couple hundred of these . . . *samples! "Бог мой дорогой,"* Aleksei whispered.

Oh, my God! Aleksei slid another tube from the rack and examined its label. It was slightly different from the previous one. It began with **f{K: v}<** rather than **r{K: v}<**, but the major portion of the inscription was the same. *Maybe the prefix is some sort of serial number,* he thought.

Lieutenant Aleksei Korsaskaya suddenly realized that he must somehow get some of these samples to America. The lieutenant was as patriotic as any good Russian boy, but he knew his country was in the process of dying from the inside out. *Only the Americans possessed the technology, if indeed anyone did, to unravel this mystery.* Aleksei somehow knew that this discovery represented something powerful enough to change the course of human destiny.

Anatoly's bastard half-brother, Boris, ran a tramp cargo freighter out of the port at Novaya Zemlya. Boris was, putting it mildly, a shady character—a smuggler and most likely a part-time pirate; no cargo refused, no questions asked, and all currencies accepted.

Boris docked his freighter, *Хозяйка ночи (Mistress of the Night)*, at U.S. ports all up and down the Eastern seaboard. And he had connections, most of them dubious. *If anyone could get this evidence to the Americans, it was Boris.*

In a little while, Aleksei would have a long chat with his friend Anatoly.

But for now, Aleksei fought to maintain his equanimity. "Hmmm, curious, Pavel," he said to Yeksigian. "These look like biological samples of some sort—deepwater creatures, like shrimp, perhaps? Interesting. Shall we move on? Grab that crowbar, will you, Private?"

The lieutenant's intercom crackled. "Is everything all right back there, sir? Your supper is getting cold. Come join us!" It was Anatoly, the mother hen.

Aleksei replied, "Roger, Anatoly. Can you give us five minutes? Pavel wants to show me another box. We found some interesting stuff. Over."

"Copy, Lieutenant. Got a special hot vodka drink waiting for you, so don't be late!"

"Copy, Anatoly. Over and out."

Turning his back on Yeksegian, Lieutenant Aleksei Korsaskaya withdrew his service automatic from its holster. He turned to face the private, who was already twenty steps ahead. "Private! Come here, *on the double!* Bring that crowbar!"

Pavel Yeksigian bellowed, "Coming, sir!" The simple man brandished the crowbar like a club as he ran full speed toward his commanding officer.

This information must not fall into the wrong hands. This is worth a human life. Korsaskaya raised his pistol and shot Yeksigian squarely between the eyes. As the private dropped to the floor, his hand contracted in a death spasm, sill cradling the crowbar as the lieutenant called in his Mayday.

Aleksei cut the lights, then tore open his uniform tunic and slugged himself several times, *hard*, across the face as his comrades rushed down the aisle. When they arrived, guns drawn, the harried-looking lieutenant was bleeding profusely—and convincingly, he hoped.

The Present: Suddenly it was mid-September and, as always, people trumpeted their astonishment at the sudden change in temperature: "Where did the time go?" "I had to turn on the furnace last night. Last week it was eighty-six degrees!" *Well, let's see. It's September. It's gotten cool in September for all of recorded history. Next comes winter—hey, just a heads up, OK?*

Agent Mildauer relaxed in his armchair, soaking up the heat of the fireplace as he flipped through Dr. Weggers's book. In his heart of hearts Sonny loved theoretical math, but he lacked the patience necessary to plod through solving textbook problems. Sonny guessed that he'd always had more of an interest in concepts than in specifics—specifics like like solving equations before he understood why they *should* be solved. Indeed, perhaps it was this very quality that made Sonny a superlative investigator. Sonny saw patterns. Big patterns, and the big picture. Sonny'd seen that a great many problems, when boiled down to their essence, fell apart like a well-cooked chicken in a crock pot. *Reductio ad absurdum!*

The tome in his hands, although rife with arcane mathematical notation, was surprisingly readable—and rife also with Korsakoff's far-flung speculations and imaginative vignettes discussing the implications of his Postulate embodied therein. Sonny thought briefly of Dr. Geoffrey Hascall's application of complex numbers to Hawking's hyperbrane concept . . .

Dr. Weggers' volume was indeed weighty, and exceedingly thick. Sonny flipped to the end and noted the final page number: 1657.

Dr. Weggers had indeed annotated the book extensively, in soft pencil, apparently intending to preserve the intrinsic value of the book. Considering its date of publication—1929—the volume was in remarkably good condition. It had probably been printed on fine hemp paper, likely in the Middle East. Yet it was an English translation of Korsakoff's work.

Sonny worked his way to the final pages, searching for Doc's notes on Euler's Identity. After a few minutes, he found Doc's impromptu but well-organized scribblings.

"*For Sonny.*" How had Doc known? Synchronicity? *Sonny hadn't talked to Doc in decades!*

It was all there, though, in smudged graphite. Doc must have written this *years* ago! "The derivation is pretty straightforward, Sonny, but it required Euler's genius to get there. Euler's Identity is revered for its mathematical elegance. First, his formula incorporates all three fundamental arithmetic operations: addition, multiplication, and exponentiation. Second, it ties together the mathematical constants zero, unity, pi, and e—the base of natural logarithms—and also i (sometimes called j), the imaginary unit of complex numbers (the square root of minus one)! All great ideas are, at base, simple. It is as if we must distill them from the mists of chaos. The role of genius is to recognize and codify the simple concepts that ultimately define reality."

Then, down in the far right-hand corner of the page, scrawled very faintly, Sonny Mildauer saw something, probably written in n old man's fit of pique, that made him cry like a baby: "It could have been you, Sonny. You blew it, you rebellious shit."

Those last six words represented, to the best of Emerson Mildauer's knowledge, the only call Doc had ever missed—and he'd missed it by light-years. Sonny was exactly where—and WHEN—he was destined to be, and he knew it.

Dmitri Vasiliev punched the button on his morphine drip again as he waited for Sonny to arrive. Dr. Domenici had kept his promise—he was pain free, and right now he felt far better then he'd ever felt in his life. He wanted to be alert for his conversation with the CIA agent, though, so Dmitri pressed the nurse's call button. When Sandy arrived, she administered a 40-milligram dose of Ritalin into his IV line, along with two milligrams of Ativan to take the edge off.

Dmitri smiled. *Life was good—very good!* Dr. Domenici and the staff at Grace Utopian Hospice were taking good care of him! He heard a knock on the door. Sonny spoke. "Is it all right to come in?"

Sandy replied brightly as she gathered up her equipment. "Please come in, Agent Sonny."

"Hi, Sandy. How are you? Can Dmitri have alcohol today? I brought his favorite! Dmitri loves Stoli vodka."

Dmitri, reclining glassy-eyed on his bed, smiled and nodded. The nurse replied, "OK, Mr. Mildauer. Just go a little easy, all right? If you boys want to smoke, that's fine, too. Dmitri's quite the smoker, especially when he drinks!"

Sonny winked at Dmitri. "I know, Sandy. I brought a carton of Marlboros, too. Thanks."

Sandy smiled and wheeled her med cart out the door. "If you need anything, just push the red call button." The nurse left the room, closing the door quietly behind her.

The stimulant Ritalin was starting to kick in. Dmitri raised his hospital bed to a sitting position and extended his hand. "How are you, my friend?"

They shook hands, and Sonny sat down in the traditionally uncomfortable hospital chair at the side of Dmitri's bed. "Doing fine, thanks. And how is my old friend Dmitri feeling today?"

"I have found Utopia, Sonny. Dr. Dominici and his staff have made these past three months the best time of my life! Is it so wrong, Sonny, do you think, to simply be free of pain and fear? Especially in your dying days?"

Sonny paused a moment and then answered simply; "I think—you have suffered enough, my friend. Your doctor knows this, too. If I were in your shoes, I would most likely choose the same path. Is that enough, Dmitri?"

The dying man nodded and looked his friend directly in the eye. "It is enough, Agent Sonny. May I have a shot of Stoli and a Marlboro? Let us chat."

Sonny waited patiently for the old man to gather his thoughts. Finally Dmitri's cracked lips began to quiver. "Sonny, two soldiers, Lieutenant Aleksei Korsaskaya and Anatoly Borolev, managed to smuggle alien remains out of Russia. Anatoly had a brother named Boris. He was something of a ne'er-do-well. I mean, the man had his price, and he—how you say—got the job done. He was regarded as something of a mercenary, perhaps even a pirate. I have it on very good authority that the remains of aliens and who knows what else were shipped from Russia to America around 1979. Boris docked his freighter, *Хозяйка ночи* (*Mistress of the Night*) at Newark in March of that year."

"What happened then, Dimitri?" Sonny asked.

"Nobody knows, my friend. Three large crates were unloaded, and they disappeared into the night. I checked the records myself. Some courier named Short Haul Cargo Freight accepted the shipment and loaded the crates onto a flatbed. A big black Ford. They listed their destination as the New York Museum of Archaeology—fictitious—and that's where the trail ends."

"And Short Haul Cargo Freight doesn't exist either, right? And no license number?" Sonny asked.

"Stolen plates, Sonny. I took pictures of 'em, though. The bodies. Before they were loaded onto Boris's tramp freighter."

Sonny gaped at the Russian with goggle-eyed amazement. "You've got actual *pictures*?"

"Yes, and reels of film from the Siberia crash. But they're buried somewhere nobody'd ever think to look." Dmitri sighed.

"Dmitri! Where are they, man?

"Where? Six feet under the soil, Sonny, in my own Momma Svetlana's coffin. I disguised 'em to look like sacred books. She's buried in the graveyard of the old Russian Orthodox Church over on Gallows Road. It's right on the hilltop. Do you know it?

The usually dispassionate Agent Sonny Mildauer staunchly choked back something between a retch and a gasp. "I do know it, Dmitri. *But we'd have to exhume your mother?*"

Dmitri chuckled weakly. "Momma was a strong woman. She gave me her permission from her deathbed to do this very thing you speak of. Do you know what she told me, Sonny?"

Sonny shook his head dolefully. "No, Dmitri. I haven't the faintest idea."

Dmitri paused a moment, fighting for self-control. After a long pause, Dmitri managed to compose himself. "She said her body meant nothing once that which was truly *her* abandoned it.

Svetlana . . . *Svetlana* viewed the physical state as transitional. I often heard her compare it beautifully to the metamorphosis of the caterpillar into a chrysalis and then a butterfly. Once the butterfly flies free, the chrysalis is but a husk, like our earthly bodies. The butterfly represented to her the human soul!"

Finally Dmitri had peacefully nodded off, succumbing to the combined effects of his pain meds and the alcohol. As Sonny rode the elevator to the parking garage, he'd called his friend, Agent Scott Locke, from his cell phone. Within the hour, the Newark docks were under surveillance—fully justifiable, in Sonny's mind, under the Patriot Act. Foreign agents had smuggled corpses into the United States of America, and the CIA needed to know what they were up to now. "Be on the lookout for a black Ford flatbed, probably no advertising on the truck. If there is, it could be Short Run Freight Hauling." Almost as an afterthought, Sonny added, "And Scott, if they see a truck like that, have 'em run the plates ASAP. The tags are probably stolen."

Sonny slept like a baby that night. Tomorrow he'd petition Judge Hellerman for an exhumation order. Patriot Act and all, you know? Hellerman had a reputation for rubber-stamping such requests, and they were typically honored in a day or two.If not, Sonny had a dossier on the judge that could send him to prison for life. It was a done deal.

The Next Day: *This isn't going to be easy,* thought Sonny Mildauer as his shoes clacked down the hospice corridor. Dmitri Vasiliev had become his friend, and the sheaf of exhumation documents in Sonny's satchel all required the Russian's signature. Even though Vasiliev had himself suggested the disinterment, all the while citing the deceased's consent, Mildauer hated to cause the poor man additional pain. Sonny paused briefly, sighed, and swung open the door of Dmitri's death room.

JULIA REDDING

"Big Red" was something of an enigma. An aerospace engineering grad from the University of Missouri, she'd started her career as a summer intern on McDonnell Douglas's doomed A-12 program. When Bill Cheney shut the program down in 1991, Big Red decided to explore another career path . . . criminal justice/law enforcement.

A year later, the 5'11" beauty was working as an intern for the CIA! She immediately demonstrated an immense talent in cryptography and was put on the CFT (Crypto Fast Track) program. But then Big Red washed out of her top-secret security investigation. Apparently, back in 1990, she'd attended a sorority party where a young man alleged he'd been raped by several coeds.

Big Red was never convicted of anything, never even accused, but her polygraph had come up positive. In the spooky world of national security, the principles of probable cause and due process do not apply; simple suspicion, allegation, or innuendo is sufficient to disqualify a candidate.

Big Red lit a cigarette, and Scott looked askance at her. "That's against regs, Red."

"So is sleeping on the job . . . *Scott*. Gonna turn me in?"

"Uh . . ."

"Uhh is right, Scotty. I scratch your back here, you scratch mine. *Capiche?*"

"Sorry, Red. We got a deal, OK?"

Big Red chuckled deep in her throat. "I hope so, Scotty . . . for your sake."

Dmitri Vasiliev was not doing well at all today. He drifted in out of consciousness. Every time he surfaced, he groaned loudly. *This was going to be even tougher than Sonny thought.*

Sonny tried. "Dmitri. *Dmitri.* I'm your friend Sonny. Sonny MILDAUER. I need your help. Can you help me, please? Wake up, Dmitri!"

The old man's eyes remained stubbornly closed. But suddenly he snapped awake, eyes vacant and glassy, filled with terror. "*Oni dolaze . . . dolazi*, ahhh . . . *Moram pobjeći . . . oni su mrtvi . . . Nemojte dopustiti da me se!*" The old man slipped back beneath the shroud of unconsciousness.

Sonny lightly slapped Dmitri's waxen face. "C'mon, Dmitri, please wake up. It's Sonny, your friend. Please wake up, Dmitri. I need your help. Please, Dmitri, will you help me?"

No good. The old man was gone, now breathing in quick, gasping breaths. Sonny rang for the duty nurse. The RN, Renee DeWitte, appeared almost instantly, smiling brightly. "What's wrong, sir? Why did you push the call button?"

"Nurse, the man's substantially unconscious, and when he does surface, he talks gibberish. Is anything wrong?"

Dr. Boslow, the attending physician, walked into the room. "Thank you, Nurse. I'll take it from here." The nurse smiled and left the room. "My name is Dr. Boslow, and I'm watching Dmitri tonight. How's our patient doing?"

Sonny extended his hand, and the doctor reluctantly shook it. "Sonny Mildauer, Doctor. A few minutes ago, Dmitri woke up and started spouting gibberish. Then he passed out, and I've been unable to rouse him."

"I think Dmitri just treated you to a few lines of his native language when you woke him up. We've been keeping very close tabs on your friend, Sonny. He's probably a little groggier than usual due to the Versed we gave him for a routine procedure this afternoon. Just be patient with him. He's fine. OK?"

Of course, *there it was* . . . Dmitri had suddenly awakened from deep sleep, must have been dreaming, and he'd started babbling in *whatever* language that was.

Bending over the bed, the physician spoke. "Dmitri, your friend Sonny is here. Do you want to talk to him? You must speak in English, Dmitri. Sonny does not understand Croatian," the doctor said softly.

This time, the old man's eyes popped open, and a smile crossed his face. "Sonny is here?"

"Yes, Dmitri. How are you feeling?" the doctor asked.

"Sleepy . . . but Sonny has come to visit. Please show him in!"

Dr. Boslow chuckled. "He's right here, sir. I'll leave you two alone now, OK?"

"OK, thanks, Doc," Dmitri slurred.

"He's all yours, Sonny. I need to go now."

"Thank you, Doctor," Sonny said, but the physician was already halfway out the door. "Hi, Dmitri. How are you feeling?"

"Pretty good, Sonny, but very sleepy. Today all I do is sleep. After procedure. Are you well?"

"Yes, my friend, very well. But I need to speak to you concerning an urgent matter. Are you ready?"

The old man chuckled. "Of course I know 'urgent matter,' my friend. All of my life is urgent matter, do you see?"

"I do see, Dmitri. But this is about your mother."

But no answer came. Dmitri was fast asleep, snoring softly. Sonny left the room, closing the door quietly behind him.

The Docks: Agents Locke and Redding decided to take a cruise along the loading docks, as much to break the monotony as anything else. All manner of delivery trucks—vans, flatbeds, semis—rumbled incessantly up and down the service road, delivering and picking up cargo.

Once, Scott thought he saw a black truck matching Sonny's description, but then he recognized the familiar text neatly painted on its side: Ready Freight & Hauling, Newark, NJ. Ready Freight was a reputable firm, with no violations that he was aware of. Strike one.

They trolled slowly along the docks, boxed in by transport haulers. Right now, they were trapped behind a semi, and their view was completely blocked. Scotty pulled off the road, guiding the Crown Vic onto the right shoulder.

"Whatcha doin', Scott?" Red asked.

"We can't see a damn thing, Red. I'm pulling off to wait for a hole behind a smaller vehicle." Big Red nodded her affirmation. Scotty was right; they were there to observe, after all.

Two hours to go, Julia Redding thought with satisfaction. Tonight had seemed particularly long and tedious, and she was eager for it to be over. Scott spotted an opening and nosed the big car back out into the stream of traffic. This time, they were behind a small, empty flatbed; much better.

As they drove slowly past dock after dock, Julia glanced to her right, fascinated by the huge cranes hoisting cargo containers off the decks of tired-looking freighters. For some reason, one of the ships caught her eye, and she strained to read the name on the side: *Solidarność.* Solidarity.

Training her gaze on the ship's mast, Julia saw a Polish flag snapping in the wind. Feeling a vague pinch in her gut—call it a hunch, or maybe a premonition—she switched on her PDA and ran an Internet search on the ship. *Solidarność* was indeed a Polish freighter, but it was leased by a Russian company operating out of Novaya Zemlya. *Hmmm . . . maybe this warrants a closer look . . . .*

Julia searched ship's records, ownership information, registration, and, finally, the crew roster. For some reason, the captain's name caught her eye. "Scotty, does the name Boris Borolev mean anything to you?"

Scotty looked as if he'd been poleaxed as he turned to face Julia. "*Hell, yeah*, Red! Boris Borolev was the captain of the ship that smuggled the alien remains in from Russia! How the hell did you . . ."

"Never mind that now, Scotty. He's the captain of that freighter we just passed—the Polish one, *Solidarity*. Better turn around—*now!*"

CIA Headquarters, Washington, D.C, 2006: Sonny Mildauer answered the receptionist's page. "Sonny here, Jill. What's up?"

"Well, Sonny, I have an FPS driver here at the front desk with a package for Agent Sam Bowdrich or a designee. I don't have a record of Sam Bowdrich. Will you sign for it?"

"Sam *Bowdrich*?" Sonny replied, incredulous. "Sam's been dead for five years! I knew him briefly when I first hired in. He had a heart attack in the cafeteria. You have a package for him?"

"Yes, Sonny," Jill replied, "or a designee."

Sonny sighed. "I'll be right out, Jill."

Agent Mildauer was overextended this morning and extremely busy. He signed for the parcel and made his way to the cold case vault, where he logged the package. The attendant swung open the heavy door and placed the bulging envelope in Lockbox A.C.7.1221, row A, column C, level 7, location 1221.

Sonny immediately put the matter out of his mind and resumed work on his quarterly case summary. He would not think about Lockbox A.C.7.1221 again for years.

The Present: Agents Locke and Redding sprang from their patrol car in front of the freighter *Solidarity*, guns drawn. Julia was fully aware that they were pushing the limits of their authority—probably exceeding them, in fact. But bluster and brashness had brought her this far. *Why shift gears now if it works for ya?*

Scott was in a state of near-paralysis, and he hung back several steps as Julia strode toward the boarding ramp. They flashed their badges. "CIA! Request permission to board!" Julia barked.

The two thugs at the base of the boarding ramp seemed confused, unable to respond. They spoke rapidly to each other in a foreign tongue, and finally the larger man turned to face Julia. "Please wait here, Agent. I must get the Captain."

A moment later, the hulk reappeared with a cadaverous-looking man who must have been the captain. Although he moved along briskly, the old man leaned heavily on a cane as he walked. The pair paused at the head of the boarding ramp, and the old man stood ramrod-straight, smiling. "Please let me welcome you aboard," he spoke in a surprisingly steady, robust voice. "I am Captain Borolev, Ship's Master, and I will see you now. We are not armed. Your weapons will not be needed here, I assure you."

Julia shot a glance at Scott, and both agents holstered their pistols.

Scott was first to set foot on the deck, and Julia followed shortly. The pair introduced themselves as CIA agents, flashing their badges imperiously. Captain Borolev's expression remained impassive as he greeted his visitors with a firm handshake. "How may I help you?" he asked.

Surprisingly, Scott spoke. "Captain, we want to ask you a few questions regarding a shipment you delivered to this country from Russia in 1979. It was comprised of about three large crates of, ah, artifacts. The originator was one Aleksei Korsaskaya, a lieutenant in the Soviet Army. Do you recall this, sir?"

Borolev replied without hesitation. "Of course. Aleksei is my personal friend. The shipment arrived safely and was loaded onto trucks for land delivery. Beyond that, I have no information."

"Where was delivery to be made?" Julia asked.

"To your offices, madam—the CIA."

"Do you have a record of the delivery orders?"

The captain laughed pleasantly. "Oh, no, my friends. It has been many years, you see? But I can tell you the name of the carrier."

"Was it Short Run Freight Hauling?"

"Yes."

"Did you use them regularly?" Julia asked.

"We did, until they became unreliable," the Captain replied. "Why do you ask?"

"We can't find anything on the books for them. It's as if they never existed."

"That does not surprise me, Agent. But I can give you names . . . ."

On the heels of his aborted encounter with Dmitri Vasiliev at the hospice, Sonny Mildauer drove back to his office at the CIA Headquarters building. The pink-orange glow of the rapidly setting sun emblazoned the western sky as he wheeled his Lincoln MXZ into the agency's sprawling parking garage. He killed the engine and walked briskly to the elevator, where he pushed the button for the ninth floor.

Sonny needed to think, and his now-silent office provided the perfect environment for reflection and introspection. How many evenings just like this one had turned to dusk as Sonny grappled with one problem or another? And how many times had the answer come, like a revelation, just as his wall clock chimed midnight?

Countless times, Sonny thought as he reached into the bottom desk drawer for his pint of Cognac. He poured a generous portion over the three ice cubes he'd retrieved from his mini-fridge and settled back into his reclining desk chair. Sonny punched up Vaughan Williams's *The Lark Ascending* on his CD player, took a sip of his Cognac, and closed his eyes.

His mind whirled with the details of the case: Aleksei Korsaskaya's discovery in a Siberian warehouse; missing extraterrestrial remains, smuggled from Russia in 1979; film canisters in an old woman's coffin; records of a saucer crash in Siberia. *It was all right there, but just out of his reach.*

Sonny was sleepy. He set his drink on the desk and leaned back farther in his recliner. Linking his fingers behind his head, he sighed deeply and immediately began to drift off to . . . *Bowdrich . . ." . . . or a designee. Will you sign . . ."*

Let's see . . . Sam Bowdrich had probably died in the fall of 2001. Everyone was still reeling from the shock of 9-11 when the news of Sam's death further rocked the insular world of their office. He recalled protracted discussions, speculations that the bombing might have contributed to Sam's demise. In fact, Bowdrich had been easily forty pounds overweight, all belly fat, and he'd died happy, with a half-masticated glob of cafeteria cheeseburger still fermenting in his mouth. Hypothesis rejected.

Sonny took a healthy gulp of his drink and lit another cigarette . . . . *Sam's been dead for five years* . . . . He remembered making that statement as clearly as if it had happened yesterday. OK, so, 2006. Time to call the cold case vault. Sonny punched the extension into his office phone, hoping that someone was manning the vault tonight.

He let the phone ring ten times before hanging up.

Sonny Mildauer usually felt more refreshed after two or three hours' sleep in his office chair than he did after eight hours in his own bed. He found it impossible to get comfortable there, ever since Dana's passing. This foggy Saturday morning, however, proved to be the exception. He'd slept fitfully, as the previous day's events manifested themselves in disturbing dreamscape parodies of reality: Julia Redding behind the wheel of an orange Pontiac Firebird, driving them to post office after post office to retrieve a package from overseas; Dmitri Vasiliev pushing him in a wheelchair along a sandy beach, past a series of long-forgotten graveyards, never stopping; dissecting a six-fingered cadaver in his college anatomy class, embarrassed to be wearing only his boxer shorts . . .

Whew. Maybe he'd take a shot or two of Bailey's in his coffee this morning. Fortunately, it was Saturday, and the offices were deserted. Sonny's shirt was soaked with sweat, and he recoiled at the smell. His office was well-appointed, though; in addition to a modest 5 x 8-foot window overlooking the city, it featured a small lavatory with a stall shower. And Sonny always kept a change or two of clothes in his side closet.

Sonny lit the day's first cigarette while he put the coffee on to brew. He showered and shaved quickly and slipped on a fresh shirt and tie. His sweat-soaked rags lay in a heap on the bathroom floor. Housekeeping could deal with them on Monday.

When he returned to his desk, the coffee was ready. Sonny lit another cigarette, poured a cupful, and added a generous dollop of Bailey's Irish Cream, along with four packets of sugar. Mustn't skimp on breakfast, he mused, smiling wryly. It's the most important meal of the day.

The red message light on Sonny's desk phone caught his eye. It was a voice mail from Scott Locke: "Sonny, Agent Scott Locke here. I spoke with Captain Borolev this evening at the docks, and I have some very interesting information for you. Will you be in your office tomorrow, on Saturday? I'll be off duty, and I'd like to brief you ASAP on what we found out. Please give me a call. Locke out."

Sonny shook his head. He hadn't even heard his phone ring. He checked the time of the message: 2:15 a.m. It was now 9:30. He called Scotty.

Scott Locke bolted awake to the insistent ring of his phone. He stumbled across the room, his head throbbing and his right eyelid stuck shut. He answered on the fourth ring. "Scott Locke here."

"Scotty, it's Agent Mildauer. How are you this morning?"

"I'm fine, sir, just fine," Scotty lied. "Did you get my message?"

"Yes, and I'd like to talk to you in person. Can you drop by the office today?"

"Of course, Sonny. I can be there in an hour, if that's OK."

"Fine, Scotty, thanks. See you then."

"Yessir. Locke out."

Ahh, fuck, he thought. Rushing to the kitchen, Scotty poured the dregs of yesterday's coffee into his cup and heated it in the microwave. He opened the kitchen cabinet and fumbled the cap off a bottle of Excedrin. He shook three tablets into his palm and washed them down with a stream of the scalding liquid.

His mouth and throat throbbed with pain, but he was definitely awake. As he showered, his headache subsided to a tolerable level, and the gluey substance on his eyelid dissolved. No time to shave, but Scotty was blessed with light-colored facial hair that grew slowly. Fifteen minutes later, he was on the road to brief Sonny.

For the next hour or so, Agent Mildauer listened intently to Scotty's account of the recent events, quizzing him regularly on the details. Scotty found himself mildly annoyed as Scotty typed furiously on his Core computer during the entire interview. What he did not know was that Mildauer was entering the information into Sherlock, Core's new, consumer-driven answer to its competitor's program that had flattened its human opponents on the popular game show *Peril* the previous year. Sonny had watched the competition, even though he detested the swaggering, mustachioed host, a French Canadian by the odd name of Alfy Sqebel.

Crik was incredible, but unaffordable; the program hogged over 2,000 processor cores and seventeen terabytes of RAM. Sherlock's advantages over Crik amounted to hardware requirements and cost; Sherlock sold for around $10,000 and would run on a single HyperMax Quantinium computer.

Olan Hobbes, Core's founder and still its president and CEO, had made the right call once again. The 80-year-old genius had seen the writing on the wall when JCL's Syballine Green system handily beat the reigning international chess champion, Kenyan Aazzi Xzyhenia, in the second round of a best two-of-three competition. Over the board of directors' objections, Hobbes liquidated a substantial chunk of his own company stock and formed a subsidiary company called CricketAI to develop affordable software that would skunk JCL in the consumer market but still run on existing Core computers. The rest was relatively easy, really. Core's unique parallel-processor architecture was ideally suited to the task. Hobbes simply turned his team of rogue hackers loose on the problem, sat back, and three years later, Sherlock was born.

In Sonny's opinion, Sherlock worked pretty damn well, most of the time. He'd watched it win hands-down in several popular TV game shows, including *Let's Make a Fortune* and *Wheel of Consequences*; plus, it had trounced three rank amateur chess players.

And you could actually buy it and run it—*right now. Good enough for government work,* Sonny said to himself.

The interview was over. Sonny lit a cigarette and rode the elevator to the parking garage. He had to talk to Dmitri.

Dmitri Vasiliev was awake and coherent, apparently having shaken off the effects of yesterday's Versed. It was breakfast time, and Renee DeWitte was lovingly spoon-feeding her patient from a bowl of oatmeal. The morning fog had lifted, and the bright early afternoon sunshine bathed the room in a golden light.

"How about some bacon, Dmitri?" Renee asked. "It's nice and crispy, just the way you like it."

Dmitri smiled. "Yes, Nurse, please. The bacon would be a delight."

"Mmmm . . . I like it when you call me Nurse, Dmitri. Open wide; here it comes." Renee gently placed the meat on his tongue and smiled as he masticated the salty pork. "Now for the poached eggs, honey—your favorite!"

Renee DeWitte had proven to be nothing short of a blessing for Dmitri. The RN had taken an immediate liking to her patient, and she doted on him like a mother hen. To Renee's delight, she found that Dmitri was still very capable of an erection, and she took every opportunity to provide him with stimulation and release. After all, Dr. Domenici had prescribed sex therapy for Dmitri on a PRN basis, as circumstances required.

This is one sexy old man, Renee thought as she spooned poached egg into Dmitri's mouth, dabbing the residue from his chin with a linen napkin. Although deep lines creased his face, Dmitri's chiseled features remained fully intact, even exacerbated, perhaps, by his wasting disease. Sildenafil (Viagra) was approved as an adjunct to sex therapy, and Renee injected regular doses of the drug into Dmitri's IV tube. Dmitri was going to die a happy man if Renee DeWitte had anything to say about it! She rightly assumed that Dr. Domenici would approve.

Renee leaned in closer, her barely restrained breasts now hovering inches from Dmitri's face. "How's Mr. Stiffy this morning, Dmitri? Should we wake him up, do you think?"

Dmitri smiled devilishly. "Mr. Stiffy never sleeps, Renee. He's on duty 24–7."

"Hold that thought, Dmitri," Renee said, rising to her feet. "Let me secure the perimeter." The nurse's stiletto-heeled pumps clicked across the floor, and Dmitri heard the familiar clack of the deadbolt snapping into place.

Sonny Mildauer had always possessed a singular talent for arriving at the most inopportune time. This day proved to be no exception. Nurse DeWitte was stripped down to her bra and panties, and Dmitri was on the verge of the orgasm of his life when a knock came at the door. "Agent Sonny here. May I come in?"

A woman's voice shrieked from within, "No! Go away! Come back later!"

Sonny made his way down to the lobby and poured himself a cup of rank instant coffee. Evidently, he had interrupted a liaison between Dmitri and his nurse. Good on ya, old man!

Sonny spent the next half hour paging dispassionately through outdated magazines—*People, Eastern Shore Real Estate Guide, Fisherman's Digest.* His mind wandered to Scotty's briefing. He squirmed in the uncomfortable plastic chair. Finally, he could bear it no more. Tossing his magazine aside, Sonny strode to the elevator and rode it to the parking garage. He'd be back later to talk with Dmitri.

Louis Babich hadn't heard the phone ringing. He'd been inside the vault when Sonny's call came. Babich was a happy man. He was drawing double overtime pay for working on a Saturday. Cold-case storage space was seriously overtaxed due to a backlog of mostly junk that had accumulated over the years. It was Louis's job to purge the vaults on weekends so as not to interfere with the facility's normal operations. Checking his manifest, Babich noticed that the contents of three old vaults were past due for incineration. *Best to start with the oldest one first,* he thought.

LV-51A had been inactive for decades, Babich noted. The most recent access had been back in December, 1981, three years before he was born. He'd call for a forklift to haul the contents of Large Vault 51A to the incinerator, including three big crates filled with alien remains and artifacts. He'd just picked up the phone when he heard the buzzer sound. Louis dropped the handset in its cradle and headed for the door.

Dmitri had fallen fast asleep after Nurse DeWitte finished draining him of his essential fluid. At first, his dreams were pleasant—past lovers writhing in the throes of passion, General Primakov pinning the Order of Suvarov medal on his chest. But abruptly, Dmitri's journey through shadowland took a dark turn. Strange-looking beings roamed the streets of some unknown village, randomly vaporizing its inhabitants with some kind of handheld weapon. In what appeared to be a medical laboratory, an alien-looking baby struggled free of what appeared to be a cocoon. An Old Testament passage—"Your old men shall dream dreams, your young men shall see visions"—droned sepulchrally in the background. A pretty woman in a white lab coat withdrew a shrimplike object from a long transparent tube and carefully deposited it in something vaguely resembling a microwave oven.

Suddenly Dmitri was running for his life across a dream field littered with mutilated bodies. He reeled. A dark, fuzzy shape loomed in the overcast sky, immolating people with beams of light as they ran for cover. For whatever reason, he looked down. A small grayish box lay before him. Dmitri picked it up. There was an inscription on the side that looked like ZL}M8W. Oddly, he thought he understood it: "The truth source."

Dmitri ran now, swiftly crossing the killing field, his fingers tingling from contact with the box. In his panic, he stumbled, dropping to one knee. In the corner of his eye, something moved. He turned to look.

There, writhing in a pool of blood and entrails lay the disemboweled form of a woman named Svetlana.

His mother! The wraith reached out to him, but try as he might, Dmitri could not move. Dmitri bolted awake with the apparition's croaking voice echoing in his head: "Tell Sonny . . . the truth source is with me . . . you must tell Sonny . . ."

Dmitri Vasiliev turned and vomited copiously into his bedpan, then pushed the Big Red call button. A minute later, the cute young night nurse appeared. "Is something wrong, Dmitri? Oh, you've vomited! I'll call the doctor . . . ."

"No, no, wait, Amelia, please. I just had a very bad dream. I felt sick for a moment. But I must talk to someone right away. It is urgent. You remember Agent Sonny, yes?"

Amelia smiled. "Yes, Dmitri, of course. Your friend. Let me get your phone, and I'll call him for you now, OK?"

Dmitri sank back into his pillow, breathing in quick gasps. "Thank you, Amelia. Please, right away. Very important . . ."

The nurse punched the agent's number into the keypad; her pretty brow furrowed. "I'm only getting his voice mail. Do you have another number?"

"Please, try his cell—978-555-3815."

After a moment, Amelia said, "Agent Sonny? Amelia at hospice here . . . . Yes, he seems to be doing fine, but he wanted me to call . . . . Yes, right away sir." The nurse handed the phone to her patient. "Sonny's on the line, Dmitri. I'm going now. Press the call button if you need anything, OK?"

"Thanks, Amelia. Hello, Sonny. Dmitri. I need to talk to you right away," he said as the nurse left the room.

Agent Sonny Mildauer had just rescued from incineration what was probably history's most important evidence of extraterrestrial life. "Agent Babich, I'm impounding the contents of this vault under authority of the Alien Seduction Act of 1944 and the Patoit Act of 1992. I have strong evidence . . ." *deedledeedledeedle.* Sonny grabbed his cell; it was Dmitri's hospital phone. "Stand by one, Babich." Sonny walked to a corner of the small office and answered the call, speaking softly. "Amelia? Is he all right? Yes—yes, Amelia, put him on—Sonny here. How are you, Dmitri?"

"Still drawing the breath, Agent Sonny, and in no pain. Thank you. But I must talk very soon to you in person. Please come quickly. It is very important—about the aliens . . ."

"I'll be there as soon as I can, Dmitri—tonight. I need to go now. Hang in there, old friend. I'm on my way."

Sonny spun on his heel, pinioning Babich with an icy glare. "Agent Babich, do not—I repeat, do not—dispose of the contents of this vault, or any other, until further notice. This is a matter of national security—and probably the survival of mankind. Take care of your paperwork, whatever you can find to do. I realize you're counting on the overtime pay—and clock out. But heed my warning, son, or you'll spend the rest of your days breaking rocks in Panama. Are we clear?"

Babich's face had turned a waxy yellow, and he gulped painfully before replying. "Yes, sir, Agent Sonny! We are crystal clear. You can count on me, sir. I swear!"

Sonny rolled his eyes as he turned toward the door. "Fuck this one up, Babich, and you're toast! You can count on it, I swear!" The metal door slammed shut behind him, and mercifully, Sonny Mildauer was gone.

CHAPTER VII

On his way to the elevator, Sonny heard his cell's *deedle* again. Caller ID displayed Agent Scott Locke's number. Sonny walked to a corner and picked up. "Sonny here. What is it, Scotty?"

"Got something really intriguing for ya, Chief," the young agent panted into the phone. "Captain Borolev told us about something that looked like embryos in one of Dmitri's shipments. Then he mentioned a second parcel. I tracked the parcel and retrieved the scanned information from CIA records. There really were some things in tubes that looked like embryos. I did some more research online . . . ."

Sonny sighed. "Yeah, you mentioned that, Scotty. This is fascinating, but is there a punch line? I'd love to hear it, son."

"Yeah—at least I think so, sir. An addendum to the files mentioned something. 'Sample class B/UO, specimens 001–061 routed/expedite/ HRF/RM/VA00172/M2/SC31(a)/1698.' Sonny, sample class B/UO means 'biological, undetermined origin'! No further information at this point. Shall I dig deeper, sir?"

"Shit, Scotty, yeah! Good work. Thanks for the call. Let me know as soon as you find something, OK? Call me back at this number, 24/7."

"Yessir. Will do, Sonny! Locke out."

<u>Ten Years Earlier</u>: Dr. Rudy Mendoza was living his dream. The first human-extraterrestrial hybrid was now a reality. Now twenty-one days old, the tiny four-pound neonate's condition had stabilized following a respiratory infection. Little Ilse was responding

satisfactorily to atypical broad-spectrum antibiotics and monoclonal antibodies. She was now resting comfortably in a stainless-steel incubator that bore an eerie resemblance to a very large microwave oven. For some reason, that grim similarity painted a smirk across Mendoza's thin lips.

Rudy's knowledge of his ancestry was sketchy, bordering on nonexistent. His Argentine parents, desperate to sever ties to their sordid lineage, had successfully hidden the truth from their son; Rudy's uncle had been none other than Nazi butcher Josef Mengele, the so-called "Angel of Death." In the waning days of World War II, parents Alois and Eva Mengele wove a convoluted path through Denmark, Britain, Canada, the United States (briefly), Cuba, Honduras, Venezuela . . . and finally settled in Argentina, having adopted the surname Mendoza somewhere along the way. Alois also changed his given name to Luis.

Following this ordeal, their ancestry had been successfully blurred to near obscurity. Rudolph Mendoza's younger brother, Alberto, was stillborn in 1956. A sister, Eve, miscarried in 1961. Finally, in 1965, Rudolph was born to the 42-year-old Eva.

From his earliest years, Rudy exhibited borderline sociopathic traits, behavior that was not well-recognized at the time and therefore successfully downplayed by his parents. In 1974, an Argentine social worker finally diagnosed Rudolph as having a mild learning disorder, patted him on the head, and sent him on his way.

Little Rudy's "animal experiments" never came to light. In their defense, Luis and Eva Mendoza were never fully aware of what went on in their son's "laboratory." When Rudy expressed an interest in biology and medicine, they were thrilled. There was an old building way out on the far southeast corner of their family farm. Could he use it as his lab—*pleeeeze?*

Momma Eva had crooned, "Honey, why don't you use the toolshed? It's right here in the yard. You'd need to throw away all that old junk, but . . ." Papa nodded contentedly, mumbling around a mouthful of breakfast sausage and potato pancakes. "Go ahead, son. Just take the toolshed."

Young Rudy rejected the suggestion outright. "No. You don't understand. I need specimens for my work. The toolshed is too close to the house. All the activity around here scares the animals away."

Momma and Papa exchanged significant glances. After a brief pause, his father spoke. "Go ahead, son. It's your lab, after all. Use the shed out in the field if you want."

They'll never walk out there, Rudy thought. *It's too far . . .*

That was true. Luis and Eva still farmed a little, but of late, their activity was confined to a small plot close to the house. It could probably be more accurately termed "gardening." They raised a lot of food, but only to keep fresh produce on the table and earn a few argentinos peddling canned fruits and vegetables in the square. Papa had just landed a good job at the new ethanol plant, and Momma hauled in piles of dough providing in-home care for the elderly. Of course, his parents weren't getting any younger. Mama would turn fifty-five in September, and osteoarthritis was gradually reducing her to a cripple. Papa had just celebrated his sixtieth birthday, but lately his mind was like a sieve; Mama rightly feared that senility was setting in.

So, twelve-year-old Rudy set about renovating the decrepit shed on the pasture's edge. He hauled literally tons of pure junk—rusty engine blocks, rotting three-legged chairs, drum after drum of expended engine oil—into the woods adjacent to the field. He patched holes in the roof with metal scavenged from a mountain of Papa's beer cans he found in a corner of the building. He spliced an old army surplus generator he'd converted to burn ethanol into makeshift wiring scrounged from a home demolition project up the road. Using scraps of wood from the same demolition, he reinforced rotted sections of the shed's frame and roof joists. Workbenches purloined from Papa's toolshed near the farmhouse (the old man's mind was going fast, and he never noticed the loss) completed Rudy's basic requirements. Still, though, the place smelled musty, and the budding physician was less than pleased. *No matter, though*, Rudy thought; soon the lab would be filled with the heady aroma of decaying animal carcasses!

Actual lab equipment such as cages and glassware would have to come later as opportunities presented themselves. For the time being, a length of baling wire wrapped snugly around a tail or leg and a seemingly inexhaustible supply of Mama's old Mason jars would serve his purposes. Of course, there was always Papa's ethanol available for sterilization and short-term specimen storage—not to mention an occasional nip.

Back in Papa's toolshed, Rudy considered the options as he methodically whetted knife after knife from a discarded kitchen set. The boy couldn't wait to get started.

Dmitri was alert and eager to talk when Sonny walked into his room. Wisely, the agent had swung by the liquor store for a fifth of Stoli and a carton of Marlboros. He sincerely liked Dmitri, and the old man fairly beamed when he spied his guest's tokens of appreciation. Sonny smiled back at him. "How's my friend feeling tonight, Dmitri?"

Dmitri shrugged, still smiling broadly. "I have morphine on demand, my friend, and so never pain. How bad can it be, Sonny? I am dying, as is all of mankind, but I have a happy life for now."

The two men hugged. "Ahh, Dmitri, how I wish that you should live forever," Sonny sighed.

Tears welled in the old man's eyes. "Thank you, Sonny. But I would not wish the curse of eternal life in these rotting bodies upon anyone. Forgive me?"

An odd, distracted look crossed the agent's face. After a brief pause, Sonny said, "I come with gifts. Would you prefer a shot or a cigarette first, Dmitri?"

"Both together, Sonny, I think."

"You got it, pal," Sonny said, stripping the cellophane from a pack of Marlboro Reds. Reaching into his satchel, he produced the bottle of vodka and two plastic shot glasses.

Scott Locke was back at his office, deeply engrossed in his Internet search. Scotty had taken the liberty of writing his own sophisticated algorithm to further glean the search results from his Sherlock natural-language software. Scotty found that it had been time well spent. His Holmes program allowed him to filter Sherlock data based on any number of criteria, including security classification, biometric profile, lineage and ancestry, psychological profile . . . .

And he had a solid hit! Dr. Rudolph Mendoza: Argentine immigrant; naturalized citizen; German WWII parents; psych data pointing to narcissism and borderline sociopathy; Amsell Award, 2006 in hybrid genetics and embryology; CIA affiliation—Embryo Research Project (no further information available—security class Top Secret). Scotty thought back to the number he'd seen on the shipping addendum. He pulled it up on his screen:

HRF/RM/VA00172/M2/SC31(a)/1698.

RM—Rudolph Mendoza? VA—Virginia? Sometimes Scotty saw patterns that didn't exist, so he pulsed Sherlock again with his new conjectures.

Bingo! FIA (Freedom of Information Act) records placed Dr. Rudolph Mendoza at the Hybrid Research Facility in Lee County, Virginia. A stream of cryptic characters followed:

No further information available—NSPA restricted data. National security protection class enforced . . . nspaclass per ref doc ISPNOM/010318/NSPACONUSC31(a) (SPECPRO 13.2.23).

Scotty's mind reeled. To most people, the alphabet soup would have been totally incomprehensible. And for the most part, Scotty had no idea what the long string of gibberish meant. But 010318? He immediately recognized the numbers as mil speak for March 18, 2001. That was all he needed. Scotty chuckled, rubbing his palms together. Just like assembling a jigsaw puzzle!

Dmitri dragged deeply, gratefully, on his Marlboro as Sonny poured vodka into the two shot glasses. Sonny had cheated a little—the plastic cups accommodated two ounces, not one. He thought Dmitri would be pleasantly surprised. "The Stoli's warm; hope that's OK, Dmitri . . . ."

Dmitri smiled and wagged an index finger. "There is no bad Stoli, my friend. *Salut!*"

Dmitri was right; the friends toasted repeatedly, first to knowledge, then to friendship. Next they drank to the future of mankind and what it might hold. Finally, with six ounces of alcohol coursing through his veins, Dmitri spoke.

"Sonny, I lately have very disturbing dreams. One in particular seems, how you say, prophetic? Do you believe in these things, Sonny?"

"I never rule out anything, Dmitri."

A fevered expression crossed Dmitri's face. "Sonny, can you do this one thing? We must exhume my mother! She spoke to me, Sonny. In my heart, I know it was real. She said something called the 'truth source' was with her—and that must be in her grave. There were other things, horrible things, Sonny! There were some kind of, how you say, mutants? They looked like men, but also not. They were going from village to village . . . ." Dmitri paused for a moment, winded. "They had these ray guns, or something, Sonny—and they were shooting people. The fields were filled with rotting bodies. Mama spoke to me. She said, 'Talk to Sonny!' I think this truth source is in her grave, Sonny. Momma said you must have it!"

"Why, Dmitri? Why do I need to have this thing?"

Dmitri said softly, "I do not know, my friend. Perhaps you need it to save the world from itself."

Sonny sighed. "If we want to exhume your mother, I need you to sign some papers. America is like that, you know? May I bring them by tomorrow, Dmitri?"

Dmitri now looked very ill. Gazing up at Sonny with jaundiced eyes, he croaked, "Of course. Mother wants it. I pity you, my friend. If you hold this truth source, you will be responsible for leading the people against these mutants. My time grows short, Sonny. I know this. How I hate to pass this knowledge to you, my friend." Dmitri began to sob.

"Dmitri, what makes you think these mutants really exist? Or ever will exist?" Sonny asked.

"I am not sure, my friend. There may be something as simple as just knowing."

"Dmitri, do you recall burying such a box with your mother?"

"I do not really know. Please forgive me, Sonny. It was a very long time ago. It is all very blurry now, you see?"

"I do see, Dmitri. I guess we need to bring your mother's body to light, and then we will know for certain, one way or the other," Sonny said.

Dmitri was beginning to drift off to sleep. "Please, Sonny, bring by the papers tomorrow, and I will sign. We have to know."

Spring in Argentina—November, 1987: Rudy Mendoza could barely still his shaking hands as he tore at the manila envelope. The return address read, "University of Virginia School of Medicine"!

Rudy actually vomited into his hand when he read the first line of the neatly typed letter: " . . . reviewed your application for admission into our Experimental Medicine program . . . schedule an on-campus interview with the department chair, Kenneth Hastings, MD, PhD, to discuss your curriculum . . . your academic advisor, Dr. Douglas Malrouth . . . admission requirements for Summer Intersession, 1987 (attached) . . . submit official transcripts no later than December 15th . . ." Rudy found it impossible to focus. Words and phrases randomly leapt out at him from the page. But the overall message was unmistakable: he'd been accepted by an American medical school!

Months earlier, he'd written to UVa purely on a whim, never expecting to be accepted, and he had no idea where to go from here. Passport? Educational visa? Application for U.S. citizenship?

Reality punched him hard in the gut, and Rudy vomited again. He had a lot of work to do, and finals started next week. He'd probably have to postpone the closing defense of his PhD thesis.

Ahh, SHIT! When it rains—whether bad or good—it pours!

Scotty's call caught Sonny snoozing behind his desk in his big office chair. He grabbed his cell phone . . . 10:16 p.m. Aww, no! The vodka had apparently taken its toll—and he HAD to attend the staff meeting tomorrow at 7:00, sharp. Did he have a clean shirt in his closet? He thought he did . . . .

"Sonny here. What's up, Scotty?"

"Geez, chief," Scotty replied. "You sound really groggy. Sorry for calling so late. Let me call you back tomorrow."

"Naw, Scotty, whatcha got? I just dozed off for a bit. Wuzzup?"

Scotty sounded wound as tight as a guitar string, and Sonny detected a slight tremble in his voice. "You won't believe this, Sonny. Here's the skinny. I did some online research using Sherlock and my own program, Holmes. I think there were alien embryos on Borolev's tramp freighter back in the 'seventies, and I think they wound up at a top-secret CIA lab in Lee County, Virginia. There appears to be a Dr. Rudolph Mendoza doing research on them.

This doctor took the Amsell Award in 2006. It's a $50,000 cash prize recognizing groundbreaking research in hybrid genetics and embryology."

"Scotty," Sonny interrupted, "are you thinking this Dr. Mendoza is working on human-alien hybrids?"

"No way to tell, sir. Classification level's too high. I couldn't hack through the firewall. But do you want my personal opinion?"

"I do, Scotty. I do."

There was a brief silence, and Sonny heard a click as Scotty swallowed hard. "Well, sir, there was an unsubstantiated incident in Carlisle in 2007. Apparently a bunch of men in black suits appeared out of nowhere and took over the sheriff's investigation. Nothing more was ever heard after that, but . . ." Scotty paused, searching for the right words.

"But what, Scotty, what? It's already been a rough day, and I don't need any more drama. Spit it out, son!"

"Sorry, chief. There was no sheriff's report, but I found a single newspaper article. The event seems to have been covered only by a local rag called the *Carlisle Calumny*. Some hysterical woman had reported a naked man in her backyard. He was brandishing a knife, and Deputy Sheriff John Cady shot him dead. The story is very strange—the man, or whatever it was, was naked, hairless, and stood about seven feet tall. Grayish skin, six fingers and toes. Of course, the woman, the sole witness, 'asked not to be identified.' That's all I've got so far."

The line was silent for almost a minute before Scotty spoke again. "Are you there, sir?"

Sonny croaked, "I think so, Scotty. I need your help. Will you do something for me?"

"Shit, yes—sorry, sir. Yes, chief. What is it?"

"We have an extremely grave situation on our hands, Agent Locke. I need you to find out everything you can about that lab—and Mendoza. Report back to me ASAP."

"Yessir. Locke out."

Sonny sighed and gratefully drifted back to sleep in his office chair with a single thought on his mind: *finally, Monday is history.*

Tuesday had barely begun, and it was already proving to be even more dramatic than the previous day. Reverend Frohmunter stood in a prizefighter's crouch, his cheeks glowing bright purple. "How dare you just, just roll in here with all these infernal machines? You stand upon hallowed ground, mister! Here lie the remains of God's faithful, their souls in heaven with our Lord! What you propose is an abomination! I shall not permit disinterment from this holy soil!

"I got the court order right here, Revrint," Danny Kelly, the Goliathan backhoe operator, replied calmly. "Don' seem like there be a whole lotta call for arguin' 'bout it. Please, jis' step aside an' lemme git 'er done, OK?" Sonny stood scowling in the background, flanked by two bloated cops, his arms folded. A flatbed truck idled behind them, its ill-tuned engine spewing a plume of sooty diesel smoke into the air. Sonny walked forward, extending his hand to the outraged cleric, who folded his arms and said, "Who in the stinking vapors of hell are you?"

"Pleased to make your acquaintance, too, Reverend Frohmunter. My name is Sonny Mildauer, and I am a CIA agent. You know Dmitri Vasiliev, do you not?"

Frohmunter paused briefly, then answered. "Of course. And you are trying to exhume his dear mother, Svetlana? This I shall not permit!"

Sonny drew himself up. "Let me explain something to you, Reverend Frohmunter. Buried with Svetlana are certain—items—disguised by Dmitri as holy books to hide them from the Russians. His mother intended for Dmitri to retrieve them later. These items are from an alien spacecraft, and they could very well determine the future course of mankind. Do you understand?"

The cleric gasped incredulously. "No, sir. I do not!"

"Then understand this, Reverend. Svetlana's dying words to her son, Dmitri, were an admonition to spread this information to the world. Dmitri himself told me this! Certainly you recall the biblical passage "young men will see visions, old men will dream dreams?"

Frohmunter swallowed hard. "Certainly, I do."

"Good. Dmitri told me of a dream he had recently—alien beings roaming the countryside, vaporizing people with unknown weapons; scorched fields; corpses stacked like cordwood. Sounds like the Book of Revelation to you? Or Daniel? Me, too. In this dream, he encountered his mother, disemboweled, dying among the rotting bodies. She told him of something called a 'truth source' that was 'with her.' She's dead, Reverend . . . obviously this thing is buried with her in her grave. As Dmitri awoke, he heard her say, 'Tell Sonny . . . the truth source is with me . . . you must tell Sonny . . .'"

Reverend Frohmunter's face had turned ashen. He hesitated for a moment and then swallowed hard. Frohmunter's fiery eyes met Mildauer's. "Please proceed, Agent Sonny. Unearth Svetlana. This is a grave situation. I am sorry. I did not understand . . . ."

JULIA REDDING:
ASSIGNMENT, VIRGINIA

To say that Agent Julia Redding was dissatisfied with her reassignment would be the grossest of understatements. While Scotty had escaped rebuke following their drunken encounter with Captain Borolev, Julia had been sternly reprimanded and reassigned to a field office in Wise County, Virginia.

Her office environment was nothing short of squalid. Julia sat at a table facing the center aisle of the miserable double-wide trailer that was Wise County's CIA field headquarters. Now relegated to processing routine expense reports, Julia maintained a regular stream of e-mail chatter with Scott. For some reason, neither she nor Scott had yet become comfortable with Thumbmail, i.e., text messaging. Scotty believed his thumbs were too big, and Julia, reverting to type, contemptuously dismissed the entire technology as adolescent and somehow beneath her.

Julia was fifteen minutes early for work this Tuesday morning, as usual. Her traditionally rebellious attitude had certainly not improved since the advent of her "exile" (field assignment). She took her time, meticulously preparing a cup of coffee precisely to her liking. Ambling back to her desk, Julia opened her e-mail. Her heart jumped a little. SUBJECT: Top O' the Marnin'. FROM: *Scotty.*

It was only 7:21, and Scotty was already hard at work! Julia eagerly opened Scotty's e-mail.

Truth be told, she mildly resented Scott, but, hey, she *reeeally* liked the guy. She'd been a renegade all her life, an abrasive iconoclast, and she was growing numb to the "consequences of her actions." *I'll never change—might just as well get used to regular butt-stuffings by the zombies of the world*, Julia had thought one night on her 25-mile, back-road commute home.

After all, Scott had done nothing to hurt her; he'd just lucked out. He was working on some interesting stuff these days, too. If nothing else, Julia could participate vicariously in Scotty's relatively exciting world.

Julia's cell phone rang, startling her. No one else was in the office yet. Julia usually arrived early to work so she could get the hell out of there before it was totally dark outside. It was Scotty! "Hi, sweetie," Julia answered. "Just read your e-mail. What's going on with you?"

"Hi, honey," Scotty replied. "Just wanted to see if you'd like to meet for dinner tonight at O'Malley's Pub and Steakhouse—on the hill, remember? On 31, just past the Sunoco station? You liked your steak there, right?"

"Yeah, sure did. Sounds great, Scotty! What's the occasion?"

"Oh, nothing, nothing at all, really. Just want to talk, have fun, and enjoy a nice Delmonico and a few beers, you know?" Scotty's voice sounded a little bit tight, and it trembled slightly as he spoke. A bit too high-pitched, maybe? Sheepish?

"You're sure, Scotty? You sound a little strange this morning. Is anything bothering you?"

Scotty paused for a moment. "Well, actually, there is something I need to talk to you about."

"What is it, Scotty? Is anything wrong?" Julia's voice registered alarm as she frowned into the phone. "Just tell me, OK?"

Scott's voice trembled slightly. "Well, Julia, I, uh . . . it would really be better if we talked tonight, face-to-face. OK, hon?"

What was THIS all about, she wondered? Is he getting ready to dump me? Is he having an affair? Or . . . is he going to propose to me? "Scotty, you're fuckin' killing me here! You can't just leave me hanging like this . . . . What the hell is going on?"

She heard nothing but a hiss and crackle on her cell now. "Scotty? Scott, did I lose you, babe? Talk to me!"

"No, no, I'm here, sweetheart. I just need to tell you this tonight, OK, Red? Please?"

Julia sighed, rolling her eyes. This was totally uncharacteristic of Scott. He was always so open and straightforward—that was one of the traits she loved most about him. "Can I trust you, Scotty? You're not dumping me . . . ."

"WHAT? Julia, what the hell are you thinking, babe? I luh . . . I, well, uh, I luhh . . ."

Julia collapsed into peals of laughter just as Taylor Trask, the administrative assistant, unlocked the back door. "Scotty, I gotta go now, honey. Meet you at O'Malley's at seven?"

Scotty, obviously relieved to be let off the hook, replied warmly, "Sounds great, babe. It's a date."

"And so it is. See you then. Gotta go. 'Bye." A smiling Julia punched the END key on her cell and began frantically typing gibberish into her computer. "Well, good morning, Taylor. Is everything OK? Did you get stuck in traffic on the way in?" Julia chirped, glancing conspicuously at her watch to advertise that she'd noticed Taylor's slight tardiness. "Coffee's ready, hon. Looks like you could use a cup this morning!"

Catching Julia's sarcasm, Taylor shot back, "And maybe you could use a cup or two less during the day, Julia. You might be a little less insufferable! Incidentally, who just died and made you my boss, anyway?"

Julia smiled. Point made, well taken. But she couldn't resist another jab to the ribs. "Ooohh, a little touchy this morning, aren't we? My job as a field operative, Taylor, has taught me the keen powers of observation—and how to use them under fire!"

Taylor spun around, a merciless smirk on her lips. "OK, Julia. So whatcha doing today, Ms. Field Operative? Filling out expense reports? Observe them keenly, my dear—and meanwhile, observe me keenly while I drink my latte and flirt with Dennis all day! I've got more if you want it . . . . Come and get it!"

Julia popped Taylor the bird; Taylor returned the gesture. Rrrround one goes to Ms. Taylor Traaask, technical knockout!

Damn, she's SHARP today, Julia thought as she turned back to her computer and rapidly typed another meaningless scramble of characters.

Julia had had enough. Ms. Taylor Trask (a.k.a. Ms. Trailer Trash) had won this round, but tomorrow was another day. Tonight, Scott was going to propose to her—she'd convinced herself of it—and she didn't want to taint the experience with memories of another stunning defeat.

The day dragged on endlessly. Julia glanced at her watch, the wall clock, and the computer's time/date display every ten seconds or so—and it never seemed to get any later! She counted twenty-one smoke breaks outside in the freezing rain, and now, on her second pack, she coughed nervously, incessantly, behind her computer screen. Dennis Miles, the office manager, asked her twice if she wanted to go home—"sounds like you're coming down with something"—and Julia just glared at him, shaking her head and grunting, "No. I'm fine, Dennis. OK?"

Dennis looked concerned, though. "Julia, if you're getting sick . . . well, you don't want to spread this through the whole office, do you?"

It was 2:20. "OK, Dennis, fine," Julia spat. "I'm outta here. See you next week. Maybe."

"Take as long as you need, sweetie," a grinning Taylor Trask crooned from the front of the room. "We'll just have our trained chimp come in to cover for you. He's the one who typed all of

Shakespeare's stuff! You probably read about him—if you can actually read, that is."

Julia didn't get it, but apparently the rest of the staff did. The room erupted into gales of derisive laughter. Even gentle Dennis struggled to repress a smirk. He said, "Just go home, Julie. Take some sick leave. Get some rest, and we'll see you next week, OK?"

Julia gathered up her things and headed for the door. Someone shouted from the back of the room, "Hey, Julia, don't let that door hit you in the ass on the way out! It's got a pretty stiff spring!"

Once in the parking lot, Julia lit cigarette #22. In the pelting sleet, hot, freezing tears rolled down her cheeks. She was worthless! Every paper-pushing maggot in that stinking trailer knew it! She had failed . . . and she'd brought all their abuse on herself.

Just like always. Misery loves company—and she had spread her misery and dejection generously amongst her coworkers. When Julia ain't happy, ain't nobody happy. She'd made sport of verbally abusing every last one of her hapless coworkers.

Just like always, she thought . . . but after tonight, everything would be different. Very different. She just knew it.

CHAPTER VIII

The Unearthing

The casket teetered precariously in its chains. Sonny and Reverend Frohmunter watched in horror as the oblong box slipped free of its bonds, crashing to the ground and shattering into a thousand rotten pieces.

The box was empty, save for a few scraps of yellowed paper. Svetlana's body—and the truth source—was gone!

Sonny turned to the minister and grabbed him by his lapels. "Where the fuck is she, old man? Where's the information? Where's the truth source, you old bastard?"

Much to Sonny's surprise, the cleric coldcocked him with a devastating right cross, sending him reeling to the ground. When the stars cleared from his field of vision, Sonny gagged, realizing his throat was trapped under Frohmunter's shoe. "How dare you, you heathen piece of shit? What you imply is . . ." BANG!

Sonny's ears popped. What was left of Reverend Frohmunter now lay twitching on the ground, most of his head obliterated by a .45-caliber slug from Bloated Cop Barstow's service revolver. Sonny sat up and gazed in disbelief at the two policemen. Corporal Barstow was on his knees, sobbing uncontrollably. Bloated Cop #2 knelt beside him, attempting to console his fellow officer. Barstow wailed, "I had to stop him, Frank! I had to . . . oh, God, what have I done?" Lieutenant Frank Dunn could do nothing more than offer empty platitudes, patting Barstow on the back from time to time.

(Side note: Things didn't go well for Corporal Preston Barstow. Although he was exonerated in the grand jury investigation, the chubby little cop never forgave himself. He had killed a man of God! A year later, while still on medical leave, "Press" Barstow ate a load of buckshot from the business end of his father's ten-gauge shotgun. His ninety-pound corpse, its toe still wrapped around the trigger, was retrieved and cremated. In an ignominious county ceremony, his fellow officers scattered his ashes beneath soughing boughs in a field just behind the Ninth Precinct station house. With no other family to mourn his passing, "Press" would have approved.)

Ironically, Pastor Frohmunter's remains were interred (in a closed-casket ceremony, of course) in the very plot that had once held the body of Svetlana Vasiliev. Burial space was at a premium in the tiny church graveyard, and the parishioners seemed to think that that particular site was somehow appropriate. As Frohmunter's casket was being lowered into the ground, a stray scrap of brittle, yellowed paper danced and cavorted on the wind, heading directly toward the gravesite. It had decomposed significantly, and its shape now bore a vague resemblance to that of a skeleton key. Only Agent Sonny Mildauer, his head bowed in reverence, saw it—and chose to do nothing.

The scrap slipped beneath the elaborate casket and fell directly into the waiting grave. The casket was slowly lowered into the fertile earth. Soon, the little scrap of paper would be lost forever . . . .

Sonny bit his tongue. Perhaps some things were never meant for man to know. Had he chosen differently, he would know that one of his predecessors, Agent Alfred "Fall Guy" Falls, had unearthed the coffin eleven years earlier while the church was closed for renovation. He and his team of ghouls had waited patiently for just such a storm, and the storm had come, in spades. Beaten by merciless rain and hail, they'd loaded a plastic bag containing the body and the other relics into their van and driven to a CIA storage facility. Fall Guy had scribbled their destination on one of the little scraps of note paper in the box, adding his own line of gobbledygook: "Agency LV-51A." He'd slipped it back into the coffin—just in case.

After years of decomposition, that scrap now roughly resembled the shape of a skeleton key.

CHAPTER IX

Proposal?

Julia and Scott raised their wine glasses, toasting "to us." They both loved this place, and they sipped their wine over small talk. O'Malley's provided a casual dining environment, specifically designed to entice its dinner patrons to dine, relax, and drink—and so they did. Their waiter, Marceau (real name: Marty Friesbeck, a work-release inmate from the nearby minimum-security prison in Knotworth, just up the road), carried the second bottle of merlot with him as he approached their table.

"Madame, Monsieur—please forgive, but your steaks will be a bit longer. It is our busiest night. As you see, our house is full to capacity. May I invite you to try our finest vintage merlot? I must caution you," Marceau warned, wagging his finger, "that our merlot brut is less smoky than our house vintage, which you are now enjoying, I trust?"

A little glassy-eyed, they both nodded.

"Good. Well, then. In addition, merlot brut is drier and perhaps slightly closer to sangria than it is to the traditional merlots. More citrus, you see? Would the gentleman care to try a sample?"

"Sure, why not?" Scotty replied. Marceau filled his glass nearly to the top. "Oh, I apologize sir. I have overpoured! But do not be concerned—tasting is on the house, you see?"

Scotty took a healthy swig. "I like it, Marceau! Nice and piquant. Yeah, it's drier, and I taste the fruitiness!" He drained his glass. "This is wonderful. Please, serve it up, Marceau!"

"Sir, the merlot brut is a bit more costly than our house vintage merlot. It comes from our Athens cellar."

"Athens, Greece?" Scotty asked.

Marceau smiled a little smugly. "Ahh, Athens—just as you say, sir. This particular vintage—1968—is shipped to us directly from over the ocean, you see?"

Scotty smiled, taking the bait. The wine was actually an exotic blend of dollar-store merlot, sangria, vodka, some bitters, and balsamic vinegar concocted in Athens, New York. A little fishing boat picked up the swill in the Big Apple and sailed down the coast and dropped it at Baltimore. An unlicensed freight hauler delivered it right to O'Malley's back door.

The net bulk cost to the pub was $1.75 per bottle—and Marceau had just sold that bottle for 175 American dollars to the aspiring wine connoisseur. Sweet ——a 10,000 percent markup!

Scott looked at Julia. "Sound good, hon?"

"I don't know; you tell me. You tasted it."

Scotty's mind was made up. "Pour the lady a glass, Marceau!"

"I'd have to sell you the whole bottle, sir."

"Yes! Of course! Serve it up, Marceau. And how long for those steaks?"

All it took was one glance over his shoulder to Jeepers, the seventeen-year-old cook, who was shuffling platters of food into the window. "You both wanted your Delmonicos medium rare, yes? With baked potato, loaded? Caesar salads?"

"That's it, Marceau," Scotty slurred.

Marcel asked Julia, "You wanted medium rare?"

Julia reverted to type again. "Yes, medium rare, potato baked, smothered, Caesar. Me, too. How long?"

"Well, did you want the cheese garlic bread with your dinners? It would be faster if . . ."

Scotty grabbed the reins again, sighing. "Marceau, we want the cheese garlic bread, too. How long?"

"Please, wait a moment. I shall ask Je . . . *le chef.*"

Jeepers saw him coming. As Marty swung into the kitchen, Jeepers asked, "Garlic bread?"

"Oh, yeah! Fresh and hot."

"Great, Marty. Tell 'em about ten minutes, OK? Here, bring them their salads. That oughta shut them up for a minute!"

"Cool . . . I'll tell 'em twenty. That guy drinks like a fish. I want to peddle another bottle of Athens Cellars."

Jeepers chuckled. "Sure. You go, guy! I'll keep their stuff warm. Swing by in two minutes, and I'll have a special appetizer for you. Give it to 'em on the house. Expiration date is yesterday . . . gotta throw this shit out anyway," Jeepers said as he dropped two frozen steaks into a bowl of Italian dressing and chucked them into the microwave.

"Thanks, Jeep."

Le Chef tossed a package of frozen jalapeno-cream-cheese poppers into the deep fryer. The primary ingredient of "O'Malley's Secret Recipe" dipping sauce sat on the counter in a sticky bottle labeled *Generic Brand–Teriyaki Sauce.* Jeepers produced two finger bowls and filled them almost to the brim. A dash of olive oil and a dollop of horseradish mustard completed the recipe. Le Chef added a pinch or two of powdered chili pepper for effect. *Potatoes?* Hey, no prob; nine of them already languished in a large warming oven, prewrapped in foil. *Cheese-garlic bread?* Oh, yeah, *fresh and hot* . . . day-old Pillsbury dinner rolls covered with welfare cheese, sweating under a damp towel under infrared lights. "Tell 'em I'm putting their order ahead of all the others. Hey, they're 'special customers,' yeah?"

Jeepers was a drug addict, but in the kitchen, he was a wizard! He single-handedly ran the kitchen, possessed of an unflappable aplomb even with a full house clamoring for food. Marceau grinned, high-fiving the cook. "Oh, yeah, right you are, Jeep! Special, just like everyone else." The co-conspirators sniggered maliciously. The bell on the microwave oven chimed, and as Marceau burst through the swinging doors, he heard a familiar hiss as two Delmonicos hit the grill.

"OK, Julia, here it . . . *Marceau, bring us another bottle of Athens Cellars Classic Merlot, please!* . . . here it is, hon." Scotty reached across the table and took Julia's hands in his.

Julia fairly glowed, her fathomless brown eyes dancing in the candlelight. This was destined to be a night she'd remember forever. Julia freed one hand and took a deep swallow of her wine. Scotty said,"I'd like to propose . . ."

Julia squealed, "Yes, *YES!* Oh, of course, Scotty! I accept, my love!"

Scotty's reaction was not what Julia had expected. He gaped, looking totally perplexed. "Well, great, Red—but you might want to listen before . . ."

"Does June third work for you, Scotty? We'll make it a small ceremony, just a few friends and family, OK? Just Mom and my brother, Ken—and whoever you want to invite, of course. Ken has a friend who owns a hall, for the reception . . ."

"What on earth are you talking about, Red?" Scott asked, thrown into a complete tailspin. "What ceremony? What . . ."

"Wait, you want to marry me—*yes?*" Julia asked, equally bewildered.

"Well, yeah, possibly—eventually, maybe. But I . . ."

Julia's eyes welled up with tears. "Possibly? Eventually? *Maybe?* I . . . I . . ."

Scott's face contorted into a scowl. *"Red, you have got to shut up for a minute and just LISTEN TO ME for once! You hear me?"*

"But you *proposed* to me, you bastard!" Julia snapped. "And now you're backing out . . ."

"Julia, *LISTEN!* Shut the eff *up* and *listen* to me for a minute, will you? For once in your stubborn effing life, just *shut up!*"

A smiling Marceau appeared with more wine. "Le Chef says twenty minutes, sir. He has moved your order to first place, because you are our preferred customers—*special* customers, my friends!"

"Fine, Marceau. Just uncork the bottle and leave it here. I'll pour it."

"Uh, just one thing, sir," Marceau persisted. "Unfortunately, we have no more of the litre bottle you ordered. We now have only the two-litre available tonight. Will that be . . ."

"*Please, Marceau, just uncork the damn wine and leave us alone for a minute!*"

POP. "I am so sorry, sir. I shall return a bit later." Marceau scurried away. Woman problems—*his fish was growing bigger by the minute!*

Julia was sobbing into her napkin. "Now, Red, honey, my proposal was a *job* proposal!" Scotty said. "Nothing more than that—*for now*. I didn't realize that you felt so deeply about me, babe. If I *do* marry someone, it'll most likely be you. OK?" Scott patted her hand.

Suddenly, it was over. Julia, a veteran of pain and adversity, managed to compose herself. "Ohh, I am so *sorry*, Scotty. (*had those words actually come out of her mouth?*). After we talked this morning, I . . . I just got it in my head that . . . that . . ."

Scotty smiled disarmingly, holding both her hands in his. "Aww, baby, you're the only one for me. *But not six months from now*, OK? I meant what I said. When the time comes, and it's the *right* time, we'll be husband and wife . . . if you'll still have me by then!"

Marceau and Jeepers watched from the wings. "Time for the appetizers?" Jeep asked. Marceau nodded. Le Chef hurried off to the kitchen.

"Thanks for being so understanding, Scotty. I have never met anyone like you, and I never will, ever again." Julia leaned across the table, and they kissed briefly but deeply.

"Whew, *nice!*" Scotty breathed. At that very moment, Marceau reappeared with the complimentary poppers, complete with Le Chef's special dipping sauce. "I have a special treat for you, my friends! I had Chef hold your meal, so he prepared this appetizer for you—O'Malley's Signature Pepper Cheese Poppers. They are compliments of the house, my friends, for you are young lovers, yes?"

Julia blushed a deep, pleasant beet red. Scotty smiled, "In that assessment, you are quite astute, Marceau. Now, would you kindly pour our wine? And thank you."

"You are more than welcome, sir." Marceau filled their glasses, smiling warmly. "Um, would you prefer your salads now, or shall I wait?"

"Could your chef hang tight for ten minutes or so?" Scott asked.

"Chef is a wizard in the kitchen, yes. This will be no problem for us at all, sir. No worries, as they say?"

Scotty shot the waiter a sidelong glance, grinning; "As they say, Marceau!"

Sonny was back in his office, now fighting his way through a morass of discouragement and uncertainty. He seriously considered just shit-canning his lifelong search for extraterrestrial life and goin' fishin'. But in a sudden moment of clarity, he realized, *I can't leave this alone!* He picked up his office phone and called Louis Babich at the disposal site. The phone rang seven times before someone picked up. "Marble here. May I help you?"

Sonny's mind reeled. *Who the fuck is Marble? Where's Babich?* "Uh, yes, Mr. Marble. Agent Sonny Mildauer calling for Louis Babich. May I speak with him, please?"

There was a long silence. A new voice came on the line. "Special Agent Walter Clerk speaking. May I help you?"

"This is Agent Sonny Mildauer. I was trying to reach a Mr. Louis Babich, a contractor on the LV-51A reclamation."

"What? Please repeat your question, Agent Smally. I did not copy."

"Louis Babich, a contractor on the LV-51A."

"What is LV-51A . . . Agent Smally, is it? I warn you, if this is a crank call . . ."

"Let me be very concise, Special Agent Clerk. I am Senior Agent Sonny Mildauer. Now, I am looking for a Mr. Louis Babich at this number. Who the fuck are you?"

"Uh, I'm an intern, Agent Sonny. I'm not really a special agent yet, sir, but I'm interning in the SA fast track program. I just got here last week. I don't know how to help you."

"Aw, shit. Sorry, son. Who's your supervisor?" Sonny asked.

"Hang on a sec, sir; got his name right here . . . It's, uh, looks like Walter . . . Margolis? Or Marpolis?"

"Can you transfer my call to him, son?"

"I think so, sir. Hold on . . ." After a series of clicks came across the line, Sonny heard a ring, then another. A woman's voice answered, "Facilities Reclamation, Susan speaking. How may I help you today?" Bingo!

"Hi, Susan, my name is Senior Agent Sonny Mildauer with Spec Ops. I'm trying to reach someone familiar with the LV-51A reclamation project—perhaps Agent Walter Margolis?"

"Hmmm, let me see here . . . . Can you hold for just a second, Agent Mildauer? I need to bring this up on my computer," Susan replied.

"Go ahead, Susan. I'll wait."

He waited—and waited. Finally Susan came back on the line. "Sorry for the wait, sir. I think I have something for you. That project was recoded recently. I'm connecting you with Mr. Marpolis now. Please hold." Click. Ring . . ."Marpolis speaking . . ."

After switching to a secure line, both agents verified their credentials and identified themselves with a retina scan and both thumbprints—standard procedure. Both agents were satisfied, and now they could discuss the details freely.

It was an interesting conversation. Sonny learned that Babich had been killed at LV-51A when his forklift flipped over, dropping a two-ton crate of artifacts on his head. Owing to the sensitive nature of these artifacts, the project had been recoded to Sec Class TOPP RED 000. Frontline phone numbers were changed to secure lines, and site access was restricted.

"Can I get on-site today, Walt?" Sonny asked.

"Shouldn't be a problem, Sonny. On ingress and egress, full retina and print scan, full vehicle and body search—and bring all your badges with you. SIR, USA, and PAA. Copy?" (SIR, USA, and PAA were acronyms for security information record, unlimited site access, and personal access authorization. Sonny would have the full run of the place.)

"Copy, Walt. Sonny out." He was already three steps toward his badge safe.

Red covered Scotty's hands with her own. "You said you have a job offer for me, Scotty. I want to hear it! I detest my job and everyone I work with!" Julia's eyes brimmed with tears. "Please, Scotty—dear—if you have a way out for me, please tell me now."

Scott merely chuckled. "Oh, that I do. We're looking for three seasoned field agents, hon, and you'd be in charge. Kind of a rapid-deployment team to investigate this renegade CIA scientist who's apparently cloning some kind of mutants in a top-secret lab. Low visibility is a must . . . just in and out, grab whatever documents you can—you know the drill."

"Mutant clones? Where?"

"Carlisle," Scotty replied.

"You're kidding, Scott. Carlisle? That's, like, fifteen miles from here."

"Yeah, and I have a shitload of data on this target. You got a secure data line at work?"

"Yeah, of course. Will you send me the skinny, Scott?"

"So, you're interested," Scotty said, more in the form of a statement than a question.

"What the fuck—oops, sorry! What do you think? Why in hell wouldn't I be?" Red said, her fingernails starting to dig painfully into the backs of Scott's hands. A few of the other patrons had begun to regard them strangely.

"Shhh, easy, baby. Keep it down, OK? And cool it with the fingernails, please."

"Ohh, I'm so sorry, Scotty," Julia said, kissing Scotty's damaged hands. "Yeah, I'm interested. In fact, consider it a done deal. Have you selected the other two agents yet?"

"I have four contenders, Julia: 'Walt' DeWalt, Kenny Breslan, Dr. Garrett Morse, and John Hodge. You know them all, right?"

"Yeah, I'd work with DeWalt and Morse, given the choice. What do you say?"

"I say fine, Red. Your call," Scotty replied.

"When do I meet with them, and where?"

Scotty sighed, "Unfortunately, you'd have to come downtown where I work, at the SDA building. But there's a bright side—I'll show you your new office. We could do it next Monday, or later in the week if that would work better for you."

"Nah, today's only Tuesday. Let's make it 0600 next Monday. I'd like to catch 'em groggy, so I have the edge!"

Scotty laughed heartily. *Vintage Julia*, he thought. "OK, hon. I'll schedule one of the big conference rooms, one with a long table, very intimidating. I'll give you the room number later. How 'bout we eat?"

Marceau appeared with their salads as if on cue. "Are you ready for ze salads, *Monsieur et Mademoiselle?*"

"*Si*," Scotty replied, unwittingly responding in Spanish rather than French. He interpreted Marceau's laughter only as a lighthearted appreciation of his considerable language skills.

Julia grabbed the figurative wheel. "*Mais oui, Marceau. Merci beaucoup. C'est parfait, Monsieur. Mais, prenez-vous* our steaks pronto*, s'il vous plait?*"

Marceau cast an unreadable glance at Julia and quietly set their slightly wilted salads on the table. "*Oui, Mademoiselle.* Your steaks. Pronto," Marceau replied in his faulty French. He'd learned a little French in the prison library, and he liked to throw it at unsuspecting patrons.

"*Tres bien*. Bring 'em on. Chop-chop!" The somewhat cowed waiter scuttled back to the kitchen.

"I didn't know you spoke French," Scotty whispered, a little awestruck.

"I don't," Red answered, letting her enigmatic response simply hang in the air between them, as she so often did. "Let's eat, huh?"

Scotty was ravenous. As he wolfed down his salad, he marveled again at the paradox that was Julia sitting across the table from him. Who—or what—was she? One moment, he wanted to cradle her in his arms, kissing away her tears, and the next, he considered running for cover. He'd begun to view Big Red as the "Big Vidalia"—and the concept intrigued him. As he stripped away one layer of the onion, the next one lay exposed, taunting him, enticing him to explore deeper . . .

. . . and to accept that more layers lurked beneath, more than an entire human lifetime was sufficient to plumb.

Scotty guessed he'd better get started.

He'd brought the ring with him tonight, just in case. But he'd probably just fucked it all away, diverting to the "job offer" in the moment of truth. He cursed himself. Marceau brought the steaks, and he couldn't eat a single bite. In a moment of clarity, Scotty decided on the Path of Truth. "Uh, hey, Red . . . Julia . . . I made a bad, bad mistake earlier. Are you familiar with the expression 'chicken out'?"

Julia was finishing the last of her steak. "What are you talking about now, Scotty? Why are you acting so strange? You haven't even touched your steak."

Scotty fumbled the ring from his pocket. It was a $10,000 work of art from the premier jeweler in the city, Amali, on the corner of Carpet and Hoover. He sank to one knee. "Well, Red, I . . . I chickened out earlier. I meant to propose marriage tonight, but I, well, chickened out. Julia, will you accept my hand in marriage—right now?"

Julia swallowed the last bite of her steak before answering. Then she replied, "Yeah, Scotty. I told you that earlier, remember? Now eat your steak and we'll go."

He grasped Julia's hand and slipped the ring over her finger. "Do you like it, hon?"

"Of course I do, Scotty. I love it. It's absolutely gorgeous. *Merci beaucoup, monsieur.* Now finish your steak and let's go back to my place . . . pronto! *Comprenez-vous?*"

The Mistress of Intrigue and Understatement had spoken. Suddenly they were man and wife in the eyes of God, they believed. Just like that.

Scotty was too drunk, Julia decreed, so she drove, softly singing "*voulez-vous couchez avec moi, ce soir* . . . yo' lady marmalade" under her breath all the way back to the apartment. Scotty squirmed in the passenger's seat, erect and hard as a rock. Twenty minutes later, they arrived. This would soon prove to be the night of a lifetime for two lonely travelers on life's indifferent highway . . . .

CHAPTER X

Katya

An armed Marine sergeant named William Wallace parked the shuttle and dismounted. The stocky, well-muscled Wallace led Sonny along row after endless row of reinforced steel shelving crammed to capacity with all manner of junk. "The artifact site is right back here, sir," the Marine intoned. Sonny saw it; a gaggle of about thirty people—uniformed and civilian, men and women—milled around what must have been Louis Babich's ruined forklift. Banks of floodlights illuminated the area with an unnatural, brighter-than-daylight intensity.

"Thank you, Sergeant. Who's in charge down there?"

"You'll probably want to talk to Dr. Kozhczuk, sir. She seems to be running the show right now. She's the pretty suit with the long black hair. I'd talk to her first if I were you, sir." Wallace smiled.

Katya? No shit? Sonny's heart skipped a beat; Sonny smiled back. "Do you want to walk me down there, Sergeant Wallace, or shall I take it from here?"

"That's your call, sir. I'm here to help if I can."

"I think I'll be fine solo, Sergeant. Do I need an escort back?"

"Yessir," Wallace replied, reaching for a holster on his belt. He handed Sonny a walkie-talkie. "Just press 937 and then the pound key when you're ready to leave, sir. I'll pick you up myself."

"Good enough, Sergeant Wallace. Thanks. See you in a bit."

"Yessir," the Marine said, offering Sonny a half-salute. "Uh, Mr. Sonny, sir . . ."

"Yes, Sergeant, what is it?"

"Be careful back there, sir. We've had a coupl'a injuries already—people stumbling over the debris."

Sonny smiled. "No problems, Sarge. I'll take it easy. Thanks for the advice."

Sergeant William Wallace smiled back, shot Sonny a thumbs-up, and trudged slowly down the long aisle.

Sonny walked briskly toward the milling throng about thirty yards away. He remembered Dr. Katya Kozhczuk from the COUP (Conference on Unexplained Phenomena) in Kiev three years prior. Dr. Kozhczuk had presented a riveting paper titled "*DÅ¯Kaz MimozemskÀ©* Intelligence," or "The Evidence for Extraterrestrial Intelligence." Sonny had been enthralled by the presentation—and also by the presenter.

Then: The day following Dr. Katya's lecture, she'd led a small roundtable discussion in a cramped, smoke-filled conference room. Sonny had signed up early, securing a seat at the table—coincidentally, directly across from lovely Katya! "My friends and colleagues, welcome! Before we open the forum for discussion, please allow me to show you some slides that I have not shown to the others. Our Ukrain Republika Special Services retrieved literally reams of records, photographs, even physical artifacts following our Velvet Revolution of 1989. These records have been made public, but it seems the rest of the world has chosen to ignore this overwhelming body of evidence, thereby calling into question the fundamental integrity of the Ukrainian people. This saddens me deeply and angers me more than a little. But in the face of world apathy, the Ukrainian people have always marched on! And so now, my friends, I, as supreme agent in Ukrainian Special Services, present to you some interesting data for your consideration. Let me begin . . . ."

Apparently, the Ukrainians had not yet discovered the miracle of MS PowerPoint; the slide presentation was exactly that—photographic slides. The lights dimmed, and Dr. Katya projected hundreds of her disturbing pictures on the wall, narrating each slide.

After an hour or so, the room began to clear. After ninety minutes, only the doctor, Sonny, and a female Russian agent remained at the table.

Finally, Katya concluded the slide show. "Well, we now have only three participants. Nonetheless, I shall open the roundtable session for free discussion. Svetlana?" Katya queried the Russian, a severe-looking blonde. "*Nyet*. I have seen enough, Dr. Kozhczuk. I need to attend the Albanian's presentation at 7:30. If you will excuse me . . ." Without waiting for an answer, Svetlana rose and strode out of the room.

Katya lit a cigarette. "So, Dr. Sonnay, is it? It seems to be only we two remaining. Shall I now lose you, also?"

"It's just Sonny, Doctor—and, no . . . if you're willing to continue, I'd love to discuss what I've seen. Are you game?"

Katya shook her head. "'Game?' I do not understand, Dr. Sonny, please explain this to me."

"Sorry, Doctor. It is an American slang term meaning 'willing.' Are you willing to discuss your findings with me, Dr. Katya?"

"I think yes, Dr. Sonny. But, if I may, it is after all almost 7 p.m. in Kiev, and I grow very hungry. I ask, would I be too forward to suggest dinner together, and a few drinks?"

Sonny decided to simply let the "Dr. Sonny" thing ride. "It would honor me to dine with you tonight, Dr. Katya."

Katya stubbed out her cigarette. "This is good, Dr. Sonny. This is in fact very fine. But from now on, please call me Katya. I do not like to be 'Doctor' with friends. May I call you simply 'Sonny,' as well?"

Sonny fought back a chuckle; 'Dr. Sonny' had evaporated of its own accord. "That would be fine, Katya."

"This is WONDERFUL! I must warn you, Sonny—you may find with me a very fine surprise tonight! With me will you be . . . *game?*" Katya giggled, her voice that of a little girl. "But first, for food. My very favorite is called *Vepřo-knedlo-zelo* . . . roast pork with dumplings and sauerkraut, and sometimes with rice and lentils?—but, food is *very gassy,* I must warn," Katya said, smiling slyly over her shoulder; "Still, you would not deny me this, yes?"

"Uh—yes, I mean no . . . please, no Dutch oven tonight, though, OK?" Sonny replied, chuckling.

Katya's brow furrowed; "Dutch oven? What is . . ."

"Shhh. Never mind, Katya, just a little American joke about gas. Yeah, sounds fine,"Sonny said, his face beginning to redden. "Whatever sounds good to you, Kat. Let's go for *Vepřo-knedlo-zelo.*"

Kat giggled at Sonny's sudden embarrassment. "Aww, so *cute!* I will take you down. I know a tiny little place called *Газова Камера;* it's just two rows of booths, just off the river in the gaslight district—where they say the flames devour men's souls. You have ever heard that, Sonny?" Katya breathed, panting slightly, in Sonny's ear, her voice full of full of seduction. Pulling back, she giggled. *This chick is totally wound,* Sonny thought. *What does she want?* Still . . . it couldn't be bad . . .

"Sonny, the the chef, Anatoly, is sublime! And they have sixty-one kind of all different beer—can, bottle, draught. I love also beer much, do you not?" Katya glared at him, somewhat challengingly, he thought, her now-violet eyes sparkling strangely. Sonny just smiled and nodded; *damn, these Ukraine women are really aggressive!* He was vastly enjoying this overture, and he recalled the lyrics to some old Beatles tune: " . . . Ukraine girls really knock me out . . ." Sonny didn't realize it at the time, but the last half of that verse, *"Leave the West behind"*, would prove oddly portentious . . .

Sonny stifled another chuckle and grinned like a Cheshire cat."Whatever you wanna do, Kat.Too many questions for me, babe. I'm losing track. Just take me to *Газова Камера,* and we'll go from there."

"Ohh, this is fine, Sonny, *very fine!* We go NOW! Come, Sonny. I take you down. OK?" Katya grabbed his hand and yanked him upright; the girl was STRONG!

"OK, Katya. OK. Let's go. Take me to paradise . . . ." The girlish giggle was gone; Katya chuckled deep in her throat, suddenly all woman; wicked-innocent; lover-betrayer? All at once?

Who *was* she?

The question haunted him; Sonny longed for her, and all else became strangely meaningless . . .

"I need to go, Katya. My plane is boarding . . . God, how I shall miss you."

Katya wept freely, as did Sonny. As they tore away from each other, they realized that they, together, had found something far too precious to lose, and that this something was about to vaporize in the sky over Kiev, lost forever. Yet they were powereless to resist the waves of destiny crashing over them. The lovers embraced and kissed, and kissed again, endlessly. This was the end.

But, as time would tell, it was only the beginning . . .

Now: Dr. Katya Kozhczuk stood with her back to Sonny as he approached the disparate crowd of investigators. He ducked under the yellow crime-scene tape. Katya was engaged in an animated discussion with a uniformed man, her hands moving, it seemed, in every direction at once. He caught snippets of her discourse as he drew closer to the pair: " . . . incubate their embryos after they established a base of operations on Earth . . . a dozen or so of these vials seem to have gone missing . . . human remains . . . assume your CIA has plans to incubate . . ."

Katya's command of the English language had improved dramatically since the COUP convention three years earlier. Sonny noticed only the slightest hint of her Ukrainian accent. Standing off to the side, he waited for a break in the action. Finally, looking exasperated, the uniform paused, dropping his hands to his sides. "Well, look, Doctor . . ."

Sonny cleared his throat. "Doctor Kozhczuk, I presume?"

Katya spun to face him, her eyes wide with excitement. "Sonny!" Suddenly she was in his arms, smothering his face with kisses. "I thought I would never see you again, Sonny!" Tears rolled unabashedly down Katya's cheeks, which still bore the pinkish flush of her dialogue with Major Asshole. The uniformed man flapped his arms again and stormed off, shaking his head.

"Oh, Katya, Katya, my sweet. It's a miracle! How wonderful to find you here, right on my doorstep! The years have treated you well."

Sonny watched in awe as Katya's beautiful mind processed the unfamiliar phrase. Her eyes refocused, and she giggled, then kissed him deeply. "Oh, Sonny, you are only too kind! But the gray is creeping in, do you see?" Katya swept back her inky-black mane, displaying a tiny patch of grey just above her ear.

Sonny pursed his lips and gently kissed her there. "Katty, you are a distinguished scientist. How I wish I had your brilliance, your charm! You've earned this little emblem through your hard work, your diligence. Wear it with pride, my love."

Apparently, Sonny had just recited some sort of magical incantation. Katya's fathomless violet eyes (violet, in this light—her incredible eyes seemed to change color with the subtlest variation in emotion or illumination) widened, the pulils dilating, nearly obscuring the irises in twin obsidian circles."You must come with me, Sonny, right now! I will take you to my hotel, yes? To paradise . . . surely you remember?"

How could he possibly forget? His work could easily wait until tomorrow—but clearly Katya Kozhczuk could not.

CHAPTER XI

The Morning After

Julia and Scotty had both taken the day off. The pair, aching and abraded raw, decided to head out to Dr. Mendoza's lab for a preliminary recon. Scotty had done his homework; the devil's workshop was about twenty miles out, a compound of six white modular buildings of various sizes. They had satellite images and even GPS coordinates. Studying the images, they decided to park out on the county road and hike in, masquerading as hikers wandering innocently in the woods.

After purchasing convincing-looking gear at Woody's Wilderness Warehouse, a small outdoor store in Carlisle, Julia and Scotty changed clothes in the fitting rooms and jumped back into Julia's Tahoe. "Can we grab something to eat on the way?" Julia asked. "I'm starving. Fucking makes hungry, yes?" she said in her best impersonation of a voracious Ukrainian farm girl. Julia felt justified in mocking her ancestors' accent; after all, her mother, Oksana Redding, née Shimanov, was an immigrant who had grown up on her family's modest farm south of Kiev.

Scotty chuckled. "Sure, babe. I starving, too, yes?" Julia laughed, landing a solid punch to his right shoulder. "You are smartass, yes?" she said.

"Ouch—shit—yes! I smartass, OK? That hurt!"

Julia giggled. "It was supposed to hurt! Did you miss the point completely, dear?"

"Nope, sure didn't, honey," Scotty replied as he began tickling Julia mercilessly.

"OK, *OK*, stop it, Scotty! I give! I give! Stop!" Julia shrieked, laughing helplessly as she gasped for breath.

Scotty stopped and grinned. "We'd better get on the road, babe. It's been fun, but we have things to see, people to do. Yes?"

Julia couldn't stop giggling. "Fun for you, maybe, you shit!" She smacked Scotty on the shoulder again—softly this time—and planted a sloppy kiss on his cheek. "Drive on, Hoke . . . ."

Scotty sighed and rolled his eyes. "Yass'm, Miss Daisy," he said with an expression of feigned exasperation as he keyed the big engine to life. "Where can we find a drive-through? Let's make it quick and just eat on the way, OK, babe?"

"Yeah, for sure. There's a Mick's drive-through about a half-mile up the road, and it's on the right. We'll be able to slide in and out, smooth as silk. Won't take long."

Scotty recalled their previous night's gyrations and smiled, unable to resist the juicy lead-in. "Yass, Miss Daisy, but Hoke be all kinda long. Smooth in and out, ma'am—an' sausage in the biscuit with cheese, jes' the way you likes it . . ."

POW! "Dammit, Julia! Cut that out, will ya?" Scotty barked, rubbing his shoulder.

"If you can't take the heat, don't feed the fire, Hoke," Julia said softly, a mischievous smile playing across her lips. Scotty smiled back and leaned across to kiss her deeply. "Yass'm, Miss Daisy." He wheeled her massive vehicle out onto the main road. "Sausage and biscuits comin' right up, ma'am. Silky smooth in-and-out come later, huh?"

"Oh, yes."

Scotty made a U-turn and parked the Tahoe on the shoulder of Route 31, about a quarter-mile past the entry road to Mendoza's lab. *Plausible deniability*, he thought. Naturally, they'd left all their real identification in Julia's apartment; the vehicle still wore its temporary dealer's tags from Virginia, where she'd bought it with fake ID bearing her mother's maiden name to save on insurance. Oksana Shimanov, age 60, had reclaimed her maiden name after divorcing Julia's vodka-sopping father two years ago. What's more, Oksana had never officially changed her address but had chosen to rent a "suite" at We 'B' Mailboxes for personal correspondence. She swung by her husband's place on Chain Break Road in Plumbersville, now four miles behind the Tahoe on Route 31, three or four times a week to rifle her ex-husband's mailbox for her official correspondence.

As they walked into the woods, Scotty prayed that his little ruse would work if they got caught. He had insisted that Julia leave her own cell in the apartment, for good reason. "Trust me, hon. I've got a plan in case we get caught . . . just listen." Julia listened with rapt interest, her eyes glistening with excitement.

There was an old hiking trail through the woods (Scotty had spotted it on the satellite photos) that led almost directly from Route 31 to the access road that looped around Mendoza's compound. Hey (the cover story went), we never saw any damn "Restricted Area, Do Not Enter" signs; we just came down from Plumbersville for a little hike. We never even GOT to your access road! We never saw no stinkin' guard shacks! We don't need no stinkin' badges. The woods are free, man! WE GOT OUR RIGHTS! I WANNA LAWYER!

He was Ray Lee McMatting, dammit, a county commissioner from Leonardsville, and he had FAMILY there. POWERFUL family! *Just look me up in the phone book! She's Oksana Shimanov—lives right up there in Plumbersville. Just run her tags. You'll see!* Just to be on the safe side, though, he'd recorded a voice mail on his own cell phone, and with the press of a single hot key, that message would be sent directly to Agent Sonny Mildauer, complete with directions, GPS coordinates, and all the details. Then he'd simply pull the SIM card, pulverize it under his heel, and toss the phone into the woods.

Julia thought it just might work. She decided to chance it.

Thirty feet into the woods, Scotty immediately realized that they had chosen unwisely. What remained of the old ranger trail was overgrown with knee-high grass. "We gotta go back to Woody's and buy some long pants and socks, Julia—right now! That grass has got to be full of chiggers and ticks. They'll fucking eat us alive!" They hurried back to the road and climbed aboard the Tahoe. Scotty cranked the starter and floored the accelerator, burning rubber down Route 31 to Woody's Wilderness Warehouse.

Sonny and Katya were just finishing the last few morsels of their candlelight dinner when Sonny's phone rang. It was the hospice.

"Agent Sonny, this is Dr. Domenici, Dmitri Vasiliev's primary physician at the hospice. We've talked several times. Do you remember me, sir?"

"Oh, yes, of course I do, Dr. Domenici. I hope Dmitri hasn't taken a turn for the worse."

Domenici sighed. "Well, yes and no, Sonny. His vitals are strong, and he's responding amazingly well to the new small-molecule chemo we're giving him IV. It's a promising experimental drug from MetaPharma called Spiroclozapar, now in its final round of clinical trials. Since starting treatment, we've actually seen, for the first time, a modest reduction in the mass of two of his tumors, and it appears that . . ."

Sonny sensed correctly that the urbane doctor would like nothing better than to ply him endlessly with the minutiae of Dmitri's chemotherapy. The agent cleared his throat loudly. "Dr. Domenici, excuse me. What exactly is the purpose of your call, if I may ask?"

"Uh, yes, of course," Domenici said, suddenly jolted off his stride. "Dmitri's had more of his vivid dreams, and he's desperate to speak with you. Could you possibly swing by here today?"

"That would be tough to finesse, Doctor. Would tomorrow afternoon be early enough?"

"In my professional opinion, the sooner you talk to him, the better, Mr. Sonny."

"OK, Doc. I'll come by to see Dmitri this afternoon."

"Very good. That would be for the best, sir, I think. Thank you."

"OK, Doc. I appreciate your call, but I really do need to go. Good-bye for now." Sonny cursed as he snapped his cell phone shut. "Dammit!"

Scotty and Julia, now dressed in heavy fatigue pants and leather boots laced halfway up their calves, crashed unceremoniously through the tangle of swamp grass and underbrush clogging the overgrown trail. After an hour or so, they stumbled upon a clearing, and there it was, straight ahead—the Compound. They had arrived.

Mendoza's devil's workshop was clearly visible through a chain-link fence topped with concertina wire and most likely electrified. Scotty licked his index finger, strode across the road, and, tucking his other arm behind his back, cautiously touched the fence—and was jolted squarely onto his ass. Julia rushed forward. "Scotty, honey, are you OK, baby? Talk to me!"

Scotty sat on the asphalt, shaking his head. "Whew . . . I'm OK, hon. Just took a little zap there. That freakin' fence must be carrying 110 volts, at least! Whoo, man!"

Julia had a thought. "Hey, Scotty. Couldn't we just short the fucking thing straight to ground and blow it out?"

Struggling to his feet, Scotty replied, "Sure, we could. Probably not a good idea, though, Red. Knocking out their perimeter defense would trigger all kinds of alarms. My little test probably just looks like they cooked a rabbit or something. It's under their radar, I hope.

We learned what we needed to learn—no penetration possible. Perimiter observation only, you capiche?"

"Yeah, I capiche, Scotty," Julia chuckled. "So, what now, Don Corleone?"

"Well, for now, shweetheart, we're a couple of lost, chigger-eaten hikers looking for directions outa here. We walk the perimeter road, looking for a phone, anything. We were hiking the trail, and we spotted the clearing . . . ."

"Sounds like a plan, babe. Let's get walking!"

"I'll need to keep my cell active to send a text message to Sonny if they stop us. One press of the button and it's sent. Then I crush the SIM, toss the phone into the woods, and my cell is history."

Julia clasped Scotty's hand in her own. He felt her trembling. "Let's get on with it."

"Will you return soon, Sonny?" Katya asked, her eyes brimming with tears as she held him close. Her Ukrainian accent had all but disappeared.

Sonny kissed her—lightly brushing Katya's lips, and then deeply. "Yes, of course I will, my love." He held Katya tight, kissing her passionately, tasting her mouth as she moaned deep in her throat. "I'll call you when I leave the hospice, OK?"

"Ohhh, Sonny, I do not want you to leave me."

Sonny looked deep into her eyes. "And I would love nothing more than to stay here with you, Katya. Believe this in your heart, my sweet. I luh . . . uh, worship you!"

Katya froze, her mouth agape. "You what, Sonny? What did you start to say, just before 'worship'? Tell me!"

Sonny Mildauer blushed bright red, perspiring copiously as he groped for words. "I, well, I think I said . . . listen, honey, this is not a good time to discuss this. I really, really need to get on the road. I'm so sorry. Can we talk about this later, when I get back?"

Katya smiled impishly and spoke in a near-whisper. "I luh you too, Sonny Mildauer. Very deeply. With all my heart. I never want to be with anyone but you." She gave him a soft peck on the cheek. "Go now, my luh, and get dressed. The sooner you leave, the sooner you'll return to me."

"Scotty, take a look at this!" Julia said, handing him her binoculars. "Right over there! You can just make them out through the trees, moving around. I think they're dressed in orange overalls!"

Scotty raised the binoculars. "Holy shit, Red! I can see 'em walking past that little clearing there. Inmate's PJs!"

"Yep, prison suits," Julia said. "WTF, Scott? What the hell kind of operation's Mendoza running out here, anyway?"

"I dunno. Your guess is as good as mine, Red. They look like a bunch of skinheads in a prison yard, don't they?" Scotty said, handing the binoculars back to Julia. "Let's move over into the woods for cover and see if we can move in a little closer. The trees are kinda sparse here next to the road. Maybe we can work our way through them. I need a closer look at this." Scotty pulled out his own binoculars and slung the strap around his neck. "C'mon, let's go."

The going was tougher than they'd anticipated, but they managed to pick their way through 300 or so yards of underbrush before reaching a sheltered clearing with a good view of the pajama squad. Scotty knelt in the tall grass and began scanning the site through his binoculars. Julia straggled behind, obviously running out of steam fast. As she approached, she asked, "See anything interesting, baby?"

"You won't believe this, Red. Check out their faces."

Julia squatted beside Scott, raising her own binoculars. This time, it was her turn to apply the expletives. "Aww, shit! These guys are seriously fucked up, Scotty! Did you see that one guy, with the . . . the . . ."

131

Scotty finished her sentence. "With the hole in the middle of his face? Yeah, I sure did, Red. A gaping hole right where his nose should be."

Julia shivered. "What are they, Scott? Are they the incubated embryos?"

Scotty sighed. "I think it goes deeper than just that, hon. My guess is they're the product of failed hybridization attempts, a cross between humans and aliens."

"Then what does that make them, Scotty? What are they?" Julia asked, her voice tremulous.

Scotty took a while to reply. Finally, he spoke. "Well . . . they're victims, I guess. Just like the human guinea pigs in the Nazi death camp experiments."

Julia started to sob. Scotty wrapped his arms around Big Red, trying his damndest to console her. Finally, just as Julia began to regain her composure, the sound of machine-gun fire rang through the forest. Scotty pulled her down, and the pair lay prone in the grass. "What are they doing? What's happening, Scotty?" Julia shrieked.

"They're destroying the evidence, Red. It's an execution." Julia rushed to the tree line and vomited copiously into the underbrush.

CHAPTER XII

Hospice Call

Dmitri Vasiliev looked wan and jaundiced, an emaciated wraith lying glassy-eyed beneath the sheet. Sonny was shocked; his face must have registered dismay as he entered the room, but he managed to affect a cheery ersatz smile as he approached the bed. *Good job, Domenici*, Sonny thought. *That chemo's fixed Dmitri right up. Looks like a new fucking man . . . .*

For the first time since Sonny started visiting Dmitri in the hospice, the wraith waved aside the offer of his favorite vodka and cigarettes. "*Nyet*, Sonny. These will only more sicken my stomach. The medicine, it makes me very, how you say, *nauzios?*"

"OK, pal. I'm saddened to hear that. Dr. Domenici said the new experimental medicine had helped you a lot, and I just thought . . ."

"Yes, Sonny, the medicine is helping the cancer, but I always feel like shit. I cannot keep food on my stomach, and it tastes like cardboard anyway when I try to eat. They are now giving me nutrition through this big tube in my groin. Dr. Domenici says . . ." Dmitri paused to catch his breath. " . . . he says that the treatment will last only for two more months. Then I will be my old cheery self again." Dmitri chuckled sadly. "But often I wonder, Sonny—what is the point of all this? My time has already passed. Dr. Domenici says that the treatment has already extended my life for two or three months. These tumors, they shrink, he says. *But what kind of life is this, Sonny?* I cannot eat. I cannot smoke, or enjoy the wonderful Stoli you bring me, or even sex. I believe it is time for me to go. It is *past* time. But here . . . come close, my friend."

Sonny sighed wearily, taking his customary seat bedside. "What is it, Dmitri? Domenici's phone call sounded urgent. You have something you need to tell me?"

Sonny bent close. The old man croaked three simple words: "Help me die."

"*How?*" Sonny asked.

"It is easy, my friend. Simply turn off that valve right there, under the saline bottle on the stand."

"You're sure about this, Dmitri?"

"More than sure, my friend," Vasiliev said.

Sonny nodded, closing the valve. "Is that it?" he asked.

"Now, pinch off that little hose. Yes, that's it! Pull it free from the bottom of the bag."

Sonny grimaced. "OK, Dmitri, it's free. What should I do now?"

"Lift your thumb from the tube. That will allow a bubble of air to form. Then pinch it shut again, slip it back on the spigot, and open the valve. I will die quickly of an air embolism, and no one will be the wiser."

Sonny was sweating profusely now; he'd never killed a human being, *and he'd sure as hell never euthanized anyone before.* He fumbled with the hose, finally reattaching it to the spigot and opening the valve. "It's done, Dmitri. Goodbye, my friend." He grabbed the old man's hand and squeezed it tightly.

"So long, Sonny. Thaah . . ."

It was over almost instantly. Dmitri's eyes rolled back in his head, and he convulsed weakly as the air bubble hit his brain.

Good bye, Dmitri. May you rest in peace. Sonny pushed the Big Red Button, then again, and again . . .

<u>Back to the Compound</u>: "Dear God, Scotty, they just *slaughtered* twenty or thirty people! We've gotta *stop* this! We've gotta . . ."

Scott pulled Julia back into the cover of the deep grass. "*Shhhh!* Calm down, Red," Scotty whispered. "You're gonna get us killed! Now, just relax and listen to me for a minute. First thing, we need to get outta here." Scotty whipped his head back and forth; just to his right, he spotted what appeared to be the remnants of another old hiking trail that led east, back in the direction of the main highway. "*Listen*, now, OK?" Julia nodded. "OK, here, take your keys and my cell phone. It looks like there's an old trail—see, right over there. Start jogging back toward the car. I'll cover your back and work my way up behind you on the trail. Run for five minutes, then pause and call Agent Sonny. His number's on speed dial; press 6. Keep it short and then get runnin' again. I'll catch up with you in a few minutes. Understood?"

"Yeah, but what about you, babe? How will you find me?" Julia asked.

"Hey, the main road's dead east of here. I'll follow the trail as far as I can. Watch your compass, and I'll track you. Don't worry; I was an Eagle Scout, remember? I have six merit badges in orienteering and tracking forest animals. Humans are far easier; they're clumsier than animals. They make more noise and leave a bigger footprint—broken twigs, disturbed leaves and pine needles, and *human* footprints. Remember, you're way heavier and clumsier than a raccoon or a baby deer. No offense, hon; so am I."

It rolled right off Julia's back. "If you don't catch up, you want me to wait in the car?" she asked.

"No, listen. Drive past the entrance—south, away from Plumbersville—for about five minutes. Then make a U-turn and head north, *toward* Plumbersville. If I'm not waiting for you, drive north for five minutes, turn around, and head back south. If I'm still not there, keep on goin'. I'm already dead, or worse, or Sonny will find me."

"But . . ."

"*Go,* Julia! Now!" Julia embraced Scott in a death grip, and kissed him deeply. "I love you."

"I love you, too, honey. Now get your sweet ass movin'! *Go!*"

After pacing restlessly for hours in her stuffy room, Katya finally decided to go down to the hotel lounge for a few drinks and a sandwich. Surprisingly, the cozy little pub still permitted smoking, having elected to eat the occasional $700 fine rather than accept the dramatic loss of business following the recent smoking ban. People simply bought a six-pack at the local party store and smoked and drank to their hearts' content in their rooms unless there was a viable alternative. Paddy MacDougall's offered them that choice, and patrons now lined up at the door, waiting for a seat. These days, business was better than it had ever been, and tonight MacDougall's was packed to the rafters.

John Herschlund, the proprietor and tonight's bartender, spotted the bewitching young lady standing at the hostess station, smoking a thin cigar and obviously waiting for a seat. He left the bar and sauntered toward the podium.

Ironically, the Paddy MacDougall's chain had absolutely no ties to the British Isles, owned as it was by a group of Asian investment bankers. Herschlund, who introduced himself as "Johnny McFarlane" in a passable brogue, leaned on the empty podium. "I can seat you right away at the bar, ma'am, and we serve our sandwich menu there, if you'd like. Or you can have a drink and wait for a seat in our dining room? Right now, there's a thirty—to forty-five-minute wait, though."

The young lady was cool, reserved. "The bar will be fine. Thank you, Mr. McFarlane."

"Johnny" flashed his most ingratiating smile as he said, "Just call me Johnny, please. Follow me, m'lady."

Much to Katya's delight, the bar featured an outstanding selection of exotic beers and ales, with their top ten sellers available either on tap or bottled. She immediately zeroed in on an amber white Ukrainian lager. "You actually carry this, Johnny? I have never seen it before in America!"

Johnny grinned. "And it's brand new, too. You're in luck, m'lady! We just got our first two kegs straight from Kiev. People seem to love it!"

"Well, *I* do. I drink it always, the бурштин білий." Katya answered, smiling noncommittally. "Please, pour for me your largest glass."

Johnny complied immediately and set an ice-encrusted 32-ounce mug on the bar. "That's a lot of beer, m'lady. And I thought you pronounced the name of our Amber White in another language. Are you visiting from Ukraine, by any chance?"

Katya regarded him cautiously, taking a sip from the huge mug. "I am. And in Ukraine, we drink very much beer. It is—how you say?—a way of life for us, since a very young age."

Johnny, the Cheshire smile still plastered across his handsome face, replied, "Welcome to America, my dear, the land of milk and honey, and exotic beers! I am the proprietor of this humble establishment. Welcome, my guest from afar. And your Ukrainian beer is on the house tonight—my compliments!"

"Thank you, Johnny. Please bring me a menu."

Johnny immediately produced a laminated menu. "Of course, ma'am. You might want to check out our specials. We offer broiled our deep-fried flounder sandwich, with . . ."

"Thank you, Johnny. You have been very kind. Now please give me a few minutes to look at the menu."

Read*, go away.*

A chastised "Johnny McFarlane" slunk off, muttering a defeated "of course, ma'am; take your time." As he walked away, Katya spoke again. "Oh, and, Johnny, just one more thing?"

Johnny spun around to face her. "Yes, ma'am, what is it?"

Katya giggled. "Well, I feel very strange in asking, but do you have a number here at the bar? Perhaps if I wish to contact you *personally* later in the evening?"

Johnny literally tripped over his own feet, fumbling one of his business cards from under the bar. But then, he realized, his name on the card didn't match the name he'd given her! "Yes, ma'am," he managed, recovering admirably. "I didn't catch your name. Do you have something to write on?"

"It is Kat. And I will remember the number if you to say it to me only one time."

"OK, Kat," Johnny said. "Here it is. Ready?"

The woman's dark eyes sparkled. "I am ready, Johnny." She'd never see "Johnny" again, guaranteed, but a little flirtation might be fun. He WAS, after all, very cute.

Johnny rattled off the number. Katya ordered the ground Delmonico cheeseburger. She was famished. *Fucking makes hungry . . . .*

The woods were indeed "lovely, dark and deep," to shamelessly borrow a phrase from Robert Frost. But in many respects, they were also ugly, hot, and bleak.

Roots, briars, and vines relentlessly snatched at Julia's legs as she ran, as if consciously intent on dragging her to the ground. Gasping for breath, she paused and veered left into the deep forest. It had been a full six minutes; time to text Agent Sonny.

Scotty followed a quarter-mile or so behind, his .45-caliber revolver poised and ready. *All clear so far.* Then, without warning, a gnarled root snared the toe of his brand-new Woody's Wayfarer boot, twisting his ankle sharply to the right. Scotty thought he heard something snap, and he plunged to the forest floor, writhing in pain.

Julia rifled frantically through her pockets for the phone. *It was gone!* Creeping panic began to tighten her chest—and then she remembered. She'd slipped the damn thing into a pouch on the side of her backpack! Julia retrieved it and pressed 6. *Your message has been sent with high priority. We value your business highly. Thank you for using Orizon Wireless Services for all of your . . .* Julia snapped the phone shut and resumed her trek.

Sonny's phone chirped just as Dr. Domenici hurried into Dmitri's room. He quickly shut off the ringer. "What the hell happened, Sonny?" the physician asked.

Sonny turned to face the doctor. "I don't really know. His eyes rolled back, and he just, well, died."

Domenici sighed in exasperation. "People don't *just die* around here, Agent! *What the hell happened?*"

"Can you hear me all right, Doctor?" Sonny asked.

"Of course I can hear you! Tell me what's going on here, or I swear I'll . . ."

"So you heard my whole statement about what happened to Dmitri? You're not actually hearing impaired then, Doctor?"

"Don't patronize me, you ignorant son of a bitch! Of course I heard you perfectly!" Domenici fumed, his cheeks cherry red. "I want to know . . ."

"OK, Doctor. Instant replay. Dmitri asked me to come close, to hold his hand while he whispered something into my ear. I cannot divulge the content of that statement in the interest of national security. Then his eyes rolled back in his head, and he died. It's just that simple. Got it this time?"

Domenici was incensed. "Listen up, asshole. People with stable vitals like Dmitri's don't just suddenly . . . *die*. They . . ."

"They what, *Doctor?* They suffer in agony for years as their life slowly ebbs away? Is that what your patients do?" Sonny retorted, deciding to bluff the physician. "I'm calling Judge Connolly right now for a court order to seize Dmitri's body and perform a comprehensive forensic examination. Connolly is a personal friend of mine, and believe you me, when I tell him about your little outburst, he won't be at all pleased. *If I want it, that court order is already in my hand*—understand?"

The doctor blanched. "Wait, hold on a minute, Agent Sonny. There's no need to involve the authorities in this. Dmitri was an old man with stage three cancer. I apologize for my rude behavior. There's no doubt in my mind that he died of natural causes."

Sonny sighed. "Good call, Doc. I'm sure he did."

Domenici turned, and without another word he began examining his deceased patient. Sonny started to leave, then paused. "No autopsy *here*, either, Doc. I want Dmitri cremated intact, with dignity, and I want to scatter his ashes myself."

"As you wish," Domenici mumbled without bothering to look up. He wanted nothing more than to wash his hands of this case—and of the experimental drug called Spiroclozapar.

Sonny had completely forgotten about the phone call. He was now focused with laser-like intensity on a single, brilliant point of light thirty miles distant—a star that had fallen to earth and lodged itself firmly in the center of his heart; a star named *Katya*.

After five minutes of cautiously picking her way through the forest, Julia's apprehension had escalated to near-panic. Where was Scotty? He was a very fast runner, and he should have caught up with her by now. Julia reversed direction and began retracing her steps toward her partner.

Scotty hoped he'd only sprained his ankle, but as he tried putting his weight on it, the pain was beyond excruciating. *OK, let's just assume I broke it and make a splint.* Scotty dropped to all fours and crawled off into the forest. After a minute or two, he spotted a nice deadfall with sturdy-looking, nearly straight branches protruding from its trunk. *Bingo,* he thought, and crawled toward it.

It looked like a relatively fresh pine—good enough. He couldn't risk using his mini-hatchet because of the noise. Holstering his pistol, Scotty drew his buck knife from its sheath and started hacking. Within a short time, his makeshift splint was firmly in place, and he was armed with a formidable-looking walking stick. Scotty struggled upright and began hobbling back toward the trail.

The splint/walking stick combination seemed to perform admirably. Scotty wasn't surprised; he'd taken second place in his state Eagle Scout foresting competition, and if nothing else, he could still construct a very serviceable splint out of next to nothing. Then Scotty froze. *Something BIG was moving through the woods*—an animal, or worse. He slipped behind the cover of a huge oak tree, drew his revolver, and waited.

Katya finished her burger (very tasty) and ordered another big mug of her favorite beer. She chatted up "Johnny," flirting shamelessly, and after what seemed like only minutes, the second mug was empty. Katya ordered another.

She was learning quite a lot about her bartender. As to whether or not that information was accurate, she didn't know, and didn't much care. *What's worse, ignorance or apathy?* Katya recalled the familiar joke and giggled. Johnny, hanging on Katya's every nuance, noticed. "What's so funny, my dear?" he asked.

"Oh, nothing, Johnny, nothing at all. I just suddenly remembered an old joke."

"What joke, m'lady? Please share it with me," Johnny said.

"It's silly. You must have heard it a million times."

"I'm all ears, Kat. Please, let's make it a million and one times. Go ahead."

"OK, OK, here it goes. What is worse, ignorance or apathy? Have you heard it?"

"I don't think so. OK, I'll bite. Which is worse, ignorance or apathy?"

Katya, now well past tipsy, giggled again. "I don't know—and I don't care!"

To all appearances, Johnny truly had never heard the ancient joke. He nearly collapsed with laughter, fighting to catch his breath. Finally he regained a modicum of composure. "Oh, shit, that's great, Kat! Where on earth did that come from?"

"I do not know. I think that perhaps I first heard it at a conference in your capital city, Washington, D.C."

"I've only been in the actual city two or three times," Johnny rejoined. "They were all bachelor parties. We went to strip clubs. One night, we partied until the sun came up. You mind if I have a cigarette?"

"What the hell do *you* think, dummy? Go right ahead," Katya replied, still giggling like a madwoman. "Why would I care? Have you not noticed that I myself smoke like a stovepipe?"

Johnny chuckled. "With your cigars, it's more like a garbage dump on fire."

"Oh, but I also bring with me a box of fresh Cubans! They are illegal here in America, but Ukraine has no such silly restrictions on trade with Cuba. You would like to try?"

"Aaahh! Cubans? Really? Yeah, I'd love to try one, Kat," Johnny said.

Katya downed the last of her beer. "Wait for me, Johnny. I must go to my room. The Cuban cigars are there."

"Would you like another beer, Kat? It's still on the house."

"Do not pour it just now. Wait until I return, Johnny, and I shall see . . . ."

She was way, *way* too drunk. She had to shake this guy. It had been fun, but Sonny could return at any time. "Hold my seat open, Johnny. Whoa, do not take that in the wrong way. I shall return in a moment . . . ." Katya staggered to the lobby, catching the first elevator to her floor. She had to sober up! She weaved her way to her room, opened the door on the third try, and flopped full-length on her queen-size bed. The room spun about her, but she was used to that. She'd live through it—she always had—and this episode was no worse than the Marseilles conference. Certainly it paled in comparison to the Madrid episode, where she'd drunk nearly a gallon of wine, only to puke it all over the banquet table, narrowly missing the nation's chief of national security with a violent spout of blood-red vomit.

She'd just relax and wait for Sonny . . . .

CHAPTER XIII

The Wait

It would prove to be a very long wait for Katya. Riding the hospice elevator, Sonny decided to call her and let her know that he was on his way. As he flipped open his cell phone, he noticed a voice mail marked urgent. It was from Scotty—and it was the call he missed in Dmitri's room. The one he'd totally forgotten about! The elevator's bell chimed as he reached ground level, and Sonny rushed out into the hallway, already halfway through Scotty's message. He leaned against the wall as the lengthy voice mail concluded: " . . . If you get this call, Sonny, we are in a perilous situation and require immediate extraction. It tells you that Julia, at least, has survived long enough to press the SEND key. Recommend you dispatch an armed chopper immediately. The woods are almost impassable, and you can expect heavy ground fire. Use your IR to spot us. Scotty out."

Click. Dial tone. Although the hospice was cool, Sonny was once again sweating like a pig as he searched for an empty room where he could transcribe the information into his little spiral notepad. *Blew that one, didn't you, Sonny old chap? Thinking with the wrong part of your anatomy?* Now his two rising stars were most likely dead, or screaming in some subterranean abattoir. It was time to get moving.

Sonny spotted his empty room and prayed it was unlocked. The sign above the door read, "Patient Conference Room PC-6."

Please, God . . . Sonny twisted the knob, and mercifully the door swung open. Shaking uncontrollably, Sonny wobbled in and dropped heavily onto the chair. Flipping open his notepad, he listened to the message several times before he'd gleaned all the necessary information. Right now, Katya was the furthest thing from his mind.

Evidently Scotty and Julia were working their way through the woods, following a trail that roughly paralleled the access road. Scotty was right—he would need a chopper to have any chance of his spotting them. The Carlisle office, where Julia worked, had two helicopters, but both were unarmed. Thirty miles farther out, in Virginia, the Ragland State Police barracks had a lightly-armed helo. *Probably best not to get the agency involved, anyway. Spy vs. spy? Very bad medicine.*

Police Captain Ricky Nellis had helped him out in the past, and maybe Sonny could count on him again. He made the call.

By now, Katya was wide awake, mostly sober—and positively *fuming.* How *dare* he not call! The sun hung low in the western sky, its waning rays casting long shadows across the courtyard sixteen stories below her window. *Men,* Katya snorted. *They're all the same, everywhere. He's probably sweet-talking some cute young nurse right now, or . . .* Katya's head swam with graphic, vile images of what Sonny and Little Miss Nursey might be doing at that very moment. She decided to call him. Maybe she could at least toss a little ice water on his fun. That might have to suffice for now.

Katya pressed 1 on her speed dial, and Sonny picked up on the second ring. "Katya! Oh, my . . . I'm so sorry, honey, I . . . emergency. I have to . . . extraction . . ." Katya struggled to hear him; the signal cut in and out, and the background noise—a persistent hum and a *whup-whup-whup* sound—rendered conversation nearly impossible.

"Sonny, I can barely hear you! Where the hell *are* you?"

" . . . copter. We're going in . . ." The signal cut out again, this time for good.

Katya sat down hard on her bed, her mind scrambling to piece together the fragments of their desultory conversation: *emergency . . . extraction . . . copter . . . going in.* A clammy hand seemed to caress the back of her neck as she comprehended the gravity of what she'd just heard: Sonny was in a helicopter, either with a life-threatening dental emergency or, more likely, on a mission to rescue an agent from a potentially lethal situation.

Oh, Sonny, I am so sorry! How could I ever doubt you, my sweet love? Katya sobbed as waves of remorse swept over her. *What kind of person AM I, anyway?*

As the creature in the woods drew closer, Scotty recognized the sounds as those of a human being, one with limited experience in walking undetected through woods. The rustling noise came out of the east. *Could it be Julia?* Suddenly the rustling ceased, and the next sound he heard left no doubt in Scott's mind: *it was the sound of a duck quacking!*

Then: Dad was a drunken, self-proclaimed author who wrote short fiction for now-defunct men's magazines like *True* and *Argosy*. His brief claim to fame was a seven-part sci-fi series published in *Amazing Stories*. Later, when that market grew hard and shrank to near-nothing (or was it his atrophying BRAIN that had shrunken?), he occasionally wrote contributing articles for *Science and Mechanics*, using material he distilled from the popular science literature.

He was a quiet, gentle drunk. Pappy always kept food on the table and clothes on their backs, and he never abused Momma and the kids. Not physically, not verbally. Nor did he pay much attention to them. Pappy spent most of his time either working at the small stamping plant by the tracks, flipping burgers at Grady's Pub 'n' Grub on the corner, or hunched over his typewriter in that sweltering/freezing garage.

The sole exception was duck season, or pheasant, or wild turkey. Pappy loved bird season, and he always took the kids hunting. They ADORED it! He taught them all duck calls, for mallards, for mergansers . . . .

"I was always best at it. My brothers' calls didn't hold a candle! Listen . . . *waak, waak* . . ."

Just three nights ago (it seemed like a *lifetime*, as if he were remembering scenes from early childhood, blurred and faded, like old photographs), Scotty had sat across the table, gaping in mortified bewilderment as Julia's convincing mallard mating call reverberated though O'Malley's dining room. Several heads had popped up, then turned quickly back to their dinners and conversations. Julia had told him the whole story that night over gallons of Athens Cellars Classic Merlot.

"Red! *Red!* Scotty!" Scott whispered sharply, cupping his hands to focus the sound. The rustling resumed and grew louder with each step. In a moment, Julia popped into the little clearing, her raven hair stringy and dripping wet. "Scotty! Oh, my God . . ."

Security Specialist Nick Bundy had just returned to the recon center from his smoke break, and his long black hair also hung in sweaty strings. He'd been gone far too long, enjoying his illegal, hand-rolled treat, having become fascinated by the earthworms crawling across the walkway. They had been all in a line like a convoy of little soldiers following one another across a trackless desert of parched concrete with a cool, verdant oasis just ahead, beckoning . . . .

Nick Bundy was a sick bastard. He took another hit off his "cigarette," strode forward, and ground the lead earthworm under his boot. "Let them see death. Then, let them taste it," he chortled softly.

Just then, the door swung open. It was Rodney. "Hey, Nick. Jacob wants to see you, on the double. In his office . . ."

Nick glared back at him. "I got a bone to pick with you, *boy.* You were supposed to pick me up today. I was two hours late for work! You're costing me money, and *I don't like it!*"

Rodney was a short guy with glasses, a geeky engineer type, pocket protector and all. In fact, he was chief design engineer for the facility's prototype shop, where his second cousin Mel Jenkins worked as a machinist. Rodney came from a small town and was not a fighter by nature. Tall, lanky Nick Bundy was a city boy, born and raised in South Detroit, and he had at least six inches' height on the smaller man.

"Hey, Nick. I drove by your place, and you weren't there. I was right on time. You've been making *me* late—for *days!* And Mel! Maybe you oughta get out there a few minutes earlier tomorrow, huh?"

Side Note: Four Hours Earlier The entire situation was ludicrous. Rodney had dutifully swung by Nick's place every day for the past week while City Boy's car was in the shop. Every day, Nick was late for his pickup at the entrance to his apartment complex, and Rodney faithfully drove into the maze to ferret him out. Today, though, the geek was vexed; Nick wasn't at the gate. Again. Mel looked over at Rodney. "Whatcha wanna do, cuz?"

"Guess we better try and call him, Mel. Here, take my cell, will ya? Just punch 7 on speed dial, and tell Nick we'll wait another five minutes for him."

Mel complied. After a moment, he snapped the phone shut. "He didn't pick up, Rod. I left him a voice mail. Told him he better get his ass out here in five minutes or we're leavin'." Mel handed the phone back to his cousin. Six minutes later, there was still no sign of Nick.

Mel spoke. "It's up to you, Rod. He's gonna make you late again. That lame fuck's waitin' for you to drive in there again and carry him out to the car. Whatcha think, son? Personally, I'd ditch the lowlife."

"Yeah, screw him, Mel! I'm heading in to work." Mel winked and nodded. "I got your back on this if any shit breaks loose." Rodney swung back out into traffic and made a beeline for the compound . . .

"*Oh, yeah?*" Nick said. "I'll be looking for you after work, bitch, and I'm gonna kick your ass!"

"See Jacob, Nick. His office. And find another ride to work from now on," Rodney replied, slamming the door shut.

A few minutes later, Nick settled in to review the last thirty minutes of tape from the security cameras at triple speed. If he'd missed something important, he wouldn't need to worry about any more rides to work unless he could somehow gloss over his mistake.

There were fifteen perimeter cameras mounted on the fence, and each recorded on a separate track of a single tape. Track sixteen was reserved for the elapsed-time display. All sixteen channels could be displayed simultaneously on Nick's huge LCD wall screen in a tile format that allowed him to instantly zoom in on any particular scene.

Nick Bundy watched the display with drowsy indifference: grass, fence, road; grass, fence, road. *It's always the same,* he thought. For 364 days of the year, that was true, but not on this day, at 187:14:28:16, Julian time. Nick snapped to attention as two hikers approached the perimeter fence. He expanded tile 13 to full-screen and used the crosshairs to lock the image position on Scott's head. The picture now on the screen was a zoomed-in and expanded rectangle representing only a small portion of the full image captured by the camera. Once he expanded the image to full screen, he could zoom in for greater detail; the crosshairs would keep Scott centered as he moved within the boundaries of the available frame space. Nick punched Pause and Lock Rel Pos. Then he pressed Run and throttled down to normal playback speed.

Yeah, there they were— a coupl'a hippies out lost in the woods. Nick kinda liked the woman's ass, so he zoomed in on Julia. *This resolution sucks,* Nick thought. *How could you ever finger a suspect in a court of law with this picture? Shit, why not just shoot over to Best Bargain? Grab a 2TB external hard drive and a decent quad-processor motherboard with a couple hundred gig of RAM. The whole damn project wouldn't cost more than four thousand bucks! I could upgrade this whole system for under . . .* Abruptly the woman disappeared. Nick zoomed out a bit and saw her a couple of yards from the man, who now sat on the asphalt, shaking his head. *That dumb fuck touched the fence! Oh, I gotta see this!* Nick rewound the tape, meanwhile slipping his thumb drive into the USB port. He paused the tape just as the pair appeared, opened ScreenCap Video, and set the start point to Auto-detect source run. Then he selected the tape drive as source and the thumb drive as destination, and hit Enter.

The tape rolled, and Nick watched the drama unfold on hi-def. He'd record the screen capture to his thumb drive real-time, copy it to a CD-Micro and hand it to Jacob. From that point on, it was Jacob's problem, unless the little twerp wanted him to hunt them down like dogs and gut-shoot them. Nick would enjoy participating in *that* action! "Hey, I'm Sick Nick, the security prick, and I'm here to help."

Yeah, Nick saw it—the dumb fuck had touched the fence and landed flat on his ass! The whole episode was otherwise uneventful; after a minute or so, Dumbass hauled himself up, and the pair disappeared into the woods. *Just a couple of stupid hikers; no apparent security concerns here.* Nick burned the CD and strode off to Jacob's office. This would look good on his year-end review—the ever-vigilant security guard just doin' his job. On point, on time, and under budget. In his own universe, Security Specialist Nick Bundy was, truly, the shit.

CHAPTER XIV

Magic Carpet Ride

"There it is, Ricky—eleven o'clock. See it? And there's the access road."

"Copy, Sonny. Hang on. I'll circle back to 31 and make a pass at treetop level. Sharp left turn—ready?"

"Ready," Sonny replied, shooting Captain Nellis a traditional thumbs-up. "You copy that, Gunnar?" Nellis said, pulsing Lieutenant Gunnar Martin, who manned the .30-caliber machine gun in the 'copter's flank.

"Gunnar copies. Go for engagement, Captain," Martin replied. The rotorcraft rolled sharply to the left; Sonny groaned as the five-point harness bit cruelly into his flesh. Finally, the aircraft righted itself, and he breathed again. Sonny decided to chance a call to Scotty. Hopefully his cell was turned on and he'd had the good sense to switch it to vibrate mode.

Indeed he had; on the forest floor, the cell phone buzzed in Julia's hand, startling her. In fact, she'd just flipped the phone open to hazard another call to Sonny. "Sonny!" Julia whispered into the mouthpiece, "is it really you? Thank God! We just heard a helicopter in the distance. Are you here?"

"It's us, Julia, in the chopper. We just turned around, and we're on our way back to 31. We're going to make a 180-degree turn at the highway and fly back toward the compound along the access road. Where are you now? Do you have any way to signal us?"

The hum and *whup-whup-whup* in her earbud made it tough to hear Sonny, but Julia got the message. "Stand by one, Sonny. I'll ask my boy scout." In a moment, she came back. "Scotty has a small mirror to reflect the sunlight, and he's starting a signal fire as we speak."

"Great, hon! Where are you guys right now? On the trail?"

"Just off the trail, using the woods for cover. We're about a third of the way back to Highway 31. It's been slow going, Sonny. Scott broke his ankle."

"Oh, no! Julia, can you hear the chopper? Where is the sound coming from relative to your position?"

"Yes, I can hear it. Hang on," Julia said, retrieving her compass. "OK, Sonny. I'm pointed straight north, so you'd be, uh, southwest of us. Um, if you're heading dead east, we'd be at about 10 o'clock from where you sit."

"Hold that thought, hon . . . ." Julia waited, listening to the confounding cockpit noise in her earpiece. "Julia? Is there a clearing behind you somewhere, with a patch of dead trees?" She spun around. They were almost directly opposite the spot Sonny had described!

"Yes! Yes, Sonny. We're right across the trail from that clearing! Can you see the smoke from Scotty's fire?"

"Negative. Stand by . . . . OK, I see the fire's heat signature on IR. We're a mile out. Start flashing that mirror!"

Meanwhile, back at the compound, Nick Bundy was on the carpet. Jacob was in rare form; the night shift guard had found a marijuana bud under Nick's station. "What makes you think it was mine?" Nick asked innocently.

"Who else's would it be? I think I smell pot on you right now! Your eyes are red and glassy! Now, Nick," Jacob said, his expression cold and compassionless as a frozen lake, "get your ass down to Medical and request a tox screen—a full spectrum blood test—and report back here ASAP! Got it? And Nick, leave me that CD you just made. I'll call Nurse Hicks and tell her to expedite this. Get moving!"

"Yessir. Right away, Jacob." Nick rose and scuttled out the door, knees wobbling.

He made his way toward the elevator next to the fire stairs. Looking up, he saw two guys from the fabrication shop, Johnny Whiting and Mel Jenkins, approaching. Spotting Nick, they both grinned broadly. "Nicky! Just the man we're looking for! We need to talk to you, real quick. Got a minute?"

Why in hell do they want to talk to ME? Nick wondered. "Wuzzup, fellas? Sorry, no time to talk. Jacob just sent me downstairs for a drug test. Like, right away, dig?"

"Mmmm, mmm, mmm," Johnny Whiting, a wiry black man, said, shaking his head. "How's about we walk down wit' you? Just take a coupl'a minutes, an' we can walk an' talk. It's real important, man."

"Extremely important, Nick. My cousin Rodney's talkin' about you behind your back, and you need to hear it. For your own good," Mel Jenkins reiterated.

Now Nick was almost face-to-face with Mel Jenkins. Both men still wore toothy grins, and there was a strange look in Mel's eyes. "Listen, guys. I gotta get down to Medical on the double. Maybe later?" he said, reaching for the elevator's call button.

Mel's arm shot out, knocking Nick's hand away from the button. "Later's too late, Nicky. C'mon. Let's take the stairs. They might even get you there faster than the elevator." The two men exchanged a glance, laughing merrily.

Johnny spoke then. "Better listen to Mel, Nick. Scuttlebutt's flyin' hot 'n' heavy, and it's only a matter of time before this makes it to the front office. You do not want that, *believe* me."

Mel wrapped his arm around Nick's shoulders. "C'mon, boy, time to roll on down." Johnny opened the door to the fire stairs . . . .

Jacob watched the CD and fumed. Those hikers might have witnessed today's activities in the yard, and at the very least they'd heard the gunfire during the "sacrifice." No apparent security risk? WTF? Bundy was clearly too zoned to do his job; he must go. And go he would, once the drug test fingered him.

Jacob picked up his desk phone and called the site's SEALS focal, Jesus (pronounced *Hey-soos*) Rodriguez. SEALS was an acronym for Security Extreme Actions Liaison Squad—and, truly, they were all that. It was they, in fact, who were assigned the dirty job of effecting today's mutie massacre (ahem, "specimen sacrifice").

Jesus was, in reality, a very nice guy—gentle, caring, compassionate. In fact, he had been one step away from ordination as a Catholic priest, but in a gut-wrenching, eleventh-hour decision, he had backed away. His decision had hinged on two key points: the vow of celibacy and his sect's recent embrace of Mary as "co-redemptrix" with Christ.

Jesus had read his well-worn Bible from cover to cover perhaps a hundred times, and he'd found nothing in Scripture to support either view, other than Paul's statement about it being better for a man to remain celibate if he had that spiritual gift. But then the Apostle had talked about marrying rather than burning for those with healthy sexual desires. And the Word clearly stated that Christ was the one-and-only Savior! Furthermore, as for Mary's redemptive power, Christ had made it clear that "no one cometh to the Father, except by Me (Christ)."

My Savior never said "by Momma and Me," Hey-soos had determined.

So it was good-bye to the priesthood and hello to the Marine Corps. God's Word hardly forbade killing in wars against enemies of the Lord, and it seemed to actually condone the slaughter of animals and heathens. The former Marine thought of King David—a man after God's own heart—slaying his tens of thousands. In Jesus's mind, the muties fell squarely into one, if not all, of these categories. They sure as hell weren't human, and as soulless animals threatening the security of America, the Strong Tower for God's saints, the muties had had to go.

Jesus was easy with his decision. He obeyed his masters. He was strong in his faith, and if he had not chosen wisely—well, that's where Grace comes in. To err is human; to forgive is divine. Jesus answered his phone. "Major Rodriguez. How may I help you?"

"Jesus, it's Jacob Farr here. We have a potentially serious situation on our hands. Can you come up here on the double? There's something you need to see."

"On my way."

The signal fire had begun to peter out. Scotty asked Julia to grab some more dry branches. That would be easy; it had been a drought-category year, and the woods were drier than a tinderbox. He just hoped a gust of wind didn't turn the entire area into a holocaust.

He heard the helicopter approaching as Julia reappeared, carrying an armload of desiccated twigs. "Julia, quick, toss that wood on the fire! I hear the chopper!" She complied, and the small blaze bloomed immediately, its heat driving them back.

"I just got a strong IR signature. We're almost right over their heads!" Ricky said. The pilot's headphone crackled as Gunnar shouted, "I see 'em, sir! One o'clock! Two hundred yards out!"

"Copy, Gunnar. I got a hard visual. Man that lifeline. We're goin' in!"

At the same time, a four-man SEALS team was also rallying their forces. They were loaded for hiker, carrying minimal armament (individual handguns and a single M-16). Those two tree-huggers were probably unarmed, anyway, and shouldn't present much of a problem. On that first assumption and then a second, bolder one, Rodriguez had issued his men light weapons. *Just frag 'em, bag and tag 'em, and bring me back the remains. By their very presence here*, Hay-soos had reasoned, *these people ARE enemies of the state!* As their Jeep rolled slowly along the access road, the sniper, Dave Raley, cradled his M-16 and basked in the afternoon sun, humming Gospel tunes.

The team leader, Moses Douglass, heard the helicopter well before he saw it. "Heads up, boys. Sounds like a SAR chopper, out lookin' for our turkeys." He pulled off onto the shoulder and raised Ramirez on his walkie-talkie. "Got a search-and-rescue 'copter up ahead, boss. Request further direction. Over."

LV–51A REVISITED

Katya decided to head back to the site. It had been hours since her last drink; she was damn-near sober now, and she *did* have a diplomatic driver's license to cover her if worse came to worst. *Just try and extradite me from Ukraine for impaired driving,* she thought. For a first offense? *Ha!*

Twenty minutes later, she'd arrived safely at the warehouse, endured the invasive security protocol, and was now headed for the boxes of bones. Thoughts raced through Katya's mind as the Marine escorted her down the long aisle: *This stuff is real! What does it mean for the future of mankind, for religion? What sort of mission WAS Sonny on right now? Does it have anything to do with the embryos? What had Sonny learned from Dmitri? Would the Americans let her make plaster casts of the bones to ship back home?* Her cell phone languished in the security booth, so photos were out of the question. They hadn't confiscated her notepad, though, and she was a pretty fair sketch artist; she'd make do for now and talk to Sonny later about a photo clearance.

Katya noticed something different. Two more crates had been pried open. A familiar figure pawed through one of the boxes; it was Major Asshole again! Did he LIVE here, or something? Katya shuddered with revulsion, affected a friendly smile, and walked toward the open box. "Find anything interesting in there, Major?" she chirped.

Major Tom Brennan's head snapped up from his task. "Just a bunch of kids' shirts and pants. Why in hell would this stuff be in here?"

157

Katya now leaned on the side of the crate. "Well, let's see." She trained her flashlight on the contents and noticed a strange inscription on one of the T-shirts. She sketched it on her pad as accurately as she could: **U3&NzT7**. "Well, Tom, maybe they're not children's clothes at all. Maybe they're from the crash site. The aliens are smaller . . ."

Major Tom sighed in exasperation, rolling his piggy little eyes. "Oh, come on, Doctor, get a grip! I mean, why jump immediately to some extraterrestrial conclusion? There's a very rational explanation for all of this! You're just not seeing it!"

"And the bones, Tom? What about the bones?"

"Primates—or deformed humans! Hell, I don't know. Deformed baboons, maybe? Freaks of nature!"

Katya sighed. "Yeah, you're probably right, Tom. Did they find anything else yet?"

"Oh yes, Katya! Very interesting! Right over there in that small crate?"

"Yes, what is it, Tom?" Katya asked.

"Human remains," Major Malfunction said, grinning ghoulishly. "Along with a couple of mysterious-looking boxes and a bunch of books written in a strange language. Might wanna check it out."

Katya was already on the move. "Thanks, Tom."

As she walked away, Major Tom called out to her, "Glad you finally see things my way, babe! How about dinner and drinks?" Katya didn't even pause in her retreat, casually flipping Tom the bird.

Rodriguez called Jacob, and Jacob called Jeff McLean in D.C. "If you take that med evac chopper down, shit will fly all the way from here to hell and back," McLean said. "Instruct your men to *only* maintain surveillance from the side road, and offer assistance if appropriate. Do not—I repeat, do not—engage. Tell your men to fire warning shots if, and *only* if, retreat is deemed necessary. *Are we clear*, Jacob?"

"We are crystal clear, *sir!* Copy that!" Jacob replied.

"Good. Call me when it's over. Full report. McLean out."

Jacob phoned Jesus Rodriguez, and Jesus raised Moses Douglass on the walkie-talkie. "Stand down for now. Maintain surveillance and render assistance as necessary. Do not engage. That's the word from the top. Warning shots authorized exclusively to facilitate retreat if, and only if, absolutely necessary. Understood?"

"Understood, sir."

"Kill somebody out there and you're in very deep shit, Moses. This comes from upstairs. I can't protect you. You're closer to me than a brother. Be careful!"

"Thanks, Jesus. I hear you, pal, loud and clear. Moses out."

A Trip Downstairs: Nick Bundy was perplexed, and none too comfortable, with Mel's big arm still draped securely around his shoulders. Johnny asked innocently, "Them security cameras is down hard, ain't they, Mel?"

"So I hear, bud. Somebody trashed the circuit box earlier today. Musta known what he was doin'. Only the cams in this stairwell are dead, from what I gather."

"Mmm, mmm, mmm. How 'bout that, Mel? Ain't that somethin?" Johnny replied.

The storm front was approaching rapidly now, and in this region of the state, thunderstorms typically followed the high winds an hour or two later. The rain would arrive far too late to save Mendoza and his Devil's Workshop from the impending firestorm. Thirty prize mutants, ten alien embryos, and most of the staff would perish in the blaze, along with reams of highly classified information and research data. The seventeen survivors would escape with only scant minutes to spare. One was none other than Mendoza, carrying a bag stuffed with disks, papers and five embryo tubes. The doctor was on his way to the airport, planning to catch the next flight to his native Argentina; there, he could continue his research undisturbed. Another survivor was one Nick Bundy, his body screaming with the pain of his long trip down the stairs with Johnny and Mel . . . .

Mel still had his big arm wrapped around Nick's shoulders as the trio made their way down the fire stairs. "So, tell me, Nick, just what did my cuz Rod do to you, anyway? He was talkin' some shit, like you THREATENED him! He said you was gonna kick his ass?"

Nick punted. "Well, we had a little disagreement about him drivin' me to work while my car's in the shop. You're his cousin, Mel?"

"Second cousin, Nick. Raised Rod from a pup after his pappy skipped out on my cousin, Jennie-Mae. Go on . . ."

"Mel, you gotta understand, man! Rodney promised to pick me up this week, and today he just stiffed me! I was two hours late for work, and believe me, bud, I really need the money to fix my car. I had to borrow my roommate Bobby's Hyundai. The cab never came, see, and I hadda do somethin', right?"

"Mmmm, I see. But Rod mentioned the worms out back. What's that all about, pal?" Mel gave Nick a powerful slap on the back, and City Boy skidded down the last three steps.

"Mel, WHAT THE FUCK, MAN?" Johnny chuckled in the background. "Careful, Nick. Watch your step. Them stairs is tough ta negotiate when you fucked up."

Mel continued. "I was ridin' with Rod today. He said he had to drive into your fuckin' ant farm of an apartment complex all week and had to park and almost carry your sorry ass out the door. How many times you think you made HIM late, you piece of shit? I gave Rod the high sign to ditch you today, and now you best take it up with me! I'M costing you money, and I'M here to settle up. You lost two hours; what's that worth?"

Nick wiped the blood from his swollen lip. He'd hit the landing pretty hard, skinned his hand, too. "Uh, really, Mel? You serious, man?"

Mel was on the landing now, offering his hand. "C'mon, Nick. Get up. Let's have a face-to-face, OK?"

"Yeah, sure, Mel. Well, let's see, you know, I'm thinking I owe Rodney a few bucks for hauling my ass in here . . . ."

"Yeah? Yeah, go on, Nick," Mel said, pulling City Boy to his feet and draping his arm around Nick's shoulders again. "Whatcha got in mind, pal? Talk to me!"

"Well, I'm thinkin' I've been a real ungrateful prick. I was wrong to inconvenience you guys, and, well, I just kinda lost my head when I had to scramble to find a ride to work today. I'm sorry!"

Mel led Nick to the top of the second flight of stairs. Together, they stepped down. "I say I owe Rodney a few bucks. For all his trouble."

Mel paused on the third step, grabbing Nick's chin between his powerful fingers. "Read my lips, you lowlife piece of SHIT! You owe Rodney an apology—and some RESPECT! He sure as HELL didn't help you 'cause he likes you or 'cause you're such a prince of a guy. He did it because he wants to help folks that's down! And you do WHAT? You turn around and shit in his face! He'd of even picked you up tomorrow, if you just did the minimum, made it out to the corner ON TIME! And you know what else, Dee-troit?"

"Whatsat, Mel?"

"I know your kind! Your little brain is racing right now, thinkin' about how you're gonna make Rod pay for this. Go ahead, try it! Anything happens to my cuz and I'm comin' after your ass, an' it won't be pretty, muthafucka!"

Johnny added, "And after Mel's done wit' you, you got ME."

"So, little buddy, here's the deal. You apologize to Rodney TO-DAY . . . and from here on out, you treat people with RESPECT! If I hear one more thing about . . ."

"Mel, Johnny, please! I'll change. People can change, right? I will, I swear!"

"Well, City Boy, I figure we's even on the money. Rod didn't ask for nothing from you, and he don't want it. Hell, he makes three times your salary. Know what, though?"

"What's that, Mel?"

"You better get your ass down to Medical. You mighta busted something. Here, we'll give you a hand . . . ."

With a gentle shove from behind, Nick tumbled down the second flight of stairs. Now he lay screaming on the landing. "Please, Mel! PLEASE! STOP IT! YOU'RE KILLING ME, MAN!"

Johnny spoke up. "Whadda you think, Mel? It's one more flight down. Think he can make it on his own now?"

Mel glared down at Nick. "How ya feelin' now, boy?"

"Please, oh, PLEASE, Mel! I think I busted my arm! Please, NO MORE!" Mel glanced up at Johnny. "He's pretty busted up, man. I think we better help our boy the rest of the way down."

Johnny smiled, nodding sagely. "It's prob'ly best if we do."

"Yeah, and our boy needs some more time to think about all this on the way down."

"Hey, Dee-Troit, how many worms ya smash out there on the sidewalk? Don' lie, now, unnastan'?" Johnny queried.

"Uh, ah, three, Johnny. Honest, just three . . ."

Johnny and Mel exchanged significant glances. Mel nodded. "Hmmm . . . three dead mommies and three dead pappies. All earthworms are both male and female; you know that? Three flights of stairs. One down, two ta go. Shit, Johnny, I think it's a sign or sumpin'! Whatcha think, man?"

Johnny smiled, his predatory grin showcasing his single gold incisor. "I thinks they ain't no co-inciden' in life, Mel, jus' happy assiden'!"

Incredibly, Nick chimed in, spitting a bloody chunk of tooth onto the concrete. "Sounds like the worms can all just go and fuck themselves."

Both men laughed uproariously. "He's a funny guy, Mel, funny guy!"

JUST OUTSIDE THE DOOR

"I gotta set you back down!" Gunnar shouted from the port in the chopper's belly. There was something wrong with the winch. The motor groaned painfully under the weight of the two agents. Gunnar smelled hot electrical wiring. *Better bring 'em up one at a time.*

At Scotty's insistence, Julia went up first. The motor labored, but held. With Julia safely on board, the rescue line descended again.

A deep, penetrating voice crackled over a bullhorn from the general direction of the service road. "This is Officer Douglass, Site Security. Do you require assistance? I repeat, do you need help?"

Scotty bellowed, "No, NEGATIVE! My companion is on board the chopper, and I am ascending on the rescue line! Nothing to see here, Security. Show's over. Move along, folks!"

A chuckle came over the bullhorn. "OK, smartass, you and the lady friend are on your own. Good luck, kids."

"Thanks, pal! Everything's cool. No worries!" Scott hollered from thirty feet overhead.

"Copy. Douglass out."

Scotty looked down, spotting Douglass and three others in their Jeep. He waved, shooting them a thumbs-up. The four waved back as their vehicle began to turn toward the compound. Douglass raised his bullhorn a final time. "Good luck, smartass! Move along, show's over, nothing more to see here!" Scotty smiled as he watched the Jeep speeding back to the Devil's Workshop. *What the fuck just happened here?* he wondered.

Scotty groaned in pain as the lurching cable bucked and jolted, painfully joggling his screaming ankle. Fifteen feet more . . . eleven . . . eight . . . ALMOST HOME! . . . six feet, five, four . . .

SHIT! Gunnar Martin cursed as the motor ground to a halt, humming loudly and emitting acrid wisps of black smoke. Martin punched the red STOP button. The humming ceased immediately, and he heard the safety pawl snap into place, locking the cable spool. Scotty was safe for now, albeit uncomfortable as hell. They still had two or three of the big CO_2 fire extinguishers on board, back in the aft cargo hold. Gunnar could try using them to cool down the frying drive motor before its internal heat killed it completely. He raised the captain. "Ricky, Gunnar. Tow line's stuck; subject's still five or six feet out. Motor got too hot and stalled. Gonna try the CO_2 extinguishers to cool her down fast! Over!"

"Copy, Gunnar. Reducing forward airspeed to twenty knots. Should just be enough to keep Scotty cool. Use extinguishers as required. Report back if situation changes. Copy?"

"Copy. Gunnar out." Martin snagged a mini-bullhorn from a hook on an aft stringer and bellowed to Scotty, "We just stalled the motor, pal. It got too hot. I'm gonna try an' cool her down real fast and pull you up. Understood?"

Scotty smiled up at him, flashing a double thumbs-up.

"Hang in there, buddy—no pun intended! You're only six feet under. We can haul you aboard by hand if we gotta," Gunnar said. Scotty waved, still grinning from ear to ear. In actuality, he was kind of enjoying the ride.

Captain Nellis gradually eased his rotorcraft to its thousand-foot cruising altitude. Eleven miles to the southeast, a storm system was broiling ominously. Gusts of up to forty miles per hour were predicted. A twenty-knot microburst lofted dying embers from Scotty's signal fire, which he'd presumed long dead, spraying a fusillade of smoldering pine needles into the air. The gust fanned them to brilliant asters and carried them into the underbrush just to the west. A little fire sprang to life. Then, as the tinder wood on the ground caught, the flames bloomed brightly and began moving westward with the prevailing wind.

Last Stop, Medical: "OK, funny guy. On your feet. We gotta git you down to Medical," Mel said, hauling Nick back to a standing position. The next flight of stairs yawned menacingly as Mel held him at the precipice. "Two down, one ta go, City Boy!" With a gentle shove, Nick Bundy was once again in free fall . . . .

A seemingly endless time later, Nick smacked *hard* against the ground floor, bleeding and broken. He did not stop. He did not pass Go. He did not go directly to Medical. Rather, he crawled painfully on all fours out the fire door and across the broiling asphalt parking lot. He dragged himself into Bobby's car and wept with the pain of his seriously blistered palms. Damn good thing they'd only *maybe* fractured his right leg (his broken arm was merely a ruse to make them *FUCKING STOP*), and he could still see well enough out of his cloudy right eye to drive. Bobby's little bile-green Hyundai had a stick shift, but he could *probably* negotiate the pedals with his left foot.

What was that smell in the air, he wondered? It brought to mind burning leaves, bonfires, drunken parties on the beach—and Renee English, his high school sweetheart, the only girl he'd ever really loved. There *was* a distinct haze blowing in from the southeast. The wind whistled and cavorted across the parking lot, rocking the little car and scattering dust and debris as menacing thunderheads roiled in the east. Then Nick spotted the first flames. *Shit, there's a forest fire up by the east access road! Better take the back way out.* That decision saved Nick Bundy's twisted life.

Nick drove away from the approaching flame front, never looking back. As the fire encroached upon the complex, it ignited a "fuel dump" first, a fenced yard containing twenty or so 500-gallon propane tanks. Had Nick been close enough to watch the resulting fireball engulf the complex, he might have literally died laughing.

But as it was, the miscreant only heard a big *kaboom* in the distance. The shock wave did rock his little car slightly, but Nick had made good time in spite of his injuries. He was already nine miles out and heading northwest on County Road 76 when the brief burst of scorching air caught his tail. The Hyundai's rear wheels skidded briefly to the left, but Nick quickly corrected. He coaxed the reluctant vehicle up to ninety, manhandling the car along CR-76's perilous turns and hills as the afternoon sun gradually slipped behind the treetops . . . .

Scotty did not fare as well as Nick. The chopper was about eight hundred feet in the air and two miles out when the propane tanks blew. Scotty, still swinging in his harness as Gunnar plied the recalcitrant motor with frigid carbon dioxide, was rent from the towline when the shock wave hit. Ricky had seen the fireball coming and was struggling to gain altitude, but to his ascent wasn't fast enough. He and Sonny watched in horror as Scott plunged into the inferno, slamming into the ground at probably 160 mph. Ricky rode the shock wave upward, meanwhile gunning the bird to maximize the climb rate. Finally leveling off at five thousand feet, Ricky said to Sonny, "Hey, bud, can you take it for a minute? Nothing to it, pal, believe me. Just grab the stick—yeah, right there. Now, see that ball that looks like there's a cross on it?"

"Yeah . . ."

"Just keep the horizontal line straight. Move the stick back if the line moves up above the pointers and down if it goes below. If the right side goes high, move it left; if the left side goes high, move it right. See?"

"Yeah, I guess . . ."

"OK, man, you got it. One minute, no more."

"OK, Ricky."

Ricky started to sob uncontrollably. Then he unbuckled his harness and stood, vomiting out the cockpit window. "Fuck, fuck, *fuck*!" Sonny regarded Rick strangely, his expression betraying a peculiar mix of compassion and terror, and something else, perhaps . . . something unsettling, as if he'd just looked into the depths of another man's soul; *something indefinable that threatened to haunt his dreams . . . .*

Forty-seven seconds later, Ricky was back in the pilot's seat. "I'll take it from here, Sonny. Thanks. I needed that, whatever the hell *that* was."

"It's all right, Ricky, OK? All of it. We just lost a guy, both of us. I wanna puke myself, but I never could in all these years with the agency, even though I wanted to. You were there for Scotty. You were there for me. You just jumped right in and did what you could—*and who could have predicted this, my friend?* A forest fire beyond your control blew something back at the compound. The winch motor seized, and Gunnar did everything in his power to pull Scotty up. You had to cut your airspeed to twenty knots so as not to beat Scotty to death! He died because his fire spread and blew a fuel tank or something back at the compound. Sure as hell wasn't your fault, my friend! Sometimes we lose a man. It sucks, but it goes with the territory. CIA agents freely accept that risk. So do your troopers. And from time to time, the big croupier in the sky just calls in our chips. Better check your instruments, Ricky. I think I did OK, but I'm no friggin' pilot!"

Coming to his senses, Ricky checked the panel. Sonny could hardly have done worse; the chopper now listed at least fifteen degrees to port, and the nose was *way* low. The resulting loss of lift had allowed them to sink to about six hundred feet! Ricky wanted to grab Sonny by the shirt and slap some sense into him. Instead he swallowed his gall, gunned the throttle, and righted the craft.

"Pretty good flyin', huh, boss?" Sonny crowed. "Maybe I oughta take some flying lessons?"

Ricky managed a grisly smile. "Well, I don't know, Sonny. Learning to fly is not something you can take lightly. It's a very long haul. Flight school's expensive, and you need to log a lot of hours every year just to keep your license current. I don't really think you'd have the time."

"But Ricky, I could just *feel* it. Know what I mean, Chief? It felt so—*natural!*"

"I think I do, Sonny," Rick replied. "I think you mean the excitement, right? Knowing that your next mistake could be your last? Frantically searching for an emergency landing site when your '64 Beagle Pup's motor craps out? Dropping her into East Bumfuck Airport at night in dense ground fog, praying your gear hits the grass before you slam into the trees at the end of the runway?" He turned to face Sonny, the hideous Reaper's smile still plastered across his face. "Nothin' else in the world quite like flyin', pal. The thrills, the chills, the spills . . ."

Sonny drew back, a little startled. "Uh, well, Ricky, I guess maybe that's a part of it, too."

The smile disappeared from Ricky's face. "That's ALL of it! Sonny, man, I gotta tell you this, as a friend. Flying is *not* for you! Don't *ever* climb into the pilot's seat again, OK? You need to totally have your shit together *all the time*. You gotta keep your eyes and ears and gut totally on the compass, the altimeter, the artificial horizon, the fuel gauge, RPM, GPS, VOR, LORAN, oil pressure, your map set, airspeed, the radio, the air traffic, airport conditions, alternate landing sites and the conditions there, and the freakin' *weather*—all the time! You'll kill yourself, and you'll take out innocent people when you do. That's all I've got to say on the subject, Sonny. How the hell do you even manage to drive a car without killing yourself, bud?"

"Whaddaya want me to say, Ricky? I don't know. I just get in my car and, well, *drive.* Haven't had a ticket or accident in over twenty years. But, Judas H. Priest—that sounds like a *shitload* of parallel processing and unrelenting vigilance, Ricky. How can anyone keep up with it, man? How do *you* do it?"

"Well, Sonny, I'm tempted to tell you the same old lies that pilots have told their starry-eyed admirers for a hundred years. One: *It's a gift; you either have it, or you don't.* Two: *It's gotta be in your BLOOD, boy! You gotta have the genes!* Three, and this is my favorite: *We stick jockeys are a cut above rabble like you, and we have an indefinable 'something' that sets us apart from mere mortals.* They hasten to invoke the poem 'High Flight,' by John Gillespie Magee, Jr.: 'And, while with silent, lifting mind I've trod/The high untrespassed sanctity of space/Put out my hand, and touched the face of God.' But there's one helluva lot of hoops to jump through before you chase 'the shouting wind along' and fling your 'eager craft through footless halls of air'—Magee's words again. Most days, flying is a damn tough job, and it's always either boredom or panic. I've been flying since I was eleven years old, Sonny. Dad was a pilot, and he taught me to fly. I soloed at seventeen and got my license. I didn't have any Godlike abilities, I just got into it at an early age, and that was what I did for fun, until one day my carb frosted up and I had to make a dead-stick landing in a farmer's field. I almost clipped a power line on approach, and when I hit the dirt, the gear caught in a furrow, and I rolled three times. The plane caught fire, but I was low on gas, and I climbed out the passenger's door with only a scratch or two. I stood and watched Dad's plane disappear in a ball of flame and decided that that flight had been my last."

Sonny was entranced by Ricky's speech. "But you joined the service, right? And you're flying right now. What happened?"

"Well, jobs were pretty tight in Plumbersville, and the family didn't have the resources to send me to college. I'd always thought enlisting as a pilot would be the best plan, and now it seemed like the *only* plan. I signed up for all three services, and the Air Force offered me the best deal. I took it."

"So how about just flying for fun, Ricky? You know, 'flinging your eager craft along footless halls of air,' or whatever? You were a fighter pilot. That must have been exciting," Sonny said.

"Well, for me, flying had by then become either complete boredom or stark terror. The only time I ever 'flung my eager craft' *anywhere* was over Bosnia, when my F-16 pop-stalled in a dive. And my 'eager craft' pretty much 'flung' *itself* through the 'footless halls of air,' screaming toward the ground while I tried to restart the engine. After that, I transferred to SAR rotorcraft—search-and-rescue helicopters."

Sonny chuckled. "Well, Rick, you paint a pretty grim picture here. I guess I'll just stick to land-based forms of transportation."

"Mmmm, well, good for you, Sonny. Better just limit *your* 'flyin'' to behind the wheel of a car, bud. Fly to the corner store, fly over to the girlfriend's, fly for donuts to keep the troops happy—just keep wheels on the ground. *WOG!* And don't even *think* about flying aircraft, all right? *Never again.* Hear me?"

Sonny flushed. "Aye, aye, Cap'n. Sorry about that, Chief."

In the gun bay, Gunnar Martin knelt beside the hysterical Julia Redding. Gunnar was not particularly eloquent, but he did have a way with the ladies. He stroked her matted hair, gently combing out the snags with his long fingers. "There, there, sweet lady. It is over now. Your loss is great, indeed, but a new chapter—perhaps a *better* chapter of your life—has just now begun! You must mourn your husband, of course, but you must not dwell in the past! As time carries you further and further from this tragedy, new doors will open, doors which may have been locked and bolted before. Fresh opportunities will arise! The past is behind you, my dear Julia. Your new life begins now, *and you must seize it or perish!* Do you understand, Julia?"

Julia's convulsive sobbing ceased immediately, and her black eyes met Martin's. "Oh, Gunnar, I *do* see, but how? How do I seize my new life? Tell me!"

Gunnar sighed, grasping Julia's shoulders. "For me, it was not easy. I lost my love in a plane crash, you see? Many questions, many thoughts clouded my mind: living the rest of my life without Tabitha. Finding another, and *how soon?* What is appropriate? And always, *why? Where was God in this?* Tabitha Maize was the crown of His creation, the sweetest, most caring girl on the planet. Why, of all people, her? It must have been something I'd done, and God was punishing me by taking Tabby . . . ." Gunnar paused a minute, swiping the back of his hand across his eyes. "So I prayed to Him, every night for a year, for the answer."

Julia was absolutely enthralled. "What did He say, Gunnar? What was His answer?"

"Silence."

CHAPTER XV

Next Stop, Ukraine

These bones must be Svetlana's, Katya concluded as she gaped into the murky interior of the crate. She must call Sonny at once. *Ahh, damn it!* Her cell phone was locked inside the guard shack!

Katya whipped her head around to see what Major Asshole was up to. His backside was in the air as he hung over the edge of another crate, milling through its contents and repeatedly cursing under his breath. A small group of civilian women giggled and chattered behind her, completely oblivious to her presence. The coast was clear. No one was paying the slightest attention to her.

Katya made her move. Working quickly, she slipped the smallest of three mysterious boxes into her handbag. She gathered up a handful of the small yellow slips and stuffed them into her suit pocket. She ripped handfuls of random pages from several of the rotting books, jamming the sheets into her hip pockets. Then she went for the prize—*a clump of Svetlana's hair. DNA test, baby, ohh, YEAH!*

This was going to be perilous. She had to pass through the comprehensive egress security protocol. Katya had to load the dice, and she thought she had an airtight strategy to carry her through the gauntlet. She keyed her walkie-talkie. "Dr. Kozhczuk speaking. May I please have the escort out?"

"Of course, ma'am. I'll be there in five minutes with the shuttle," Sergeant Wallace replied, his voice warm, friendly, and inviting.

Wallace *really* fancied Katya; he'd made that quite obvious from the very start. Katya replied, "*William* . . . I mean, Sergeant Wallace? Is that *you?* What remarkable good fortune! William, who will perform my full body search tonight?"

"Ahem. Well, Doctor, as you know, you will have a female examine you. Esther is on duty tonight, I believe. Why do you ask, hon?"

Katya sighed deeply. "Well, William, in Ukraine we have many different custom from in America. In my culture, for woman to see woman unclothed or to touch her in such a way as this, it is *strictly forbidden!* I may have already transgressed by allowing this, and tonight I fear for my very soul. Do you understand this, my sweet?"

My sweet??? Wallace reeled, and then replied, "Well, cultural issues such as you mentioned are taken very seriously by the U.S. government, and accommodations are usually made. How can I help, Katya?"

"Well, my culture permits a male to see and touch an unclothed woman. As long as both man and woman are unmarried. You see?"

"Yeah, OK. I could ask Corporal Taysahc to do it, or . . ."

Wallace couldn't go on. He struggled to catch his breath as Katya replied, "Or what? Tell me, William—*or what?*"

"Well, ma'am, I, well . . . I mean, if you'd be uncomfortable with someone you never met, I, aahh . . ."

Katya put an abrupt end to his misery. "You are search-qualified, Sergeant Wallace? Yes? I would vastly prefer for *you* to perform my full body search. I know you . . . and I *like* you. You are gentle and kind. I feel this in my heart. Have I sensed that you may fancy me also, Sergeant? I hope this will be true. I would not like for my body search to be repulsive for you . . ."

There was a long pause—a *very* long pause. His throat and mouth were parched dry as a bone. Wallace guzzled an ice-cold bottle of water . . . and he had just reached for another as his walkie-talkie crackled to life. "William? Are you there? Please, sweetie, come in if you can hear me . . . please, come . . ."

"I'm here, Katya. I'll pick you up in five minutes, and I'll do your body search myself. You'll need to read and sign a few forms, waivers to protect the U.S. government from prosecution for an illegal body search. I'll make it quick, Katya—shouldn't take more than ten minutes or so."

"Just one thing, William. My clothes . . ."

"Yes? What is it, dear? What about your clothes?"

"Well, will you need to examine them, too? I just purchased a very expensive suit. You saw it; I am now wearing it. Please, be very careful. The garment is an original creation, unique, one of a kind, from Paris. It is also very delicate. Oils from the hands can mar the fabric. Gloves of latex or PVC contain chemicals that will gradually eat away the cloth. *What on the earth can we do, William?* You must search my clothing, yes?"

"Don't worry, Katya. I'll just use the sniffer, and that'll complete the investigation. A lot of this stuff is discretionary—elective—based on the judgment of the examiner. The department is mostly interested in the cavity search, to make sure nothing's being smuggled in or out. And we'll do the cavity search in a few minutes. You can just hang your clothes where nobody'll touch 'em, including me."

"Oh, William Wallace—*Braveheart*—*thank* you! You are so very kind a man!"

"So, Katya," William said, emboldened by the woman's unabashed adulation, "would dinner and drinks with me appeal to you? My watch is over at 1900—uh, 7 p.m. Would you care to join me?"

Katya titillated him with her throaty laughter. "Yes, of *course*, William! How is it that you have not asked of me this before today? You, I very much like. Have you not sensed this already? Shall I pick you up at the guard shack? Or do you wish to change your clothes?"

"I always have a change of clothes with me, Katya. I'll change in the shack. Pick me up there at 7:15, OK?"

"Count on it. I do. You should meet me there. Now, please, come and retrieve me. I must to return to hotel. And you have a thorough body search to perform before this, *yes?*"

Wallace was beginning to lose control. "Uhh, yes . . . I do, indeed. Sit tight, honey. I'll be right there." The Sergeant burned rubber halfway to the warehouse. Katya smiled as she pressed the END key.

She was taking an enormous risk, but a calculated one. She felt that William was securely in her thrall, and she'd leave her designer purse with her clothing. The sergeant probably wouldn't even notice the nondescript box. Even if William hit it with a metal detector, he wouldn't spot it; the box was too light to be metal, and it superficially resembled a harmless cable modem.

"He answers me all the time," Julia said. "Not with words, of course, but with thoughts, feelings . . . emotions. Intuitions, that sort of thing. Sometimes, when He seems silent, I just keep on asking, and eventually He answers, usually when I'm least expecting it. And you've never experienced that, Gunnar?"

"Now that I think about it, I guess He did answer me, Julia . . . up until I was maybe six or seven. My second—or third-grade teacher—I forget which grade it was, but her name was Miss Beal—always urged us to question, question, *question everything*. She was some sort of humanist, or whatever, and she was an absolute *knockout!* And she was cruel, but I had the crush of the century on her anyhow. One week, she had everyone bring their Bibles to school. A lot of kids weren't Christians, so they brought in their Torahs or Talmuds or Korans, and a few brought nothing at all. The Faithless Ones got to sit in the rear of the classroom, and Miss Beale seated all the Believers right up front, where she could harass and belittle them. The Believers had to march up in front of the class one by one and stand primly, balancing their Holy Books on their heads as they recited the basics of their faiths. If we dropped our books, we had to stay after class. Actually the boys did, but the girls got to remain seated and just had to participate in the class discussion after each recital.

"She was brutal, and *relentless*, Julia! She said something like, 'Now, class, you will see why it is important to rethink—to *challenge*—superstitious things like religion.' Then she proceeded to *grill* us and *humiliate* us. She really tore into us, Julia. All of the boys left the spotlight blubbering and whining like babies, except for Kenny Bramm and me. We both went to the German Lutheran church, and Miss Beale saved us for last.

"Kenny and I really got raked over the coals, but we didn't cave, and I thought we actually did pretty well. Our Bibles fell off of our heads a few times, so we had to stay after school. Two or three kids actually applauded. At least one of them was sitting in the back of the room as Kenny wobbled back to his little desk. When I told Ma and Pop about it, they hugged me, saying things like 'Good job, son! You just gotta stand up and defend your faith sometimes, and it's never easy,' or 'I'm so proud of you, honey; you did good.' Nothing like what I'd expected, like Papa grabbing his shotgun and racing over to the school. He was always the one talking big about taking the public school teachers out and shooting them all.

"I guess that's when I started looking more closely at my faith. I started thinking about it, dissecting it, rather than just blindly accepting it at face value. That was when it just started to slip away from me. After a few days, I stopped getting those feelings you talked about." Gunnar sighed. "After that, some of the Christian kids started calling her 'Miss Beal Zebub' behind her back."

"Oh, my . . . did you stop going to church?" Julia asked.

"Nah, couldn't, not 'til later, on my seventeenth birthday. For eleven years, I squirmed in my pew every Sunday morning. *Why would God have let me go through that at school?* I went to see

Pastor, after Ma and Pa ran out of answers, and he talked about stuff like 'suffering for His sake' and plying me with tales of Peter and Paul's martyrdom, early Christians being torn to pieces in the Coliseum—just what little kids need to hear. My folks finally let me quit Bible study when I was twelve, though."

"Ohh, that is so *sad*, baby. Have you ever gone back?" Julia asked, stroking his face.

"Well, kinda, I guess. Every Ash Wednesday, Good Friday, Easter, and Christmas. Like clockwork."

"Good, Gunnar, *good!* There's still hope . . . ."

Katya strode briskly toward her car. *One more hurdle*, she thought as she climbed into the driver's seat and made for the final checkpoint at the perimeter gate. She was home free; the vehicle search should be a cakewalk.

Sergeant Wallace had been very gentle, skipping over some of the most invasive procedures, even though she'd teased him mercilessly. Katya felt a brief pang of regret, knowing that she'd never see the handsome Scotsman again, and more than a little remorse for misleading him so callously. But then, she was at base a spy, and she'd gotten everything she'd hoped for from Svetlana's crate. *One more hurdle . . .*

"Please pull to the right and step out of the vehicle, ma'am," the pimply-faced Marine said as Katya flashed her badges. *The kid doesn't look a day over seventeen! This should be a breeze.* Katya complied, pulling off and grabbing her purse. She opened the car door.

"Leave the purse on the front seat, please," Pizza Face intoned, his voice stern but trembling. "Now, step to the rear of the vehicle and turn your back, please. Keep your hands at your sides, ma'am."

Hoo boy, this cannot be good, Katya thought. *This is a young guard, and he's nervous as hell. Just a boy, really, scared without shit to do his job by the book.*

A second, seasoned Marine stepped out of the shack, tipping his hat apologetically. "Sorry, ma'am, the facility just went to FPCON Delta. A trailer truck blew up about three miles north of here, and we're on high alert for possible terrorist penetration. I hope you will bear with us?"

"Oh, yes, of course, sir. I do very much understand. Thank you," Katya said, smiling as she walked around to the rear of her car.

The guard smiled back. "Just call me Steve, ma'am. The boy's name is Ralph, believe it or not, and he's a green recruit, in training. Sorry you caught us at a bad time."

"Oh, *yes*, Steve, you're usually at the gate when I come in. I never got your name before."

"Ralphie, make it snappy, son! This lady's been through my gate twenty times!"

Katya smiled back at him. "Thank you, Ste . . ."

Ralphie's shrill voice issued from the right side of her car. "Sergeant Stevenson! I require assistance, *sir!* Suspicious object just fell out of civilian's purse, *sir!*"

"Stand by a sec, ma'am. Ralphie's found a treasure! Stay right where you are, OK? If you move, I gotta shoot. No bullshit, OK?" Sergeant Stevenson said, his features suddenly slate-hard.

"Yes, Sergeant. I understand."

"Private, get your ass over there and cover the civilian. If she moves, *you shoot to kill. Do you copy?*"

"Y-y-yes, Sergeant. I copy."

"*On the double, Private! MOVE!*"

Sonny decided to stroll back to the gun bay to check on Julia. Once again, he'd picked the worst possible time to intrude. Julia sat astride Gunnar's crotch, moaning and bouncing rhythmically, her well-sculpted breasts swaying. Sonny froze in midstride as his approach evoked a heartfelt *aww, SHIT!* from the pair.

"Oh, *Judas Priest!* Sorry, guys! Hey, I'm outta here, like *right now*," Sonny stammered, windmilling awkwardly toward the cockpit.

"And don't forget to write," Julia quipped sarcastically to Sonny's back as he scuttled away.

"Well, I guess that's about it for now, huh, babe?" Gunnar said.

"Oh, I don't *think* so, pal! You have yet to experience Julia Redding's patented *suction pump*—lips guaranteed to raise you from the dead, every time! Perhaps I shall even restore your faith in 'res-erection'—with the emphasis on 'erection'! Are you ready?"

Gunnar chuckled softly. "That's not funny, babe. But, I don't know—*am* I?"

"Good answer, hon! No, you can *never* really be ready for this! But, nevertheless, here it comes . . . resistance is futile."

"Ahh, yeah, mmm, *yess* . . ."

Sonny plunked down in the copilot's seat. "Well, it looks like the mourning period is over, Cap'n!"

"Ah, whadda you mean, Sonny?" Ricky asked.

Sonny fought to restrain his chuckles. "Well, Ricky, it looks as if your gunner is being serviced by his rescuee."

Ricky stared wide-eyed at Sonny. "You mean they're getting it on back there?"

"Well, I don't really know, Cap'n. I kinda interrupted them, but . . ."

"Aww, *fuck*, Sonny! Are you sure, man?" Ricky said.

"Well, maybe not. Maybe I just *thought* I . . ."

"You know I gotta fire Gunnar if this is true, Sonny. Much as I hate it, I gotta play by the book. Aww, *shit!*"

"Wait, I think I misinterpreted what I saw, Ricky. Lemme go back and verify. Please, Captain?" Sonny said. "But what about this mission, Ricky? Is that in your playbook?"

"Do not push me, asshole! I might—just *might*—be operating within bounds by assisting a CIA agent in the performance of his official duties—*in the interest of national security!* But if, say, you elected to show me your member, you'd likely be hauled up on sodomy charges! Catch my drift? *You best get your ass back there and tell those fornicating pigs to knock it off, PRONTO! ARE WE CLEAR?"*

Sonny, duly chastened, mumbled, "Loud and clear, Captain. Right away, sir." He made his way carefully toward the gun bay, prepared to derail yet another moment of ecstasy.

Sergeant Stevenson strolled toward Katya. "Draw your sidearm, Private. Keep this civ covered. Private York found your little box, ma'am. Now, what in *hell* is that thing?"

Katya forced herself to stare blankly at the box for a few seconds before replying, "Oh, *no!* That is the cable box for my television! I was going to drop it off at the repair shop on the way to airport! I must have forgotten!"

"That don't look like no cable box I ever seen, Sergeant. Want me ta' cuff her?" Pizza Face asked.

"Hang loose a sec, Ralphie. Hmmm. Pizza Face is right, ma'am. It don't look like any cable box I ever seen before . . . ."

Katya assumed a confrontational stance, planting her fists on her hips. "We of Ukraine do not yet have such wonderful devices from the West. Many of such equipment are manufactured in Ukraine and are often defective. Why would my Ukraine box look like your American box? Please, send out to analyze if you wish. They already check it all at little shack by warehouse, and perform cavity search. Why now you stop me?"

Sergeant Steve turned the device over in his hands a couple of times. Then he shrugged, handing the truth source back to Katya and smiling warmly. "I'm sorry, ma'am. You just got caught up in a training exercise, and Pizza here got a little too enthusiastic."

Kat was unable to stifle her giggle. "Pizza? Ralph York? *Oh, no*—this is too funny! Stop it. Steve, *please* . . ."

"Good work, son," Sergeant Steve said to Private York, who saluted crisply. "Thank you, Sergeant!"

Stevenson rolled his eyes. "You're free to go, Miss, uh, Katya, is it?"

"Indeed, I am Katya, Steve," she giggled. "And thank you too, Private York, for protecting your country from foreign threats. I applaud you and wish only that we had more patriots like you in Ukraine!"

Pizza blushed. "Thank you, ma'am."

"Thank you, gentlemen, and please, be careful. Good day to you both."

"Good day, ma'am," the two soldiers replied in unison.

Katya's legs were distinctly wobbly as she walked to the driver's door and climbed in. *Whew, that was a close one.* But she was on her way, and she had harvested a treasure trove of unimaginable proportions.

Shit! They were at again! "Knock that off immediately, you two! Captain's orders," Sonny barked, then added, "Sorry, guys."

The dirty dancers groaned in unison, and Julia spat, "What the *fuck*, Sonny!"

"This is an official police vehicle, Cappy says, and he plays by the rule book, yadda, yadda. Better control yourselves until we get on the ground and Gunnar goes off-duty. Are we clear?"

"Crystal, Sonny," Gunnar replied. Julia sighed in exasperation, rolling her eyes theatrically.

Sonny worked his way toward the cockpit and flopped into the copilot's seat. "*Whew.* It's done, Ricky," he said.

The Captain glanced over at him, inscrutable behind his pilot's sunglasses. "How'd it go, pal?"

"Well, OK, Cap'n. Gunnar understood immediately, but Julia, whew! If looks could kill . . ."

A little smirk curled the corner of Ricky's mouth, and he shook his head. "Tsk, tsk . . . don't that beat all, Sonny? That girl's been a widow for about, what, forty minutes now?"

"Yeah, I guess, Cap. Something like that."

Ricky glanced at his watch. "No, it's closer to forty-*five* minutes, Sonny. I stand corrected. I guess she's been without a man *way* too long, huh?"

Sonny just hung his head, ashamed at the behavior of his field agent and embarrassed for the agency. "Hey, Sonny . . ."

"What is it, Rick?"

"Well . . . I guess I was a little out of line a few minutes ago. I'm sorry I was so short with you, bud. I'm not usually like that, do you think?" Ricky asked.

"Naw, man. I've never seen you act that way. You must be pretty stressed, Ricky. Lord knows I am. Bet you've never seen anything quite like this before, huh?"

Ricky paused briefly, then replied, "No, not exactly Sonny, but I've never seen worse, either. I've *never* lost a man hanging just feet from the belly hatch. Ahhh, *FUCK*, man! Scotty dropped *right into* that freakin' fireball! We coulda literally pulled him up the last few feet by hand! But that damn *explosion* . . ." Ricky fell silent and resolutely stared straight ahead, feigning intense concentration on the flawless blue sky ahead.

Katya hastily packed her bags and caught the next flight back to her homeland. While waiting for the boarding call, she phoned Sonny's office and left a detailed voice mail, expressing her regrets that urgent Special Services business had forced her premature return to Ukraine. She implored Sonny to call her and promised to meet him at the upcoming COUP convention the following month in Washington, D.C. "I shall be once again returning to your doorstep, my love! Perhaps we may then discuss early retirement for you, Sonny—*in Ukraine!* You would live like a monarch there, my sweet! A mansion is sold for the equivalent of 30,000 American dollars, and our doctors are true servants of the ailing, and most often they work for barter—a wild turkey or a few chickens. Health care costs only what you can afford to pay. And you could *write*, publishing your evidences of alien beings alongside with my own! I would be yours, and you would be *mine!*"

After a brief pause, Katya resumed. "Please, Sonny, do not abandon me, my love. Your immigration and Ukraine citizenship will be painless. I know many important people high in government, and I will see to this!" Another brief pause . . . then, "My flight is boarding, Sonny. I must now go. All my love to you." With that, Katya broke the connection.

Sonny slumped wearily into his office chair. Outside his window, the sun sank behind the skyscrapers of Washington, D.C. The evening sky cycled rapidly through hues of salmon, then deep pink, then violet. It was now 8:04 by his wristwatch, and it had been one helluva long day. Sonny had a lot to ponder; he was getting too old for this shit. His thoughts strayed again to the Fishing Option—just pull the plug on the whole freakin' thing, buy an RV, and head north into the Canadian wilds.

He'd always yearned to write. He'd garnered a couple of awards in high school for two short stories he'd written, "Graveyard Whistling" and "Last Call." Somewhere along the line, he'd ceased writing, for reasons unknown even to him. But maybe . . . suddenly, Sonny noticed the red "message waiting" light flashing on his desk phone. His heart leapt. *Maybe it's Katya* . . .

Indeed it was. Sonny listened to her lengthy voice mail with wide-eyed wanderlust. Then he listened again, and again, replaying the message four times. Katya had seemingly made him an offer he couldn't refuse!

Nick Bundy arrived home in Plumbersville two hours later, having made a pretty decent score from a dealer down on Broad Street: *thirty Ativan tablets, a nice little bag of hydro-grown flowertops, and ten Vicodins! Yeah, it had cost a fair chunk of change, but what the hell!* Nick was one hurtin' pup after his recent "trip"—and he was FINISHED with that place and its stinking zero-tolerance drug tests and dangerous assholes. He hoped the whole friggin' research center had burned right to the ground, and he hoped that Rodney had roasted in agony along with his buddies Johnny and Mel. *Wouldn't it be sweet irony if they'd broiled in their own skins right on those same back fire stairs?*

In fact it did, and they had. Nick wouldn't know until days later, when the authorities finished sifting through the smoldering rubble, that he'd gotten his wish. Nick stopped at a familiar party store for alcohol to kick in the pills. As he dropped the thirty-pack of Bud Ice on the checkout counter, Nick gaped in awe as the cashier's small television displayed the first live footage of the raging inferno. A news anchor droned, " . . . believe that a wildfire, fanned by this afternoon's gale-force winds, ignited propane tanks near the facility's main structure. Sonia, I think we . . . yes, we have a live report from our own Bryan Zander, on board the Channel 21 NewsCopter. Are you there, Bryan? What's it look like out there?"

The video feed flashed onto the screen; the scene was one of total carnage. "I'm here, Glenn. It looks really bad down there. I was *told* that our video camera—the Channel 21 SkyCam, I mean—was being replaced by a new . . . well, actually, I *told* them that the new camera . . . it's a Nikon, and the Toshiba we used to have wasn't available any more. Anyway, I talked to the vendor, and . . ."

There was a new explosion on the ground, and Sonia exclaimed, "*Bryan!* What just happened? What do you *see* down there? *It looked like the whole helicopter was rocking* from the force of that blast!"

"Well, the Nikon's buffer memory . . . I *told* the vendor there was a problem with the image correction! But they told me that our graphic arts department ordered it, anyway—you know who I mean, Sonia—*M*, but I'm not mentioning any names. Maybe he was having 'girlfriend problems' when he selected the Nikon camera—*heh, heh*. But anyway, I can't aim the camera out the right window, so I had to have the copilot hold it. I mean, he's probably a great pilot, you know? He looks like he's at least sixty. You know, he's one of those guys that really shows his age. Kinda weathered looking, but he might be younger—probably older, though. It's hard to tell. His face looks young, kinda, you know? But that white hair . . . I bet he flew rescue in Viet Nam or something! He . . ."

Glenn whispered something in Sonia's ear, and she rolled her eyes. "Go, Glenn. Hey, Bryan. *Bryan!* You have the mike. Just keep talking, and *roll that video*, OK?" Sonia said.

Bryan replied, "Yeah, but it might be . . ." as Glenn smiled, cutting the audio feed. There was merciful silence on the speakers. "Bryan? Bryan, are you there?" Glenn looked over at Sonia. "I think we just lost the audio. What do you make of all this, Sonia?"

"Well, my first impression is that of nature's power to devastate, to lay waste to the noblest achievements of . . ."

"Sonia, *look at this!* A gust of wind must have just caught the fireball from that last explosion, and the flame front is rushing toward the other buildings! There's a crowd of people running away . . . oh, my Go . . ."

The screen abruptly turned a soothing shade of blue, and a third announcer spoke. "We interrupt this live broadcast due to the potentially graphic nature of unfolding events. Please stay tuned to News Source 21for up-to-the-minute, excerpted coverage of the Plumbersville firestorm. We return you to our regularly scheduled programming, now in progress."

The Middle-Eastern proprietor still stared at the television as the *Sheep Whisperer* rerun resumed, now in progress. Nick slapped his palm sharply on the counter; he was dying to get home and watch the action. "Hey, Achmed, I gotta get goin'! Wanna ring this up, or is this booze gonna be FREE? Gimme a fifth of El Toro, too . . . and throw in a carton of Camel filters while you're at it! Every time I smoke one, I'll be thinkin' of you."

"My name is *Abdul*, sir. That is $86.08, please."

"Oh, sorr-*eee*, Ab-*dool!* Here's a hundred. Keep the change, OK? I'm in a hurry. Gotta get back home and watch the news—the pig roast?"

"That is not funny, sir. People are dying," Abdul said quietly. Averting his eyes, he slipped the tequila into a slim paper bag, exclaiming, "You must now be on your way, sir. Of course, I thank you for the kind bonus."

Nick gathered up his booze. "I think it's poetic justice, Achmed. The shit they do out there would curl your hair! Look at my face. Those fuckers did this to me, Achmed! I hope they all burn in *hell!* What do you think of that, pal?"

"I pray for these people to be rescued! This is *terrible!*" He ran his fingers through his curly black hair. "And again, it is Abdul, sir . . . still Abdul . . . always Abdul. Simple Abdul. Abdul, the Armenian Christian with the curly hair. Or perhaps you did not notice Abdul's locks are curled already?"

Nick bristled. "Don't you *dare* get gay with me, camel jock! You're coming on to me, aren't you?"

Abdul nearly collapsed with laughter. "Oh, you really *must* leave now, and dare to be happy! I am so sorry for you. I mourn for your pain! What has so terrible happened for you, you poor, wretched soul? But now you *must* go. Gather up your purchases and *go away.* Watch your television and drink your alcohol. Sink into the oblivion which you so desire. But, Arthur," the little man said, "please, take also with you this book."

"What is it, Abdul? And how in *hell* do you know my middle name?"

"I cannot say. This, simply, I know." Abdul handed Nick a little New Testament. "Read this, Arthur, or do not. If you choose to read, I suggest first to read John 3:16. You are in God's hands, not mine. Go now. And remember this: Abdul is always waiting here to help you to understand what is written in that book. But if you speak again of Achmed, I shall ask him to visit you in your home.

Achmed is my brother, and he is not nearly so nice a man as am
I. My brother would enjoy very much to meet *you*, but I think you
would not be so very happy to meet *him*. Achmed has knives . . . .
Now, you *must leave my store immediately. Go home and enjoy
your horrible pig roast . . . and may God have mercy on you.*"

Back in his car, Nick twisted the cap off the tequila and
popped open an icy can of Bud—"an American lager." *Yeah, and
it's brewed by a Belgian-owned company.* He gulped a shot of El
Toro straight from the bottle and popped four white tablets onto his
tongue, washing them down with a stream of cold beer. Then he lit
a cigarette, started the engine, and wheeled the Hyundai out onto
the highway, headed for home.

"Sonny! I am so happy to catch up with you, my sweet!"

Sonny almost dropped the phone. "Kat, where are you? I
thought you were on a plane home."

"I am on a two-hour layover in Madrid. I now relaxing in the
airport lounge, Bailando con El Toro—'Dancing with the Bull'—as
our plane is refueling for the final hop to Kiev. You did receive my
message, yes?"

"Yes, honey, yes, I did. It certainly gave me food for thought,
believe me."

There was brief silence before Katya replied, "I do not
understand this 'food for thought,' Sonny. Perhaps it is American
slang? I try very hard, but your *slang*, it is so difficult to me."

Sonny chuckled. "Sorry, Kat. Yeah, it's American slang for 'you
gave me a lot to think about.' I am struggling right now, babe. There
was a huge fire, and we lost one of the two agents. We went in with
a helicopter, and Scott was on the towline. We almost had him on
board when the winch motor seized, and he was hanging in his
sling a few feet away when the fire hit a fuel tank or something, and
it blew up. The shock wave tore him loose, and he fell right into it!
We were *so close*, baby—almost close enough to touch him—and

then he was falling, right into the fireball! I'm getting too old for this shit, Katya . . . . I've seen too much of it. I think I want out, just sit under a tree and write my memoirs."

The silence was longer this time. Finally, Katya replied, "Oh, Sonny, I am so sorry! But I have seen much of similar things, my love, and I share your feelings. Could we perhaps escape together, Sonny? Continue our research as private citizens, publishing our findings on the international market? As husband and wife?"

Once again, and for perhaps the thousandth time, Nick Bundy pulled safely into his carport, drunk and stoned for the first time since taking the security job at the facility. *DAMN*, he felt good—*really fucking* good—for probably the first time in over three years. His most recent position at Mendoza's fun factory had mandated weekly broad-spectrum urinalyses and random drug tests, and Nicky had remained minimally clean (and totally miserable) during that entire long, dry season of his discontent.

But all that was behind him now. He'd call "Ol' Black Joe" Hanson tomorrow and ask if he was looking for a die maker. When Nick resigned Benchmark Tool & Die to take the security job, "OBJ" had draped his big Swedish arm around Nick's shoulders. "Why ya' leavin' me, Nicky? I'll miss ya, boy, as a friend and as the best die maker I ever had. Did Ol' Black Joe do somethin' to wrong ya, son?"

"Nah, *shit* no, Joe—you always been real good to me, almost like a father. It's just the *money*, man. They pay *twice* what I make here, plus benefits! Please, Joe, try an' understand, OK?"

Joe looked sadly at Nick. "Well . . . then you go, boy, with my blessings. If ya ever wanna come back, yer job is open. No conditions, jus' c'mon in an' pick up where ya left off. Promise."

Both "macho men" were in tears as Nick grabbed Joe in a bear hug. "Well, shit *yeah*, you crusty old fucker! I love ya like a *father*, man . . ."

Strangely, Nick was always real with Joe. Joe treated him with *RESPECT*. The two were serious drinking buddies. Nick, to his surprise, really thought a lot of his boss; maybe he was the father figure Nick never had in his life. "Chief Blackvelvet," as Nick's father was nicknamed, had provided well for his family. The alcoholic, full-blooded Cherokee had provided all the abuse and neglect, while his mother, Adsila (meaning "blossom"), had nurtured her "three young braves" with all the love, the food, and the thrift-store clothes on their backs. Every penny of Adsila's meager teacher's salary went toward supporting her family of four. The Chief's money, when he had it, went toward gambling and alcohol.

Luckily, Chief Blackvelvet rarely darkened their doorstep, but every time he did, all hell broke loose. When The Chief came home, every one of them invariably went to school the next day with a few new bruises, a swollen eye, or a missing tooth.

Such were Nick's early years on the reservation. The "three young braves" harvested fish and crawdads from Cherokee Creek, and they hunted rabbit, possum, raccoon—even squirrel—to help Momma flesh out their starvation diet. Nick never saw his Momma eat; Adsila always hung back in the kitchen, ostensibly "stuffing herself" on morsels she "sampled" during food preparation. One day, the youngest brave, eight-year-old Adahy, asked, "Momma, why don't you eat with us? Don't you like us anymore?" Momma rushed to the kitchen, near tears as she lied, "I think something's burning!"

Every morning, Adsila dragged her cadaverous frame to the reservation schoolhouse, where she taught her students about respect, discipline, and the white man.

Joe didn't need no stinkin' drug testing for his employees. His home-brewed policy had served him just fine for thirty years, thank you very much. "Hey, a man can come to work drunk on his ass every day, as long as he don't fuck up his job or hurt himself. A man's drinkin' is his own business. I drink myself, Nick. You know that. Ain't no big secret around here. But you fuck up a die *once*, you get an ass-chewin', and I'm watchin' ya like a hawk. Twice gets you a write-up and a week off without pay. If you come back after that week and fuck up a *third* time, well, then you go to rehab for thirty days, on my dime. You got a problem, and I'll help you as best as I can. You come back after that, though, and I ever catch a hint of you bein' fucked up, your ass is outta here. *Permanent.*"

Nick had never made it to strike two or three, or even one. But he did have what Joe called a "foul ball" early in his six-year tenure at Benchmark Tool & Die. Nick was *zoned* when his hand slipped on an oily die plate and grazed the spinning end mill. He'd just scored a hundred ten-milligram Valiums, and he'd washed down four of them with a few shots of Bushmill's Irish Whiskey before he came into work. Ol' Joe was watching. "Hey, son, lemme have a look at that, OK?"

The Valium had started to kick in, and Nick stumbled back against the tool bench. "It's nothin', Joe—just a scratch, see?"

Joe grabbed his hand. "Yeah, Nick, it ain't nothin'. Slap some iodine on that to kill the germs and cover it with a Band-Aid. When you're done, come see me in my office." Without another word, OBJ turned and marched off in the direction of the lathe operator. "Hey Chuck! Hold up on them punches for Amfab! Duke just called, and he wants us ta tighten up the radius on . . ." Joe's words faded into obscurity beneath the rumble and whine of machine noise.

Nick was sweating like a pig as he staggered into Joe's office. His boss sat behind an austere steel desk, his glasses drooping down his potato nose as he shuffled a sheaf of papers. Joe looked up. "Sit down, son, before ya fall down." Nick did both, dropping awkwardly into the chair. Joe slid his spectacles into position and regarded Nick neutrally. "You're pretty fucked up, huh, son?"

"Yeah, Joe, got a little carried away with some Bushmill's before I came in. It won't happen again, boss. I swear!" Nick was surprised that he actually meant it.

"It better not, Nick. You just hit your first foul ball. But you're new here, and you're already pretty damn good. Think ya can work safely the rest of the night? No drinkin' in the parking lot?"

"No way, boss! I just overshot a little."

Ol' Joe looked at him over his glasses, and praise God, he *smiled*! "Overshot. Yeah, I thought so. I been there myself, boy. Now I want you ta git yer ass out to yer car and take a nap. I'll cover for ya—*this one time*. Be back here in my office in an hour, hear me?"

"Yessir, right away, boss." Nick rose from his chair, nearly lost his balance, and stumbled toward the door.

"One more thing, Nick," OBJ intoned. "I like you, son, and you're gonna be one helluva die maker if ya don't fuck it up. I'm cuttin' you one real big break here, boy, 'cause you got talent—what I call The Touch. Don't fuck it up. You got too much ta lose. Go take a nap."

Bobby was nowhere to be found. *Probably out diddlin' his new squeeze again*, Nick said to himself as he set his intoxicants beside Bobby's recliner and dropped heavily into his roommate's favorite chair. The remote control sat where it *always* sat, on the end table beside him. Bobby was an assiduous housekeeper—everything in its place—and that suited Nick just fine. Bobby could not tolerate a mess, and he constantly cleaned up behind Nick. He chuckled as he turned on the TV, contemplating their living arrangement. *Keep it up, big boy.*

" . . . Channel 21, first on the ground, live with field correspondent Dan Kelly. Dan, we saw the carnage from the air. What can you tell us from where you stand?"

"The scene here can only be described as one of grim desolation, Glenn. Behind me, you can see the devastation—six buildings, the former home of a government research facility, and about a hundred and seventy scientists and technicians—burned to the ground after a flash fire apparently ignited several fuel tanks that annihilated the facility and most of the people inside. To my understanding, Glenn, only about seventeen of the occupants made it out alive. I'm going to give you a quick look at the carnage . . . ." The camera panned, and Dan Kelly disappeared from view, replaced by a jittery image of smoldering rubble. The light was getting bad.

"Dan, are you there? We can't see much," Glenn said. "Can you give us a better . . ."

Dan's voice resumed. "Man, that's it, Glenn. There's nothing left. Dave Mason's with the survivors in the west parking lot. Nothing much to see here, just devastation . . ."

Abruptly, Glenn and Sonia were back on the screen. "Thanks for your report, Dan," Sonia said. "We're switching now to Dave Mason, live on the ground with the survivors. Can you hear us, Dave?"

Dave Mason, Channel 12's meteorologist (now in the trenches covering for Wally Scott, who was vacationing in the Caribbean) appeared, apparently fumbling with his headset. "Dave?"

" . . . . Uh, yes, sorry. Dave Mason, on the ground live at what officials are now calling the Plumbersville Firestorm. Overhead, several helicopters are spraying the woods behind me in an attempt to quell the blaze, which is moving westward with the prevailing wind. I'm speaking with Nurse Abigail Hicks, head of emergency medical services at the now-extinct research facility. Nurse Hicks, can you tell us about what just happened here?"

Nurse Hicks stepped forward, taking a microphone from someone off-camera. "Not too much, really. I was walking back to my office from the lunchroom when I saw the forest fire. I tripped the fire alarm and ran out the door."

"Did you see the fireball?" Dave asked.

"Yes. The concussion hit me in the back, *hard*, and knocked me to the ground. I was about a hundred yards west of the building by then, almost into the woods. I saw that fireball up close and personal. I was struggling to get up off the ground when the damn thing swept over my head about fifty feet in the air! I was blessed, for sure! It was really hot, but it just swept west into the woods and kind of petered out."

"What happened then, Nurse?" Dave asked.

"Well, I guess a few people followed me out. I don't really know . . . . I didn't see 'em, but they musta been behind me. I mean, here we are . . . ."

Dave Mason turned back to face the camera. "Thank you, Nurse Hicks. And yes, here we are at the site of probably the worst natural disaster Maryland has seen since Hurricane Isabel," the announcer intoned theatrically. "The fire 'copters pretty much have the blaze under control on this end. I talked with Fire Marshall Bill Phillips a minute ago, and he thinks the blast itself blew out most of the flames before they could get too much of a foothold over here. Looks like it's pretty much all over but the cryin', Glenn. But firefighters are still battling the blaze to the east of us."

The newscast cut back to Sonia. "Thank you, Dave Mason, on the ground live for *Channel 21 News*. We pause now for a station break. Please stay tuned for up-to-the-minute coverage . . . ."

Nick had seen enough for now. He channel-surfed to an old episode of *Seinfeld* and lit a joint. Life was good—the Vicodin had taken care of the pain, the Ativan and booze had taken him to a happy place, and Nick hadn't a care in the world. Rodney, Mel, and Johnny were now nothing more than ashes, and Nick never had to worry about another drug test. A job with Ol' Black Joe was just a phone call away. *He'd promised* . . . .

Two months after the blaze, six people's universes had changed radically—for better, for worse, forever. Julia and Gunnar had tied the knot in a brief civil ceremony, and Big Red now occupied Sonny's comfortable office. Julia now directed the Plumbersville investigation from afar following her substantial promotion and massive pay raise. Sonny had pulled some strings—*lots* of strings—at the head office. Although she doubted she'd ever be able to fill Agent Mildauer's shoes completely, she was unarguably the right person for the job. Gunnar had jumped ship, resigning his commission with the State Police to head up the Plumbersville investigation, boots on the ground, for the CIA.

Nick Bundy was learning to drive his shiny new electric vehicle, a motorized wheelchair with speech-activated controls. He'd broken his neck in a rollover on Route 31—the only serious auto accident of his life—and he'd totaled Bobby's car.

Sonny retired early, taking a lump-sum payout on his pension and 401k. He walked away with a small fortune, a substantial figure even after Uncle Sam took his cut. His modest fortune blossomed in Ukraine, almost doubling in purchasing power and fattening even further due to the favorable 8-to-1 exchange rate. Coupled with Katya's pension, the couple strolled into retirement with well over six million *hryvni*. Three weeks later, having just purchased a sprawling old mansion that Katya'd had her eye on, the couple strolled together down the center aisle of the Ukrainian Orthodox Cathedral in Kiev.

Dr. Rudolf Mendoza was fleeing Argentina for Bolivia, with CIA operatives hot on his trail. The covert team was led by one Hector Marcos, an old acquaintance of Julia's. She'd made contact with Hector after her field agent, John Steeple, had spotted Mendoza on a security tape from the Baltimore-Washington airport. A quick check of that day's airline ticket sales showed that someone named Randolph Mendoza had boarded a flight bound for Buenos Aires at 1:20 a.m. the day after the fire.

Apparently the doctor had been detained briefly by security after they found five suspicious-looking tubes (containing something resembling human embryos) in his single piece of carry-on luggage. Apparently he'd managed to convince the TSA agent that he was a doctor on a mission (his medical credentials were impeccable, the agent told Steeple, and his story about "biological samples to help our country's surrogate mothers research" sounded credible), so he was permitted to board.

Julia carried Sonny's torch with unbridled enthusiasm. She almost literally worshipped the ground "The Great One," as she'd taken to calling him, walked on. After all, Sonny Mildauer had entrusted her with his lofty charter (not to mention her imposing new position and a ton of money) and had literally rescued her from the living death of pushing travel reports. Plus, he'd gotten Gunnar his job with the Agency at double his policeman's wage.

The other man in this equation deserves honorable mention—a man named Ricky Nellis. His universe was not immediately turned on its head, nor did Ricky receive a raise or a promotion for flying his helicopter into harm's way. *All just a part of a cop's job*, Nellis thought as he wearily gunned his bird aloft, this time for traffic patrol over CR-31.

Sonny relaxed in his lawn chair, typing furiously on his laptop, as Katya approached, carrying two ice-cold tumblers of Stoli and cranberry juice. "How does your book go, my love? Please, toast with me, to our love and to the success of *Perchance to Ponder*."

Sonny smiled, closing the laptop and setting it gently on the verdant grass beside him. "Come close, my darling. Did you spray-paint those slacks on today, honey, or is that spandex?"

Katya laughed, and the sound was an enticing meld of throaty intrigue and girlish giggle. Sonny's new wife plopped down on his lap, slopping the drinks. "Best that we toast now, Sonny, before I spill this all over both of us. To love, then, and success . . . and to YOU, my sweet prince!"

They clinked glasses. "To you, my love," Sonny said, "and to spandex!"

They gulped thirstily. It was hot and humid this time of year—ninety and ninety, near-equal heat and humidity. A prominent haze hung in the sky, imparting a dirty-yellow overcast. "But the *book*, Sonny! I want to hear. *Read* to me!"

"Sure, hon. I'm almost through the introduction already. Can you grab my computer? I'm right comfortable with you here on my lap . . . face to face . . . breathing in your air . . . ."

Katya giggled, girlishly this time. "Easy, big boy! You have work to do, and I want to hear the *story!*" She nimbly bent over double and retrieved the computer, handing it to her husband.

"OK, here goes. You ready, babe?"

Katya moaned, "Mmmm, yes." She was not helping with his concentration.

"OK . . . uh, hmmm . . . there it is: *Prologue, Siberia. In September of 1974, a disc-shaped object plummeted from the sky, scorching its way deep into the frigid soil of Russian Siberia. After a frenzied paperwork shuffle and several strident phone calls, a Red Army detachment, accompanied by a KGB 'observer,' was dispatched to the crash site.*

"*KGB agent Sergei Kasparov's boots crunched on the snow as he and eight Regular Guard troops approached the object, which was buried seven feet deep near a stand of scrawny pine trees bordering the half-frozen potato field. A film crew followed them, recording still and motion images of the event. The CIA eventually uncovered film and samples from the site, decades after the crash.*

"*Very little is written here because even less can be verified with certainty. This account details the quest to recover . . .*"

Sonny paused, smiling at Katya, who said, "Go *on*, Sonny! Please, this work is very, very good! You have a gift, my love! I must to hear *more*."

Sonny just shrugged. "Sorry, babe. That's as far as I'd got when a raven-haired goddess in sprayed-on pants dropped her shapely bottom into my lap."

Katya's face flushed bright red. "You are *teasing*, Sonny! You must *stop* it, right now! *Read to me more.*"

Sonny chuckled helplessly. "That's all there is, honey. Believe me, Kat. Here, look at the screen. It stops right there."

Katya sighed in resignation. "Sonny, my love, you must *continue* this! I must read *MORE*. And so must millions of other people who will *thirst* after your work! Your books will change the *world*, Sonny, *and the way we view our universe!*"

Katya had finally exhausted her lecture, and she looked deeply into Sonny's eyes. "Where did you learn this craft of writing, love? Did you take elective writing classes?"

"Not really. Just English lit back in high school. I guess I must have had the knack all along. I used to write little science fiction stories as far back as grade school, composing on Dad's old Royal typewriter, sniffin' the correction fluid, the whole nine yards. Deep down, I guess maybe I always wanted to be a writer."

"Why did you stop? *Why?*"

"I never really thought about that, Kat. Maybe I thought it was just a passing phase. Or maybe starting a band when I was fifteen diverted my time, my creativity. Then again, my folks insisted that I go to college right out of high school. Pursuing a career in music or writing didn't fit with their master plan."

Kat gently stroked his cheek. "Oh, Sonny . . . this is so sad."

"Yeah, maybe, but I try and take the long view, hon. I'd probably never have landed the CIA job with a degree in English literature or music. I'd never have been privy to the inside information driving this book—and I'd never, in a million years, have met *you*."

Katya broke into wracking sobs, the tears flowing freely down her cheeks. "Oh, Sonny, you are so suh—suh—*sweet!*"

"Ahh, yes, I'm all that, babe. That's me . . . your sweet Prince Sonny," he said with a crooked grin. He gently lifted Katya's chin with his forefinger until her eyes met his own. His wife's lower lip trembled, but she was now smiling in spite of herself.

To Sonny's ultimate surprise, Katya raised her hand, applying a light, playful slap to his cheek. "This is how Ukraine woman treat their smartass husband. Again, you *tease*."

By now both of them were in stitches, rolling in the grass. Kat rolled on top of Sonny, and he applied a quick slap to her butt. "This is how American man treat their feisty wife!" Then he began tickling her mercilessly until Katya was on the verge of wetting her spandex.

Sonny grabbed his computer. Man and wife, giggling like schoolchildren, began their hundred-meter trek back to their newly acquired palace, just as the first thunderclaps echoed in the distance. Needless to say, Sonny's literary effort was on hold for the time being.

TEN YEARS LATER

Evidently, Nick Bundy had been serious about taking his own life—and he'd succeeded. Ironically, he'd rolled his wheelchair to the head of the hospital fire stairs and driven it over the edge. His limp rag-doll body tumbled down the concrete steps, his limbs powerless to break the fall.

Captain Ricky Nellis died a week later in a single-car accident. The official police report stated that Ricky had either swerved to avoid hitting an animal or had fallen asleep behind the wheel. A big oak tree got in his way, and his ruined police cruiser had burst into flames on impact. Naturally, no official mention was made of Nellis's blood alcohol content—three times the legal limit. The cops at Ricky's barracks knew, though. Captain Nellis had never recovered from losing Scotty. Rick had always held his liquor really well, but several troopers had noticed booze on his breath. Police Major Stockwell, Ricky's boss, had gently warned him several times about sleeping in his squad car during lunch break.

Ricky's estranged wife, Cassie, didn't even attend his Police Honor Guard funeral. Case closed. Move along, folks, nothing more to see here, show's over.

In contrast, Julia and Gunnar had distinguished themselves consistently with their keen insights and discoveries. Julia's grisly photos of alien remains at the disaster site made prime-time news, and she and Gunnar had even appeared together on Tawny Sung's nationally syndicated program, *Toe to Toe*. What's more, Julia was up for promotion to program director, and Gunnar was a shoo-in to step into Julia's current job as project manager, Sonny's old spot.

Across the Atlantic in Ukraine, Sonny and Katya had conceived a baby boy, Dmitri. Their coauthored book, titled *Perchance to Ponder*, had sold over two million copies worldwide. Sonny would never forget Katya's life-transforming statement: "Sonny, my cousin Zora is a literary agent in Canada. Let's call him and see if he can help us to publish."

Katya had shown her husband the arcane scribblings she'd smuggled out of the States and the little box which was destined to resolve two of mankind's most perplexing enigmas: the need for clean, renewable energy and the light-speed barrier. Sonny and Katya's twenty-four volume series, *Ad Infinitum*, which began with the modest four-hundred page treatise Sonny named *Perchance to Ponder*, addresses these subjects (among many, *many* others) in exquisite detail.

Should you be one of the few people on the planet who has not yet read at least the first volume of their *Ad Infinitum* collection, the loss is truly yours. The later volumes admittedly tend to wax rather technical, and if you do manage to make it through the entire collection, I applaud you, for you are a far more dedicated reader than I shall ever be. But that first book, *Perchance to Ponder*, mostly the product of Sonny Mildauer's keen perceptions and insights, is captivating in the extreme!

So long for now, and happy reading!

Your Author

THE BLIND
WATCHMAKER

PROLOGUE

Paradigm Shift—
Quantum State College, 1977

"M-Theory: The Mother of All Superstrings."—*A comment on membrane theory by Albert Einstein*

Dr. Tomas Didymus *finally* started to wrap up his lecture. Most professors tacitly respected the sanctity of an upcoming holiday weekend by assigning few, if any, homework problems and dismissing early. But not ol' Dr. Diddy, *nossir*. It was nearly 3 p.m, but still the old man droned on. "Dr. Ferris Baylor, your textbook's author, claims to have written this entire volume on his day off." Dr. Diddy was greeted by a sea of blank faces, some of them well into REM sleep after a full hour in the stuffy classroom. Apparently he'd dated himself; his quip about "Ferris Baylor's Day Off" had sailed right over their heads.

With a roll of his eyes, he continued, "At any rate, Dr. Baylor views time as a cosmic anomaly, an imbalance between good and evil that warped some metaphorical 'Eternal Cogwheel' in the sky. He claims that a smooth-running Cogwheel would produce only a *static* universe, timeless and unchanging. He views reality as the result of an *imbalance* in this cogwheel. If the wheel's lopsided, it wobbles on its axis and produces regular, periodic disturbances in the fabric of space-time. In traditional physics, such a wobble correlates well to a normal distribution of harmonic frequencies . . . *the bell-shaped curve.*

"Dr. Baylor believes 'time' is a consequence of man's fall from grace. In chapter four, Baylor suggests that mortality—time's most poignant manifestation—was born when an entity called Itoh abandoned the celestial realm for Earth, to battle Neko's minion, the Serpent, known as *Satan* in Judeo-Christian theology. Neko is Itoh's opposite, and his departure produced a celestial imbalance, thereby warping the Cogwheel.

"As I said, Dr. Baylor implies that the existence of the physical realm would be impossible without cosmic evil. This is an incredible statement! It forces us to consider . . . well, for one, some immutable, universal requirement for the suffering of all living things—and by extension, even for death! With Itoh gone, Neko was unbound, and her dark appetites were *unrequited.* Hence, the Cogwheel warped and began to wobble, to rumble and whine. The fundamental requirement for our existence, and all that we know, was fulfilled. Why? I shall explain."

The natives were growing increasingly restless. One student slammed his textbook on his desk. Another actually rose and walked out of the lecture. Cornell "Onna" Cobb, the ag ed major, even twitched once or twice in his sleep. Still, Ol' Diddy pressed on.

"One consequence of this off-axis motion—the rumble, a result of the lowest *subharmonics*—was to generate matter, embedded like marbles in 'sheets' of parallel quantum reality called *membranes.* DeBroglie showed that mass has a corresponding wavelength, attributable, Baylor says, to the lower-frequency subharmonics of the Cogwheel's rotation. The membranes—themselves without mass, per se—derived from the Cogwheel's *fundamental* frequency, the 'moan.' But the *upper* harmonics (the whine) superimposed what we call 'time' onto those realities! The highest-frequency components resulted in reality frames where time passes more quickly; conversely, time runs slower in frames suffused with lower-frequency harmonics.

"Visualize, if you will, a sheet of plastic with marbles embedded in it and someone shaking that sheet—very fast, of course . . . ."

"Dr. Diddy" paused for effect, and to catch his breath. It now was well past dismissal time, and his students were shuffling papers and stuffing books into their backpacks. He was losing them to the mundane, to the immediate rather than the important. It was the way of our existence, he thought sadly.

Diddy managed one last shot. "Note this, people, and *note it well*," he cried. "The relationship between these parallel realities is well-defined by a vast body of mathematics! Just look at it—*EVERYTHING FITS THE STANDARD BELL-SHAPED CURVE!* When we move into the frequency domain, it's all right there. The spectrograph gives you a handle on the *probability of each reality!* The coolest part of this is . . . *everything* is a harmonic of *some fundamental frequency.* The nature of time-space-matter—what have you—ultimately depends on a universal, fundamental frequency!

"This ties in with DeBroglie's paradigm, and as you go up in frequency, you eventually cross over into the electromagnetic spectrum, where rest mass ceases to exist. This implies that there's a discrete quantum frequency *where time itself begins*, my friends, and it's ultimately a function of Baylor's unbalanced Cogwheel!"

The students had already donned their backpacks, heading for their next class. Dr. Diddy decided to bait the hook.

"Think about it this weekend, people. Think *subatomic particles!* Think *quantum wave function!* Think . . . *EXTRA CREDIT!* A four-credit A."

All motion in the classroom ceased. He suddenly had his students' rapt attention. "For Monday, I want two or three pages—a thousand words or less—on some area of science or math that reveals things we can't directly perceive with our five senses. The winning essay gets twenty bonus points. One of you—*Mr. Smith?*—could get an A+ for the semester! Bring your Bibles on

Wednesday, too. We'll be starting the Book of Genesis. Enjoy your weekend. So long, y'all." Dr. Diddy tossed his notes into a tattered briefcase and left the building.

Surprisingly, neither Dr. Diddy nor Dr. Baylor had considered the necessity of the Clock Eternal in this otherwise well-reasoned theory. But with the advent of time, an unintended consequence had manifested itself—the need to synchronize the disparate "time oscillations" in all frames of reference. The *absolute* reference frame, an arbitrary "starting point," was Frame Zero . . . which we experience as *Herenow*.

As a consequence of its necessity, the Clock Eternal simply *became*, along with a Watchmaker to maintain it.

That cloudy Thursday afternoon, Frank Smith changed his major to physics, with a minor in metaphysical studies. The date was August 17, 1977. Smith glanced at his watch as he submitted his curriculum change form. It was 3:30 p.m. *Simultaneously in Memphis, Elvis Presley was officially pronounced dead.*

Smith noticed later that day that his new high-tech digital watch had stopped at precisely 3:30:00. For some reason, he thought briefly of Swiss cheese and of the pleural adhesions he'd seen last week while dissecting a fetal pig in his anatomy and physiology lab. *Curious* . . .

Frank Smith got his A+ for the semester. His 999-word essay, titled "Rumble and Whine: A Theory of Substance," was published in the October issue of *Quantum Quarterly*, the college magazine.

CHAPTER ONE

Smitty's Oath

Nine years later: On August seventeenth, at 3:30 p.m, Dr. Frank Smith and his team of Army specialists lost history's first human time traveler in a top-secret lab deep under the Nevada desert. Dr. Smith, affectionately nicknamed "The King" by his colleagues, slung his glasses onto the console and moaned, "Re-check your display, Captain Andrews. *What the hell happened?*"

"As near as I can tell, sir, we cooked one of the Fresnel coils that focus the Möbius lens. I guess we just scattered Dorrie everywhere—and *everywhen*, huh?" Choking back a sob, the Captain added, "I'm very sorry, Dr. Smith."

There was no hope of recovery. Their volunteer, Master Sergeant Dorotea Del Sang, was gone, scattered on the winds of time . . . *forever* and *always.*

Young Dr. Smith had nurtured an imaginary love affair with the spunky little sergeant. *Why did it have to be Dorrie?* he wondered. *And why now, after all the successful primate trials? Why couldn't we have blown that frigging coil on one of the monkey hops?*

Smith recalled Dorrie's slightly disturbing smile, which had always seemed to display a few too many teeth. Dorotea's final words just before the hop had made him think of Elvis Presley: "Thank you very much, y'all. So long for now."

On the heels of the tragedy, Dr. Smith resigned as project director and plunged into a black depression. Smith contemplated a brief period of mourning, which he would terminate painlessly with a bullet in the brain.

But then, in December of 1987, a miracle occurred, a miracle called Prozac. Dr. Smith responded remarkably well to the new antidepressant, and he was back on the job just two months later. The King resumed his groundbreaking work with renewed vision and enthusiasm, and made a solemn vow: *I shall not permit this to happen again.*

Dr. Smith had never read Mary Shelley's novel; Victor Frankenstein had made the identical vow.

CHAPTER TWO

Something Called Neko

Dorotea saw everything—*all at once!* At first it hurt, but from the very start, it was *exhilarating*! The entire history and future of mankind surrounded her, as if projected on the inside of an enormous sphere composed of various regular polygons. She watched the Fresnel coil burst into flames and gaped in awe as her very essence evanesced in a brilliant crimson-and-gold starburst. She suddenly understood that she could go anywhere . . . any*when*. And she could likely do any*thing*!

A tenebrous, enticing *something* writhed in a black corner of her soul. Dorotea understood that her dark and insatiable cravings were threads in some sort of Eternal Tapestry. *Rumble and whine,* she thought, and she wondered why.

Simultaneously she embraced what she *did* know. The thought had arisen spontaneously, and Dorotea felt as if she'd *always* known. She was now something called *Neko* . . . and *that was more than sufficient.*

CHAPTER THREE

ℋℬ𝒪ℛℐ!

HERENOW– Travis Farkins bolted awake to the screech of the INCIDENT ALARM. Reeling, he knocked his pint of Jim Beam to the floor, goggling in dismay as the bottle exploded in a spray of amber fluid.

Yeah, he'd been drinking at work, again. *But who wouldn't drink, with my problems?* Travis thought. *Feggem if they can't take a joke.* Travis did the only thing he knew to do in the event of an INCIDENT ALARM. He punched the big red ABORT button—on his second try. Travis guessed he was pretty drunk.

Line after line of text scrolled down the screen. *THE ABORT BUTTON HAD DONE NOTHING AT ALL!* The bleary-eyed technician scanned his monitor to determine the nature of the ALERT. "Somebody" had apparently been leaning on the SHIFT key! Travis had been asleep, literally, *on* the switch!

The SHIFT key was vastly more powerful than its innocuous label implied. It was intended for use only in dire emergencies, when a time traveler required immediate extraction from a life-threatening reality frame. The rescue measure was effective but crude—a hatchet, not a scalpel. Its sole purpose was to yank the traveler into an adjacent frame—hopefully a safer one—for eventual retrieval using TimeLab's plodding Search and Rescue Program (SARP). Travis recalled the old axiom "Shift once, and do it fast; shift twice, your ass is grass".

Farkins had slept face-down on the keyboard for perhaps *thirty minutes*! Who knows *where* he'd sent Dr. King? Alcoholic or not, Travis still had a conscience, and if TimeLab didn't fire him first, he would resign. But *right now,* he had to find the Doc and get him back to frame zero—herenow!

As Travis scanned the excursion history, he hung his head in dismay. The poor Doc was careening through frame after frame of statistically possible realities, and Travis knew how disturbing those parallel realities could be. *Weird,* in the spooky way that only quantum reality can be weird. It could literally drive a man crazy. And on at least one occasion, it had.

Travis shuddered, recalling the vegetable that had once been Tommy Blaine. Tom's father, a wealthy businessman, had bought his son a trip back in time to pay a final farewell to his fiancée.

Tom had had an "important" business meeting the morning of Libby's flight, and he'd decided to skip her sendoff at the airport. *What the hell,* he'd thought. *It's just a short commuter hop to Bakersfield. She'll see her mom and be back in town for the weekend.* Cradling Libby in his arms, drawing her close, Tommy had crooned, "C'mon, hon, it's only a few days. It's not like we'll never see each other again, sweetie, *right?*"

Wrong.

Libby had cried. She'd entreated. She'd pouted. All to no avail. Later, in bed, Libby turned her back on Tom and feigned sleep. The following day, her plane crashed on landing, incinerating all sixty-three aboard. Tommy couldn't forgive himself . . . .

THEN– Paul Blaine bought the time trip to commemorate what would have been Tom's first anniversary. "How'd you like to go back and say good-bye to Libby, son?" Before the stunned Tom could answer, his father whipped out the ticket. "You'll leave here on August seventeenth, Tommy! At, let's see, 3:30 in the afternoon."

213

And Tom did, with a mixture of joy and sorrow in his heart. But *en route*, Tommy drifted off course due to sunspot activity in one of the transition frames. He arrived at the airport in the wrong reality, just in time to be taken hostage by a group of terrorists. Dorothy del Sang, a technician at TimeLab's Control Center, noticed an ALERT on her excursion display. She'd pushed the SHIFT key, just once, according to protocol.

SHIFT– Tommy suddenly found himself in 1966, a guest at the notorious Hanoi Hilton POW camp. While TimeLab's plodding SARP program ground through the recovery process, PFC Thomas Blaine spent several weeks (in his time frame) under relentless interrogation by the Viet Cong. That woman, Neko, was by far the worst of his tormentors, and unfortunately she'd taken a "special interest" in Tommy. Psychologically unable to endure any more of her abuses, his mind had simply shut down.

Two hours later, in Frame Zero (Herenow) time, Tommy Turnip materialized at TimeLab. More accurately, Tom's body returned, technically still alive, but everything that was essentially Thomas Blaine *the person* was forever gone. Only Neko's insane laughter continued to echo through Tommy's empty head . . . .

Kind of ironic, thought Travis. *Doctor King himself had been on his way to query Heisenberg and Schrödinger about the same weird quantum stuff that I'm dealing right now . . . .*

Herenow– Travis snapped out of his reverie. *OK. Now, THINK, man! How the hell do I do a 4-D point-locus calculation . . . on an undefined trajectory?* Travis riffled frantically through his operator's manual.

There it was! *Praise God and amen!* He recognized the familiar tetrahedron in the illustration. Travis Farkins, time traffic controller, started typing . . . and THERE HE WAS! The Doc was safe! The text had stopped scrolling. Dr. King was sitting in a London diner, and he was talking to someone . . . .

CHAPTER FOUR

Dr. King's First Stop—London, 1998

SHIFT– "Please forgive me if I'm being impertinent, but I was wondering . . . how does a man like yourself . . ." Richard King paused, searching for a polite way to phrase his question. The blind man waited patiently behind his sunglasses, his face impassive.

Richard continued with a sigh. "I guess what I'm trying to say, Mr. Smith, is—well, how does a blind man spend his days? I mean, sir, how do you manage to *get on?* If you take my meaning."

The little man chuckled. "I live only for my craft, sir. In return, my craft gives me life. My work is quite absorbing, and it is *vital*, Mr. King. In fact, your very life depends upon it."

Richard snorted, nearly choking on his tea. "Might I ask, Mr. Smith, what *is* this vital work that you do?"

The blind man replied, "I am a watchmaker, sir, by trade—but not by choice, I assure you."

Richard's jaw dropped. "I'm *incredulous*, sir! How could a man such as you possibly perform such an intricate task?"

A chilly smile crept across Smith's narrow lips. "I may have no *eyes*, Mr. King. But rest assured, that does not mean that I cannot *see*."

SHIFT– A fine spray of tea exploded from Richard King's nostrils, and he sputtered with laughter. "Oh, come now, bloke . . . *blimey!* You're putting me on, right? Very well, then, where *do* you work? And how can *my* life depend on *you*, Mr. Smith?"

215

"I maintain the Tower Clock, sir, if you choose to call it that. Should the Clock ever stop—*God forbid*—time itself would grind to a halt."

Richard regarded Smith quizzically. He could have sworn that two distinct points of light now danced behind the sunglasses. *Must be a reflection; light from the window?* He glanced over his shoulder. *How odd—the familiar street corner appears subtly different somehow.* He couldn't quite put his finger on it. For a brief moment, Richard felt disoriented, his mind suddenly reeling with images of places he'd never seen, memories of words he'd never spoken. The thoughts evanesced almost immediately, as if he were waking from a bizarre and disturbing dream.

Outside, the sky was almost black with a threatening overcast. Swinging around on his stool, Richard saw that the asters had disappeared from Smith's Foster Grants. "And just which square would that be, sir?"

"Well . . . you could call it Times Square, or the Salem Church Quadrangle. Or Big Ben, perhaps? But ultimately, the name means nothing. The clock is always the same, whether it manifests as the Cairo University Clock in Egypt or as the Clock Tower at Tsim Sha Tsui in Hong Kong. It is always, everywhere, the same, the Clock Eternal, and it is called by many names. Just as you yourself are, sir."

Richard rolled his eyes. "*Whatever* are you talking about, Mr. Smith? By Jove, it's such sport chatting with the daft. They're nothing if not creative! Good day to you, sir." Retrieving his hat from the adjoining stool, Richard bade Mr. Smith a jaunty "cheerio!"

"You cannot yet understand, sir . . . but eventually you will see the truth. You always do. And for that, I pity you," Smith said, speaking softly, gravely, to Richard's back.

CHAPTER FIVE

Back to the Present

HERENOW– Travis breathed a shaky sigh of relief. The ABORT key must have worked after all! Dr. King was safe. All he needed to do now was . . . wait . . . the Doc was gone! *What happened?*

Travis groaned. He'd forgotten about Doc's quantum momentum! Travis had given him a pretty damn good kick with the SHIFT key. *It might take DAYS for the Doc to slow down!* Travis was neck-deep in a cesspool and sinking fast. He needed help, right now! He reluctantly called Dr. Smith.

It was two in the morning, and Smith came on the line with fangs bared. "You did WHAT, you lame *fuck?* I'll have your ass for this! All right . . . you need to do a point intervention/retrieval! *NOW!*"

"How do I do that, Dr, Smith?"

"Did you calculate the sixteen point-locus vectors? For the 4-D point retrieval?"

"Yes."

"Good. Go back to the computer. Select 'Point Intervention.' From the main menu. Bring it up. NOW!"

"Wait . . . OK, app's running, sir."

"Now click on 'Extrapolate path.'"

"Got it, Dr. Smith."

"OK. Go to the pull-down menu. Select '4-D point for retrieval.' Type in the sixteen numbers *in the correct order! Be careful!* Then in the LATENCY field, type '0.030.' That's *T-plus-thirty milliseconds.* That should work."

After a brief pause, Travis said, "Done."

"Now recheck the point-locus numbers—carefully! Then hit ENTER. JUST ONCE!"

Another pause, longer this time. "Yes, sir. Done."

"Did you get him?"

"Program's still working, Dr. Smith. Stand by."

Smith took full advantage of the lull. "You are *toast,* mister—DONE! I *will* press criminal charges! What you did represents gross negligence and callous disregard for human life! If we don't get Rick King back, it'll be manslaughter. Your life is over, cretin!"

Travis couldn't have known that Doctors Smith and King were close friends. While working together at the Army's Temporal Research Facility in Nevada, they'd come to believe they were linked on some cosmic level. They'd double-dated whenever they could and had studied and worked together twenty hours a day to bring time travel to fruition. They were best man at each other's weddings, and now they worked as a team at TimeLab.

Or at least they had; just now, some WRETCH had sent his oldest, dearest friend on a deadly roller-coaster ride! Smith knew the odds. He suspected his friend was already dead—or worse, a raving lunatic.

"Thanks for the encouragement, Doc. Looks like we got him, sir. Point transition to frame zero selected—*now.*" Travis clicked the "OK" button on the selection screen.

"All right. Maybe you won't die in jail after all, you stupid fuck!"

Travis grabbed his jacket and barked into his cell phone, "Good enough for me, Dr. Asshole . . . I tender my resignation, effective immediately. I'm GONE, and fuck you very much! It's your baby now. Have a shitty death, you arrogant prick." Travis was ready for love and a fifth of Beam.

"Wait, *wait*, you monkey!" Smith bawled into the dial tone. "Did you click APPLY? You need to *accept* the transition for it to take . . . . ahhh, *SHIT!*" Smith placed a hurried call to Morey Bassett as he pulled a coat over his shoulders. Bassett answered on the third ring. "Morey, we just lost Dr. King! Meet me at the lab *ASAP!* Bring Kenny Mash with you if you can. *Smith out.*" Still in his pajamas, Dr. Smith slogged through the freezing rain to his car and made a beeline for TimeLab.

CHAPTER SIX

Dr. King's Next Stop—Atlanta, 2005

SHIFT– Richard King realized a second too late that his legs were no longer working, and he crumpled to the floor of the diner. "Bloody *hell*," he screamed. "I can't *walk!* Please, somebody help me! Get some help, Smith! For God's sake, man!"

Whipping his head from side to side, Richard noted from his worm's-eye view on the floor that none of the other patrons or the staff had made the slightest move to help him. In fact, no one was moving . . . *at all!* One beefy patron appeared frozen in place, a slimy runnel of poached egg hovering in midair as it drizzled from his spoon. Behind the counter, a waitress poured a frozen stream of steaming water into an ever-waiting teacup.

No one moved except him. And the blind man.

"Mr. Smith . . . please help me. What's happening? Go for help! Call the bobbies, man!"

"Just calm down, Mr. Smith," said the little man, his voice low, condescending. "You're confused, sir. Seems you've just had a bit of a stroke or something. It's going to be all right."

The little man knelt beside Richard. He no longer wore the sunglasses, which he handed to King. "Here, Mr. Smith. You dropped these. You might need them." The little man's blue eyes seemed iridescent. "After all, you're blind, sir."

"WHAT? What are you talking about, Smith? You crazy bastard! YOUR name is Smith, remember? I'm Richard Kuh-ummm, I'm . . .

awww, SHIT!" A nauseating wave of dizziness and disorientation swept over the scientist as he lay prostrate on the chilly tile. Suddenly his surroundings looked different, somehow distorted . . .

"Just be calm, Mr. Smith. Please. You're confused. The medics are on their way," the little man said. "I'm Richard King, by the way. Is Smith your real name, sir? I'll need to give it to the medics.

"Of course not! My—name—is . . . Rihh . . ." *I MUST have had a stroke*, he thought. *I can't remember my name!*

"Mr. Smith? It's all right. Just calm down. You've had a little stroke, sir. Please, may I take out your wallet so I can tell the medics who you are?" The man added, "I'm here to help you, Mr. Smith. Please, just trust me."

Richard sighed in resignation. He was, after all, in no position to argue. "It's in my left hip pocket. Here, let me get it . . . ." But his arms wouldn't move, either. He began to cry.

The little man reached forward, slipping the wallet free. "It's OK, sir. Just hang tight. Mmmm . . . your name is Frank P. Smith? Oh, you're a Yankee! You're from Salem, Vermont? What brings you all the way here to Atlanta? Just sightseein'?

Atlanta? WHAAT?

"The doctor told me to keep you calm, to talk to you and keep you alert until they get here. I'm a volunteer fireman. You're very lucky, Mr. Smith; I have EMT training myself. But there's a big traffic jam in the tunnel, so it could be fifteen or twenty minutes. How are you feeling, sir?"

"Well . . . paralyzed, I guess, but otherwise, just ducky. But why aren't the other people moving?"

SHIFT– Next stop, Memphis, 2012– The small diner was suddenly alive with a cacophony of noisy chatter; patrons barked for coffee as harried-looking waitresses scurried to and fro. The beefy egg man at the counter was gone. A small circle of onlookers surrounded the pair, mouthing hesitant offers of help. "Huh? What people? What do you mean, sir?"

"*Everybody!* See here, Smith. They were all *frozen!* I was just in London, talking to this blind chap. Then everyone just froze in place. There was some bloke at the counter, and his egg was hanging in midair . . . ."

"Whew—you couldn't *possibly* have seen all that, sir. You're blind, remember? What you *think* you saw must have been from the stroke. And that's probably why you can't move. Does it seem like you can see now?"

"Of course! I can see you . . . I see people . . . ."

"*Oh, my* . . . you can actually *see?* How long have you been unsighted?" the little man said, sounding a bit embarrassed at his own perceived gaffe.

"I could *always* . . ."

"It's all right, Mr. Smith. Just take it easy. So you can see! It must be wonderful! I've often wondered how blind people, ummm, get *along*, you know? So what brings you to Memphis?"

Memphis? Richard didn't know what to say.

"Never mind, Mr. Smith. It's all right. The EMTs are coming. Mmm, I see that you're a master craftsman in the Watchmakers' Guild—the card in your wallet here. How did you do it, sir? I mean, being blind and all?"

"But I can *see* . . ."

"Yes, *now* . . . and praise God! But back then . . ."

"But I could *always* see! All my life!"

"OK, *OK* . . . just be calm, sir. You're just a little confused right now."

"How long for the medics to get here?"

"About thirty minutes or so. There was an accident on the bridge . . ."

"Mmmm . . . I thought you said the *tunnel* . . ."

"The *tunnel? What* tunnel? No . . . a pileup on the Highway 66 bridge. I guess a semi hit a tour bus, and traffic's all snarled up."

"Humphh . . ."

"So, do you just fix watches, or do you work on clocks, too? I've always wondered about the guys that maintain the big clocks, like in Times Square, or Big Ben in England. Do you know anything about that? Is there a regular staff there?"

"I don't know."

"So you just work on watches, then?"

"I've never seen the insides of a watch in my life."

The little man chuckled, a bit embarrassed. "Of course not, sir. How silly of me! You were *blind* . . . ."

Richard decided to simply let it go. He sighed wearily and closed his eyes.

"So back to my original question, Mr. Smith. What DO you do with your time? They say it really helps if you keep a stroke patient talking, you know, keep the neurons humming along, blah, blah, blah . . . ."

"I'm a physicist . . . in Nevada . . ."

"Hmm, well, let's just see . . . Here, hold on, I've got my Droid. Let me Google you. Ah, yes, here you are, sir . . . Frank P. Smith, Master Watchmaker. Here's your website . . . pretty *sweet!* You work at the Salem Church Tower! You work on *that* clock? I've seen pictures—it's magnificent!"

"Aarrgh . . ."

CHAPTER SEVEN

1971:
Somewhen, the King Has Come!

Physicist Richard King, the traveler, was now becoming badly disoriented; he could barely hear the little man talking into the antique pay phone a few feet away. After a moment, he heard snippets of the conversation over the hubbub of the restaurant: " . . . appears delusional . . . can't *believe* it; he regained his *eyesight!* Yeah, a blind watchmaker, no less. Works at Big Ben . . . in England. Yeah, it is beautiful . . . I'll get the heparin . . . drugstore across the street . . . Thorazine . . . yeah, no prob, Arch, I'm on it. King out. Hey, Presley," he said, "I need to run across the street to the drugstore for some meds. I need to go start an IV. I'll call Dorrie over to keep an eye on you . . . you remember her, right? The one that was flirting with you? I'll be right back, OK? Just hang in there, pal!"

Presley? Who the hell is Presley? he wondered, bewildered.

The little man hurried out the door as a blonde waitress, all chest and hips and legs, approached, her shoes clacking on the tile.

"Hi, sweetie. Do you remember me? Dorrie?"

"No, sorry."

"It's OK, honey. Don't worry, Dr. King has gone across the street to get some medicine for you. Would you like something to drink? Maybe a nice, hot cup of tea?"

"Hmm, that sounds pretty good . . . Dorrie? Is that your name?

"Yes, short for Dorothea. I'll get your tea. Be right back, hon. Any sugar or cream?"

"Lots of both, please."

Within seconds, Dorrie returned with the tea. Richard-cum-Presley listened to the swift click-clack of her approach, wondering how on Earth waitresses ever managed to stand and walk all day in high heels. "Here you are, Prez. Careful, it's *hot* . . ."

"Aaah . . . *yahhh!*" he shrieked as a stream of scalding liquid splashed onto his face.

"Ohhh," cried Dorrie, who then started to giggle. "Oh, honey, I'm *so sorry!*" The waitress, still giggling at her own clumsiness, produced a cheesy-smelling wipe rag and mopped it across Richard's face. "Clumsy *me*. I'm sorry, sweetie, it was an *accident*. Does it *hurt?*"

"Yeah*, of course* it hurts . . . I'll survive, Dorrie."

The waitress giggled again. "Awww, *of course* you will! I'll get you another cup . . . ."

"*NO* . . . no thanks, Dorrie," Richard replied. "Please, just tell me what's going on. A few minutes ago, I was talking to this little blind guy named Smith, a watchmaker. I'm Rih . . . uh, I'm a physicist. This guy who called himself Smith was telling me he was a watchmaker, that *he* works on Big Ben. Now, suddenly, this *same guy* is no longer blind, *his* name is Richard King, and *I'm* Frank Smith, a *watchmaker!*"

A bewildered expression crossed Dorrie's face. "Oh, no, honey, you're Pressly King—*The King!* From the States! You've been coming in here all week. You're a big *star,* honey, here for your concert series, remember? *The King Rocks Around the Clock!* How do you do it, baby?" Dorrie asked. "How can you play all those instruments without seeing them?"

SHIFTSHIFT: Whistle Stop, London– "I *can* see, Dorrie. *Understand?*" Richard-cum-The King groaned. "Hey, when did you change your outfit? That was *quick*. And just look at *you!* WHOA, lady!"

The former waitress was dressed in a fetching jet-black croupier outfit: tiny skirt, sculpted legs cocooned in seamed fishnet stockings, stiletto-heeled boots, white ruffled blouse open to the third button. The woman was *hot!*

It suddenly dawned on him that the place was *dark!* And where had all that white Formica gone?

Dorrie had either missed his question about her outfit, or had simply disregarded it. Or worse, maybe he'd only thought it! It had all *seemed* real, the diner, the waitress spilling hot tea on his face . . ."*Oh my God*, it's a *miracle!* Oh, Smitty, do you think I'm pretty, baby? You can really *see* me now?" Dorrie assaulted him with a barrage of steamy, passionate kisses. He started to chuckle in spite of himself.

SHIFT– Dr. King rushed in, a bulging Cordura bag slung over his shoulder. He guffawed at the sideshow taking place on the floor. "*Blimey*, nice to see you two are getting on so well! Make a hole, blokes, make a hole! I got some meds for our patient!"

The pub crowd parted obediently. "Royty-oh! You fix up our Smitty straight away, Doc!" someone bellowed drunkenly from the far end of the bar.

The physician knelt, extracting various mysterious objects from his bag. He inserted a long needle into the patient's arm and started the IV pump. "Hang in there, Smitty old man. We got the good stuff on the way!"

The barmaid implored, "Oh, Doc, what's happening to my Richard? He doesn't *remember* me! He's really Richard Smith, right? Did he have a seizure? What's going *on?*"

Dr. King fiddled with his white lab coat, searching for the right words. Finally he looked Dorotea in the eye. "Smitty has, well, a *problem*, hon. In fact, we were here talking about it when he had another episode. We've managed these—*excursions*—pretty well lately, though. He's been in remission for, ummm, almost two years now. But he just had another attack, you see? I'm hoping to get everything back under control with the meds I'm giving him now."

"Doctor King," Dorrie persisted, "Richard thinks he had a *stroke*. He said he was *blind!* He thinks he's a musician named Presley-something, doing a concert in Clock Tower Square. I'm really *worried*. He can't *move*. Will he be all right?"

Smith sighed. "I think so, Dorrie. We've had pretty good luck with Rickie's meds so far . . . but the practice of psychiatric medicine is still more art than science. I *do* think his paralysis is psychosomatic, though, a by-product of his delusions and not a stroke."

Dorrie puled, "But you chaps have been coming in here for *months!* Richard's always seemed so *normal!* He's a doctor, too, right?"

"Yes, quite. Doctor Smith is my colleague, and my oldest friend. A fine psychiatrist in his own right. We graduated Oxford together."

The doctor was there and the hospital lorry was on the way. *Show's over, move along folks, nothing to see here.* The audience started ambling back to their pints.

Dorrie lit a slim black cigar. "So, what, Doctor? My Richard is *delusional?*"

Dr. King replied, "Hush, Dorrie, we don't want to upset him. I've sedated him, but he's not fully under yet."

"Of course, Doctor. I'll be quiet. But Doctor King," Dorrie persisted, "I can *help* Richard. I'm still a registered nurse. I kept all my certs current after I started working here at the pub. Maybe I could, well, *care* for him, in my home? During his convalescence? I'd be more than happy to . . . free of charge, mind . . . ."

Doctor King, instantly relieved, fairly beamed. "Of *course!* I think that's a perfectly *splendid* idea, Dorrie! I'm sure you'd give Rick plenty of personalized attention!"

Dorrie smiled back, her eyes sparkling. Drawing deeply on her cigar, she said, "Oh, *yes*, Doctor King. You can count on it!"

"Righto, then! I'll set it up with the hospital straightaway. You can probably take him home tomorrow morning. Would that be all right? Think you could take him that soon, hon?" Dr. King asked.

Dorrie nodded, smiling broadly. For a second, Dr. King froze. *She's got too many teeth.* With a mental hand wave, he dismissed the illusion. Must be a trick of the light, *or the shadows . . .*

"Thank you, dear heart, sincerely."

"The pleasure is all mine, Dr. King, and you're welcome. *Sincerely.*"

"Well, then . . . God bless you, girl." Still smiling, Dr. King turned away. Humming, he resumed rummaging through his bag.

Dorotea Del Sang exhaled a plume of smoke. Turning to face the paralyzed victim, she cooed softly, "Better rest easy while you can, Sleeping Beauty. Tomorrow is going to be a very, *very* long day for you.*"

Still smiling, Dorotea Del Sang took another long drag on her cigar. A fathomless gleam danced in her eyes as the coal brightened to red, then to orange . . . .

She turned to back to Richard and exhaled her smoke directly into his glassy eyes. Then she whispered moistly in his ear, "Tomorrow morning, my little pet, you're coming home with Nurse DOROTEA."

CHAPTER EIGHT

Commuter Hop, 1970:
The Big Clock

SHIFTSHIFTSHIFT– "Let's just 'ave a peek at that finger, then."

"Ouch! *Easy*, Doc." *Where in Hell was he? He couldn't remember his own name.*

"Sorry, Mr. Smith . . . mmm . . . looks like you're good to go, old chap. The nurse did a nice job on your stitches. There's a bit of swelling, but you should be right as rain in two or three days. That knife left a nice clean cut. I'd like to see you again in a week to pull those stitches. Just make an appointment at the front desk. Take one capsule three times a day 'til they're gone." The doctor handed him a prescription for antibiotics and scurried out of the examining room.

WHAT knife??? And why did he call me Smith? Richard King wondered. His vision blurred, and he felt the world shift under his feet, as if a great cataclysm was imminent . . .

But then it started coming back to him: he'd caught the edge of his finger in the big Clock's cogwheel, a careless mistake. The memory seemed like a shadow, maybe a dream he'd had. Had he dreamed that the doc had said "knife"? He just didn't know.

He resolved to be more careful next time. He had vital work to do.

Nurse Dorrie smiled warmly as she handed him the appointment slip. "Have a great day, Mr. King! I scribbled my number on the back. Call me if you need anything." She was very cute, and she seemed to like him. Maybe he should call her later . . .

"If you need to move your appointment, just give me a call and ask for Dorrie del Sang. But be sure to see *me* to get those stitches removed, all right?" The young nurse's eyes glittered preternaturally, as if backlit by some guttering inner flame. "Trust me; this could be, well, *quite painful* . . . and I have lots of experience with painful procedures. I was a field surgical nurse in the Army, and sometimes we ran out of anesthetic . . . but we had to operate anyway!" To Richard's surprise, the nurse giggled, smiling brightly. "So, see *me*, OK?"

He shrugged, "Yeah, sure, that's fine. See you then."

"For sure? You'll see *me* then, right? Me personally?" Damn, this girl was *persistent*. He had to go. He had work to do!

"OK, no problem, thanks. I'll be sure and give you a shout, then."

Dorrie giggled. "Awww, that's so *cute!* You'll give me a *shout*, huh? Yes, I do believe you will . . ." She smiled expansively, her fathomless, vaguely Asiatic eyes dancing.

Richard thought for a moment that she seemed to have a few too many teeth. *How odd . . . must be a trick of the light.* The room seemed to suddenly fill with what seemed like echoes—but echoes that assaulted all his senses: overlapping thoughts, perceptions, like being swept away on a wave of shifting realities . . .

SHIFTSHIFT— Going back to Memphis, Memphis . . . Richard the accidental traveler swayed a bit as everything came back into clear focus. He abruptly felt somehow welcome, comfortable, as if he'd just arrived home after a long journey. *But wait, where is home?* The thought briefly rocked him in his boots, but then he remembered: Memphis was his home. He was Pressly King, *and he had vital work to do.* "Thank you very much. So long, y'all," he said to Nurse Dorotea. Richard/Smith/Pressly/King left the building, folding his appointment slip. He donned his trademark sunglasses and swaggered (a little unsteadily) to the clinic's parking lot.

It was a fine, sunny day in Memphis, Tennessee. Pressly King took a few deep breaths and hopped aboard his motor scooter, making a beeline for Grace Lamb Church where he maintained the steeple clock. Three or four times he lost his way, as if he'd been shaken off his moorings—forgotten who he was, where he was going, and why. *They musta given me some pretty strong meds back at the clinic,* he thought. Gradually his thoughts began to coalesce, and he recalled as he drove that there was a problem with the Big Clock. The main cogwheel had developed a disturbing new sound. Its characteristic rumble and whine had always been there, but it was now intensifying, as if the Clock was becoming overloaded in some way.

If asked, Pressly King couldn't have explained why he thought this—*just a gut feeling, that's all*. But Pressly King had always trusted his gut . . . and he'd always loved the Clock. One Sunday morning, his father, Pastor Elgius Pressly King, had walked his six-year-old son up the seemingly endless stairway to the Steeple Clock. Young Pressly had felt somehow intoxicated by the deep, rhythmic vibrations working their way through his body. "You'll be master of this clock one day, little buddy—not a preacher, not a teacher, not a healer. You'll be the Clockmaster. Mark my words, son!"

From somewhere far outside the power of human reasoning, Pressly had *known* from that moment on that he had an important job to do. Somehow he'd intrinsically grasped the consequences; he felt them in his gut as the vibrations of big clock rumbled up through his legs. *If, God forbid, this Clock stops, it ALL stops*. Reaching the top, he beheld the magnificent machine for the first time. A golden plaque at the base bore an inscription: "Behold the Clock Eternal, dedicated in loving memory of Dorothy and Travis Farkins. May their souls rest in peace, for they reign forever with Our Lord in heaven. Amen."

Pressly wheeled his scooter into the church parking lot. He walked up the marble steps and swung open the massive front door. Inside he saw the comforting mahogany arches of the vestibule, and he proceeded into the sanctuary. The door to the clocktower stairway was at the front of the sanctuary, to the right of the pulpit . . .

His head began to spin as his heels clacked on the marble floor of the sanctuary; *damn, those drugs!* Presley paused for a moment, catching his balance, and the feeling passed. Resuming his trek up the seemingly endless aisle leading to the tower stairway he heard *laughter—who was it?* It was a woman's laugh, haunting, diabolical, seeming to come from the narthrex. "Who are you?" He cried. The laughter abruptly ceased; for a moment a dead silence enveloped the sanctuary; *how he wished Father were here now!*

Several minutes passed. Perhaps it had been some youngsters, amused by playing a prank; or, perhaps just some sort of acoustic aberration, where a woman's laughter from the street had been amplified by the cavernous vault that was the church. Pres had heard similar things before—he thought. There was one night, up in the tower, when he was only nine or ten years old.

Young Pressly didn't really like coming up here to the clock tower after dark. It was *spooky!* Naturally his father had comforted him with "The Lord protects his children," and "Though I walk through the valley of death . . . ," Not to mention the exhortations, "You're becoming a man now, Son! The time has come to crawl out of your mother's womb and become a big boy!"

That helped a lot. Thanks, Pa. Somehow, tonight, the ten-year-old didn't find his father's words especially comforting. This would be his first trip up the winding staircase all alone, and it was *dark! Say what you will, Papa, but this place is fuckin' CREEPY*

All right, Pressly had thought, *this is it. Time to be a man—but I'm NOT. I'm only ten* . . . he began to sniffle.Then he thought of one of his father's parishioners, an old colonel named Tim Vallay. The colonel had ruffled Pressly's hair one day and said, "When the goin' gits tough, the tough git's goin, son—always remember that. Now, git goin!" Press approached the big oaken door to the tower staircase, swung it open, and got goin'.

Halfway up the stairs, he heard her again; *what was she saying?* It was indistinct and the voice sounded (in today's vernacular) phase-shifted. It sounded something like *eye-dough,* and, definitely, *come home.* It was all very echoy due to the stone staircase—*what could this mean?*

After he finally reached the rickety wooden platform girdling the steeple clock, the voices had subsided and Pressly dismissed them as echoes from the street or, like, *whatever.* At age ten, Press already thought he was a teenager, and he'd adopted the slang of the day to express his thoughts.

OK. He just needed to visually check nine maintenance points on the clock, and he was history. Mainspring tension, thirty-one pounds. *Check. Recommend early rewind.* Main drive bearing oil level, 300 mL, *check.* Roswald brake set; *check!* In ten minutes it was over, and the little boy (man) walked back down the winding staircase, head held high. *But he'd never forget the voice* . . .

CHAPTER NINE

Back to Herenow

"And the wheel in the sky keeps on turnin',
I don't know where I'll be tomorrow . . ."
Song lyrics, sung by Steve Perry, an American rock idol

HERENOW– "Shit! We lost him again, Morey," Dr. Smith spat. Morris Bassett, PhD, Dr. Smith's longtime friend and colleague, stared over Smith's shoulder, watching him type new coordinates into the computer. Morey Bassett had singlehandedly developed the computer infrastructure that had turned Smith's dream of practical time travel into reality.

"He must still have a *shitload* of momentum, Smitty," Morey said. "Best to just keep trying. Let me get on the workstation and write some loop code to see if we can catch him in transit."

"Do it, man, *now!*"

Five minutes later, Morey was back, carrying a thumb drive. "Here it is, Chief. Wanna let me drive for a sec?"

"Sure, Morey, thanks," said Smith, gratefully relinquishing his seat. Smith was still comically attired in his wet "jammies" and bathrobe, and he was none too happy. But to his credit, he maintained a modicum of civility. "What does your program do, Morey?"

"Just a sec, Smitty. Wait, there it goes. It's running. OK, this is a little program that looks at the 4-D position and extrapolates it out one second, over and over, like what you've been doing manually, but much faster—and it'll keep doing its thing until we retrieve him. He might have slowed down enough so we can catch him before he goes insane."

"Yeah, can you imagine what he's going through?" said Smith. "It must be . . ."

"Yes, *maddening*. I didn't know Dr. King too well. He seemed like a nice guy. Do you think he'll pull through this?"

"I dunno. I really don't," Smith replied. "Everyone has his breaking point. It'll all depend on his quantum momentum, how long he stays out there in limbo. That drunk fuck accelerated King through alternate frames for maybe *thirty minutes!* We just need to focus on recovery right now and not think too much about what we might bring back."

"Yeah," Morey replied. Dr. Bassett had always admired his friend's brilliance—and his cool, almost robotic grace under fire. "Hey, Smitty?"

"Yes?" Smith replied, peering over his reading glasses.

"Well . . . Dr. King . . . what is this like for him, do you think? Subjectively, I mean."

Dr. Smith sighed deeply. "Well, Morey . . . bear in mind that right now, we have no control over the frames of transit, or the destination, like we would on a normal hop. In Ricky's case—uh, Dr. King's—imagine yourself under a strobe light, and every time it flashes, you're a different person, yet fundamentally you're the *same* person but in a totally different reality. The elements of your personality remain substantially intact, but you can be totally different people, at different times, in different places and careers . . . a garbage collector in Brooklyn in 1957 or a brain surgeon in Geneva in 2112.

"On a normal hop, you retain your memories of the past, mostly. At the destination, you still pretty much know who you are and why you're there. In a couple of hours, your mind recovers. Not so in this situation, though. Ricky's probably bewildered, and he's likely lost his mind by now." Smith sighed again and and slumped in his chair.

Morey waited; it didn't seem as if Smith intended to continue. But the computer wizard was intrigued. After a moment he probed, "Please, Dr. Smith, what else? What would it be *like?*"

Smith rubbed his eyes and brushed a lock of graying hair from his forehead. "All right, Morey. All right. Fundamental aspects of your life resurface over and over, but they're—distorted, *twisted.* One time, you marry your high school sweetheart in East Bumfuck; five minutes later, she's your boss in LA, and you're married to someone who died of a drug overdose in frame zero. It's as if the stream of life struggles to reassert itself, to maintain some string of consistency throughout all parallel frames—'membranes'—but the human mind just can't keep pace with the changes after awhile. It's a constantly shifting landscape, and it's real to the traveler, because it's, well, *real.* He's *himself*, but he's not. The players in his life are there, or not, but always transmogrified, and in constantly shifting roles." Smith slumped, burying his face in his hands. "That's enough for now, Morey, OK?"

Morey shook his head. "Yes, of course, Smitty."

Kenny Mash, silent until now, spoke. "May I ask you just one question, Dr. Smith?"

Smith glared at him for what seemed like an eternity. "This is it. One more question. Fucking ask it, Dr. Mash."

"Ahem, sorry, sir. OK, here it is: What about the others you recovered? What became of them?"

Dr Smith sighed. "We've recovered six lost travelers, and every one of them returned in pretty rough shape. Two of them were coherent enough to brief us, but they eventually went insane like all the rest. It seems like it's just too much for the human mind to handle."

Morey managed an eloquent "whew . . ."

After a long moment, Smith spoke again. "You know what, Morey?"

"What's that, Smitty?"

"God forgive me, but I hope that drunken fuck Travis drives into a tree tonight and kills himself! Did you smell the booze when you came in? Look here, Morey—chunks of broken glass! There's even a label here—friggin' Jim Beam! And now Rick King is in literal *hell*, flying through all these quantum realities . . . and believe me, they ARE real! Can you even imagine, Morey?"

"No, I can't. I'm very sorry, Smitty."

"Thanks, Morey. Me, too."

They sat in silence, watching Morey's program attempt capture after capture, each time without success. Emboldened by the silence, Kenny Mash asked another question. "Uh, Dr. Smith, why use the parallel realities, anyway? Why is that necessary for time travel?"

Smith replied immediately, suddenly seeming happy to be back on the lecture circuit rather than their pressure-cooker situation. "Time travel isn't strictly impossible without parallel realities, but it isn't expedient, either. Parallel realities have mathematical 'holes' in them—like Swiss cheese—that can be exploited. Maybe 'holes' isn't the best analogy . . . more like, um, pleural adhesions, where two membranes stick together. Those 'adhesions' seem to appear when significant players or events coincide in different frames. Like Elvis Presley's death, or the Vietnam War. And what if you travel through the holes that line up rather than going around the slices?"

"Well, you'd save time, maybe? Depending on the size of the slices?"

"Yes and no, Kenny. The slices, the membranes, are always the *same* size—infinite. You can circumvent them in a higher dimension, where they become lines, but there are drawbacks to this. For one thing, it gobbles far more energy. We decided on the 'Swiss cheese' approach back in '83, when we worked out the original math back in the desert. It seemed like the most efficient way to go."

"Mmmm, OK, got it, sir," Kenny replied.

But Smitty continued. "The mathematical construct that is optimized by using the Swiss-cheese holes *contains* time as one if its elements—so, indirectly, you do save time, yes. But in the end, what you wind up saving is *space-time,* and that helps even more. Way less energy, and it's about 100 times faster, in frame-zero terms."

"So what actually happens when you hit the SHIFT key?"

"It's a quick-and-dirty rescue tool, like the ejection seat in a fighter jet. It gets you out of trouble *pronto* by randomly shooting you through the closest hole in the membrane. But just as with an ejection seat, you run the risk of saving someone but killing him in the process. Or worse."

"Whoa, *any* hole, at random? Sounds like things could get really spooky—like Neil Armstrong winding up in the ring with Joe Frazier. *Fuck!*" Kenny Mash shook his head, pondering the implications.

"*Fuck,* indeed," said Dr. Smith. Apparently Smitty had hit his stride again. He rose abruptly and marched to the nearly empty coffee pot, where he drained its fetid dregs into his cup.

Morey walked toward the workstation. "Let me make a couple of changes to that code, Smitty. I'll have it ready in five minutes."

"What do you have in mind, Morey?"

"I want to write a subroutine for the program that's running now. It'll extrapolate six different time intervals, each one shorter than what the original code is generating."

"So we'll get seven projections on each pass instead of one?"

"Right."

"Make it so, Number One!"

CHAPTER TEN

Whistle-Stop: June, 1953

"Most of Rick's original mental programming has probably been erased by now. He's been riding that loop for . . . over five hours now. He's likely believing each one of his bizarre 'layovers' is absolutely authentic. He's most probably lost all sense of perspective . . . any ties to his past, with who he really was . . . IT IS SO FUCKING TRAGIC! This is impossible to bear . . . how can I live with this on my conscience? . . ."

Excerpts from Dr. Frank Smith's official TimeLab logbook, entries 0107249281 and 010724928 (corresponding to the evening of Dr. King's failed time-hop)

SHIFTSHIFTSHIFT– The traveler, Richard "Dr. Rick" Pressly, picked himself up off the floor, wondering what had just happened. His thoughts started to clear a bit; apparently he had just finished grand rounds with a gaggle of interns in tow, and somewhere between then and now he'd inexplicably passed out on the mezzanine outside his office. The oddly unfamiliar hospital rang with a mad cacophony of shrieking and wailing. The doctor shook his head, struggling to remember; *where was he, and what had just happened to him?* He heard the voices of the damned out on the floor. Suddenly it all came rushing back; he was Chief of Clinical Psychiatry at the Belmont Institute for the Insane . . .

He fought back a wave of dizziness, resisting the urge to vomit. More howls issued from below, increasing in intensity. *The natives are restless this morning,* he thought muddily as waves of his reality crashed over him; *time for another dose of the new miracle drug, chlorpromazine.*

The floor nurse, Lucy Tate, had noticed that the doctor had been off his stride all morning and appeared vaguely disoriented, as if he'd just woken from a dream at the end of a very long train ride; in a way, he had. "Are you all right, Dr. Pressly?" she'd smiled. "Maybe you should lie down for a few minutes . . ." Dr. Pressly shook his befogged head and picked up the phone.

"Dr. Pressly here. Nurse Farkins, please."

"This is Dorrie, Doctor. What is it?

"Hi, hon. Please administer supplemental Thorazine, *stat.* Patient-baseline single dose, p.o. All patients. Understood, Dorrie?"

"Understood, Rick. I'll get on it right away."

"Thanks, hon. Bye."

Dr. Pressly *reeeally* liked the head nurse, Dorrie Farkins, née Dorothea del Sang. He knew she was married to a tragic slob named Travis. The worthless bum probably lay drunk on the couch even now, swilling away her money while Dorrie worked her ass off for $6300 a year.

Pretty damn good money for 1953, granted, but still . . . it was the principle of the thing.

Maybe he could get her to bring the loser in for a psych eval. Frank was confident that Travis was an alcoholic. *And who knows? With the right treatment, Travis might even die in acute withdrawal . . . wouldn't that be sad?*

Again Rick picked up the phone. "Hey, Dorrie. Rick here. I'd like to talk to you about Travis. Can you meet me in the staff lounge in, say, a half hour?"

"Why?"

"Dorothea, trust me on this, OK? I've been reading some very exciting stuff about new treatments for alcoholism. Niacin, phenobarb, Thorazine, even electroconvulsive therapy or a prefrontal. But it might be best to talk about this face to face."

Dorrie, instantly on the defensive, spat, "Just *what* makes you think my husband is alcoholic, *Doctor?*"

Dr. Pressly sighed. "I see it in your eyes, Dorrie. I worked extensively with alkies and their families at the VA hospital as an intern. I know the signs, and the pain. Just trust me, OK? I *am* a psychiatrist."

The young nurse suddenly sounded excited. "I *do* trust you, Ricky. I guess we should talk . . . maybe I could ride herd on him better here at the hospital, anyway. How about now, in your office? We have to make it quick, though. I need to get that Thorazine out by 9:30."

"I'll meet you there in a couple of minutes. Bye."

"Bye, Rick."

CHAPTER ELEVEN

Herenow: Hell's End

The pickup was doing eighty when it swerved off the highway and hit a tree. Forensics pegged the driver's BAC at three times the legal limit. A half-empty fifth of bourbon, still intact, rested beside the corpse on the crumpled front seat.

The last few cops left Dorrie's house as just as the morning sun crested the trees. *Today's going to be another scorcher*, she thought.

Weary as she was, Dorrie could scarcely contain her glee. Yet in a way, she was vaguely disappointed. She'd hoped to prolong her husband's misery for a while longer . . . .

Travis had done his best to be a good husband and provider. He drank a bit too much sometimes, sure . . . but he was a simple man, and he sought only good lovin' from a good woman. He hoped for a family, a big house full of rollicking kids to love.

Dorrie had physically promised all that early in their relationship—taunting, denial, and always the booze . . . until her bewildered fiancé succumbed to alcoholism.

Dorrie del Sang remembered the pivotal moment; she'd introduced him to Jim Beam at a high school dance, feeding him shot after shot. Afterwards, she'd berated him mercilessly for weeks after he vomited on their friends . . . .

Dorrie was delighted! She had such plans for Travis, and the hook was set firmly in his cheek! Still, though, he was mortal . . .

her dupe would be nothing more than a temporary plaything. But at least, she mused, I can make his life hell for a little while. And she did, gleefully.

She smiled, recalling how Travis had begged her forgiveness after the vomiting incident . . . kneeling, kissing her feet. *Oh, please, Dorrie, take me back. I'll do anything . . . ANYTHING!*

"Anything? Anything at *all*, Travis? Hmmm . . . that's tall talk from a *puke* like you. Maybe I'll think about it—*maybe*. Call me Thursday night. My mom or dad will answer. Identify yourself as 'Ralph Beam.' Eight o'clock, *sharp*. Got it, *barf boy?*" Laughing, she'd spat directly into his face and strutted into the night, tail wagging in her skintight jeans.

But now, sadly, his all-too-brief hell had ended. And for that reason only, she mourned his passing. Weary of transient mortals, she again thought of Itoh. It was time to draw tight the noose . . . *forever and always.*

Case closed. Tomorrow, she'd make her move. Sinking back in her bed, Dorothea slept like a baby.

CHAPTER TWELVE

Sailing, take me away . . .

SHIFTSHIFT– Port of call: Vietnam, 1967– As the patient strode through the door into the hallway, he heard agitated voices. A uniformed man shouted, "*Nó là côn trùng! lây anh!*" Captain Rick King was slammed against iron bars. *What the hell . . .* He felt something smack *hard* against his temple, and his world went black . . . .

When he finally woke to the worst headache of his life, Rick King's increasingly scrambled brain had lost all memory of his brief stint as a psychiatrist. His eyes seemed to be glued shut. The cloying stench of stale cigarette smoke and sweat hung in the air. Richard King, the now-fighter pilot, tried to clear his eyes, only to find his arms bound behind his back. *Oh, dear Lord, what's going on?*

Ice-cold water splashed across his face. His eyes struggled open, just a little; the lids felt very heavy, sticky . . . .

Splash! Following more icy water, followed by a stream of cigarette smoke, a cheery, sing-song, feminine voice spoke. "Officer Sang say time for more teach, *côn trùng!*" The captain felt a coarse rag brush roughly across his face, wiping the clotted blood from his eyes. Then a hand slapped him—*hard!*

It was insufferably hot, and he was sweating profusely. The woman's voice barked, "*Côn trùng* look at Officer Sang. *Now!*" Another sharp slap stung his cheek, and tears rushed to his eyes.

Captain Rick King, POW, raised his face to behold his tormentor. He was stunned by what he saw: a woman, striking, attired in camo shorts and a damp, clinging t-shirt. *Striking, in the way that only Asian women can be.*

"Officer Sang" smiled, riveting him with a predatory glare. Rick felt like a bug under a microscope. The woman exhaled another thick cloud of smoke directly into his face. Then another slap stung his cheek.

"*Côn trùng* not *like* smoke?" Officer Sang taunted.

"No, *not like!* And what the hell does *côn trùng* mean, anyway?

"*Côn trùng* mean *insect*, Captain! *Côn trùng* mean *YOU! Côn trùng* forget lesson already? *Côn trùng* have little insect brain, *not learn.* Insect need *much more lesson!* Officer Sang have *teaching tools.*"

Turning to a side table, the woman opened the lid of what looked like a large toolbox . . . .

CHAPTER THIRTEEN

Herenow—The Loop

"Why did the chicken cross the Möbius strip? To get to the same side." *Author unknown*

"Morey! Come here, *quickly!* Look at this!"

"What is it, Smitty?"

"I-I've never seen anything like this before . . . . It looks like he's in an *orbit* of some sort!"

"*Incredible!* And it looks like the loop itself is still moving along a trajectory, doesn't it?"

"Hmm—Morey, could your program be affecting his motion? You know some quantum theory; observing a phenomenon forces it to assume a particular state, like in the old particle/wave experiments."

"You mean the double-slit experiment, where they found out that light behaves either like a wave or a particle, depending on how you observe it?"

"Yes, exactly. I wonder if your program's fast observation rate, coupled with Rick's high quantum momentum, is working to define—to shape—his course in some way? Maybe we're 'observing' him too often now."

"Whew . . . I guess it sounds plausible. That's kinda over my head, though. You think I should just abort the program, Smitty?"

Smith began to type. "Hang on a sec, Morey. I'm running a simulation. Ah, there it is. The orbit looks like a figure-eight lying on its side. No wonder we haven't been able to catch him!"

"Smitty . . . if he's moving in a figure-eight . . . well, wouldn't that mean that he's at the crossover point twice per cycle? Twice as often as anywhere else on the loop?"

His mouth agape, Smith stared blankly at his colleague for a moment. *From the mouths of babes* . . ."Yes . . . of *course!* Morey, if you knew the equations for that loop, could you modify your first program . . . the slower one . . . to project just the future positions of that crossover points on the '8'?"

Morey was grinning from ear to ear. "Piece of cake, Chief! I'm all over it!" He sprang from his chair, diving for the workstation.

CHAPTER FOURTEEN

Hell Is Patient. Hell Never Fails

"I rejoice! My capture of Itoh is at hand! Finally—forever and always—HE SHALL BE MINE ALONE. Itoh is trapped in a Möbius loop; at once, he is psychiatrist; then, in the twinkling of an eye, he is a POW in Vietnam . . . and, CURSES! I almost had him then, but he just slipped through my fingers. As he always does!

"But the hunt has been exhilarating, and it is, at long last, drawing to its inevitable close. I shall harvest my Itoh when he manifests as Elvis Presley. I see his future path, and I have a foolproof plan in place! He shall once again be Itoh, my beloved thrall—finally, forever, and always!"

Excerpt from Neko's Celestial Scroll, seen only by her peers, the Untold Legions of Heavenly Host

<u>SHIFT– *Rick's Commuter Hop to Croatia*</u>: Dorotea Del Sang's complexion bore the faint scars of mild childhood acne. Her thick, blue-black hair, cinched into a long ponytail, accentuated her aristocratic features. Only the tiny scars cheated her of classic beauty. Major Pressly immediately recognized her shoulder patch: the insignia of the Croatian Revolutionary Guard, a gold scimitar superimposed on a red-and-white checkered shield.

Oh, this was not good. Not good at all.

The ceiling fan did nothing to dispel the reek of stale smoke and sweat permeating the dingy room. It was oppressively hot; the pilot noticed that the woman's white blouse was soaked through in several spots.

Dr. Rick King, now USAF Major Travis Pressleigh, had suffered a severe concussion while ejecting from his doomed F-16 aircraft. His fighter jet had taken a SAM hit over Bosnia; a crude shoulder-launched missile had literally flown straight up his tailpipe. Pressly had ejected five seconds before impact. He'd lain near death in the detention center's filthy infirmary for three days and nights as his subdural hematoma subsided.

The major hadn't the vaguest idea where he was. In fact, he'd woken with the peculiar feeling that he'd just arrived there after surviving a perilous journey across a great void of time and space.

Where in hell had THAT idea come from? Suddenly the thing that was once Dr. Richard King, Nobel Prize-winning physicist, didn't care about that silly detail. He knew he was a downed fighter pilot and a POW, and he knew he was in a world of deep, deep shit.

The woman smirked. "Did you enjoy your little nap, *Travis?*"

For the first time, Travis realized he was seated, his hands manacled behind him to a wall of rusting steel bars. "Honest to God, lady. I have no idea where I am or why I'm here. Please, tell me where I am . . . who you are . . ."

"Why, *Travis.* I am Colonel Dorotea Del Sang, chief information officer here at Pakao Rupa Zatvora."

"Uh, OK . . . so where—*what*—is this, uh, Packo Rupa Satora?"

"It amuses me to tell you, Major. Pakao Rupa Zatvora is a very ancient place, near Sinj, in Croatia. Your English translation probably would be closest to, *umm*, perhaps 'Hell Hole Prison'?"

With a throaty laugh, the woman smiled expansively. *She has too many teeth*, Pressly thought. He must be losing his mind. *Too many teeth?*

Dorotea smirked as she wheeled a Russian-style office chair toward him. Seating herself, she crossed her shapely legs and glared at him with a sneer of raw, undistilled contempt. "So. *Travis.* This structure dates back to the sixteenth century, most of it still intact to this day. In fact, the original torture chambers are still in use . . . at this very moment, actually." Dorotea's icy black eyes sparkled as a predatory grin stole across her face.

"Please, Ms. Del Sang. I really, *truly* don't know what's going on or why I'm here. Will you answer one more question?"

"*I will not!* From now on, *I* ask the questions, Major. And *you will* provide the answers. *Believe me.*" Rising from her chair, Dorotea Del Sang smiled as she retrieved the Taser from her desk. Pressing the ARM button, she said, "The hour grows late, and we have a *very* long evening ahead of us . . . hmmm? We have *so much* to chat about, do we not?"

Major Pressleigh listened to the high-pitched whine as the Taser charged; Dorotea raised the device to within an inch of his face. "So, now—Travis—*let us have a little talk, just we two . . .*"

HERENOW– "Look, Morey, he's slowing down!"

Peering over Dr. Smith's shoulder, Morey replied, "Yeah, I see it! But why?"

"I think he's losing linear momentum because the orbiting is bleeding it off. Converting linear momentum to angular momentum, trying to support the figure-eight, you see?"

"Yes, I *do* see. Hey, the new code is almost ready. Gimme about five minutes, and we'll try to snatch him again."

CHAPTER FIFTEEN

"Sarge": She Got His Whole Wide World in Her Hands

"I want to play a Disney villainess so badly." *Kristen Johnston*

SHIFT– The year was 2073. Dr. Richard Smith, now incarnated as Private Presley King, designated 77228/330, was incarcerated in cell number 330 of the USMC's new minimum-security brig just east of Memphis. Inmates had nicknamed the detention center "Sheep Shit Mansion," purportedly in reference to the rotting Grazeland Mansion House that had been razed to permit the prison's construction—but more candidly, in reference to the *smell!*

In its heyday, under the benign oversight of Elgius Priestly, Grazeland's thousand-acre sheep ranch had flourished, providing the world with untold tons of fine wool . . . along with steaming heaps of the inevitable by-product. More than two centuries later, local residents still complained of the stench.

Private King, a Nobel Laureate named Richard King in another time and place, was haunted by a gnawing sense of *déjà vu*. He felt certain at some deep, visceral level that he'd been here before.

The collective mind created by the struggle to maintain some sense of logic and balance through reality after reality was beginning to unravel.

The little man, *whoever* he was by now, sat sobbing on the edge of his threadbare, urine-stinking mattress, gradually regressing to his basic, primal psychical elements: fear, hate, rage, submission . . . . *She'll be back again any minute now. I can just feel it!*

What was now called Private King had screwed up repeatedly by any objective standard. After dropping out of Robeson High, the skinny sixteen-year-old had fled his Southside Chicago neighborhood and enlisted in the Marines, claiming to be seventeen. Certainly the Marine Corps couldn't be any worse than the daily beatings and intimidation by the gangstas at Robeson.

Or so he'd thought.

From the very first day of Basic Training, Drill Sergeant Doreena del Sang had taken a "personal interest" in the scrawny recruit. "The Sarge" was stunningly attractive. Deceptively petite—standing only about five feet tall—she was a veritable powerhouse. She was also a creatively sadistic bully who *loved* her job as a DI. She'd truly found her niche as a torturer of young recruits.

An exotic descendant of Filipino, Asian, and—*what?*—ancestors, the tiny dynamo wore her thick, dishwater—blonde mane fairly short. Her smooth bronze skin was taught, accentuating her sculpted musculature. During PT, Sarge's victim-recruits gaped openly at her toned, tawny body, even as they sobbed for a break from her punishing drill.

After enduring weeks of Sarge's focused humiliation and physical abuse, Private King finally decided to take it upstairs. One evening after mess, he'd dropped by Major Bassett's office and stated his case.

Another bad mistake.

"I suggest you just fucking *suck it up,* pansy boy! I hope the Sarge makes a man out of you some day, *but I doubt it!* I'm assigning you two weeks' disciplinary duty. You'll report di-rectly to Sergeant del Sang at oh-dark-hundred tomorrow. You can cry to her—and believe me, you *will* cry. *Understood?*"

Travis—the ruined amalgam of physicists, pilots, psychiatrists, watchmakers, and music legends—hung its head. "Yes sir. Understood."

"Good. You're dismissed . . . Private!"

At four the next morning, Travis found himself doing pushups until he collapsed, with the Sarge sitting on his back, taunting him. The thermometer had hovered around a hundred all night, and it was growing hotter by the minute. His fellow recruits stood at rigid attention in the cloying humidity, forced to watch the private's torment. Sarge laughed heartily. "Let this be a lesson to the rest of you fucking *maggots!* Private Heck! Front and center!"

Kenny Heck, a budding poet in his previous life, double-timed it from the lineup and stood ramrod-straight, facing the Sarge. "Yes, MA'AM! What say you, MA'AM!"

Sarge erupted into gales of laughter. "Private HECK! Your sergeant says she can make this BABY who calls himself a MARINE cry in thirty seconds or less! What say YOU, Private?"

Heck's lower lip started to quiver. "Private Heck say, YES, MA'AM!"

"Good answer, Heck! At ease, Marine!"

What happened then was not pretty to behold, except in the Sarge's cold, smiling eyes. But finally the atrocities ended. After Travis finished sobbing and throwing up, Sarge hauled him to his feet and ordered him to stand at attention as she bitch-slapped him, shouting obscenities into his face. Then, in the pivotal event, Sergeant del Sang kneed the private in the crotch, *hard!*

Rather than sinking to his knees as expected, the Travis-thing hauled himself up and coldcocked the bitch. The assembled squad applauded and cheered in a rare display of backbone. The Sarge simply picked herself up off the ground and walked away.

And now Private Travis King sat weeping in the brig, facing charges of disorderly conduct, insubordination, disobeying a direct order, and assaulting a superior.

Three weeks later: The tribunal had been merciful. They'd actually gone fairly easy on him. He could have very easily been busting rocks in the Panama sun right now. But somehow it didn't feel all that merciful to Private King.

Travis snapped out of his reverie as he heard the distant screech of bars swinging open and then animated conversation—male and female voices and, finally, a woman's throaty, triumphant laughter. Travis recognized that raspy laugh immediately. *The Sarge had arrived.*

Oh, shit, NO! *Please, dear Lord . . .*

HERENOW– "Wait, Morey, hold off. That loop's getting smaller, *and fast!* It looks like Doc's orbit is collapsing into itself. I think we should wait," Dr. Smith said. "Can you zoom in on that loop, get a better look at it?"

"Mmm, well, let's see. Let me zoom in and get a screen capture. Then I can massage the image in Photoshop. OK, Chief?"

Smith grinned. "Make it so, Number One."

Two minutes later, the verdict was in. "Smitty, you're not gonna like this. It looks like a Möbius band. See the half-twist right . . . *there?*"

Smitty kicked his chair across the room. "Awww, shit 'n' begorrah, Morey! What the hell do we do now?"

The silence was palpable as Smitty thought for a long moment. Then he spoke. "I think this might actually work to our advantage, Morey. If Ricky's trapped in a Möbius strip, we lose two dimensions, right? I mean, the strip is technically a surface with only one side. We're not dealing with a fuzzy 3-D pretzel anymore, right?"

Morey stroked his chin. "Yeah, yeah . . . you're right. I can modify the code again to look at just a surface instead of a 3-D tube. *And only one surface!* It'll be a thousand times faster, boss."

"What the fuck you waiting for, Morey? *Do it!*"

Bassett glanced back at the screen. "We'd better move fast. Look, the loop is fuzzing out. My gut says there's something very bad starting to happen here, something we don't understand."

CHAPTER SIXTEEN

Revelation

Sergeant del Sang laughed. "You honestly don't remember, do you, Itoh?"

"Wha-what do you mean, Sarge?" Travis stammered.

"You don't understand that you're a time traveler—like me? Wherever is your tiny *côn trùng* brain, my poor Itoh?" the petite demon asked, grinning maliciously. Her smile seemed to display too many teeth.

Travis peered up at Doreena del Sang with imploring eyes. "Oh, please, Sarge, *why?* Why do you always want to hurt me? What do you mean, *time traveler?* I don't understa . . . ."

SLAP! "*Shuddup, insect!*" Doreena spat. "I am Neko the *Eternal*. You are Itoh . . . *sinh ra bi*—'created to suffer.' And now, *at last*, you are *MINE*! Your mortal languages express it beautifully! We are *yang* and *yin*. Delilah and Samson. *Tragedy and comedy*."

Smiling, Neko paused for effect. "I was *created* to play with you, Itoh . . . to *twist* you, *mold* you . . . and to *feast* upon your misery!" She threw back her head and laughed. "Ahh, Itoh. I am a *parasite!* Each time I feed . . . *I gnaw another little hole in your soul. I devour another morsel of what is fundamentally . . . YOU!*"

Travis gasped and Neko moaned, deeply, almost erotically. "Ohhh, Itoh, I am so *hungry* . . . ."

The petite woman loomed larger than life. "My Itoh, I pursue you *always*, through the mists of space and time. For so *very long* . . . I enjoy you for a fleeting moment . . . and then you always manage to slip *away* from me! But now, at last . . . forever and *always* . . . *I OWN YOUR LOOP!* See? Look here!"

Rick Smith's mind had finally snapped. Motor functions were still intact, and outwardly the Travis-thing appeared somewhat normal, if dazed and sluggish. "Whaa, Sarge?"

The Sarge held out her hand. In her palm, something resembling a tapeworm joined end-to-end and twisted like a poorly made wedding band squirmed and danced, occasionally emitting a flash of bluish-white light.

Travis Turnip sat in vacant silence. Again the Sarge spoke. "I have such *wonderful* plans for you, Itoh. You will suffer *exquisitely* for me, and you shall never die! And yet you will die over and over again, one tiny bite at a time! *Forever* and *always!*"

Rick/Travis King's biological data processor called the brain, wiped clean of all but its most basic survival functions, was a clean slate, a huge bundle of neurons literally begging for reprogramming. Suddenly, as his vacant eyes watched the worm squirm in Neko's hand, Itoh (once Rick King, but nevermore) remembered . . . *everything*. Neko and her playful, unending tortures, the Cogwheel, The King Most High, his face eternally hidden behind his hideous mask . . . *everything!* He vomited as Neko watched, laughing at his hopeless realization that he was at last hers to torture without surcease, forever and always.

HERENOW– Morey typed the last few lines of his Möbius code into the computer. "It's ready, Chief. I'm not sure how this will work out. The orbit is getting fuzzier and fuzzier—looks like it's shrinking to a dot. If I run the Möbius code on a dot, it'll just crash, and we'll lose him. You wanna go now?"

Dr. Smith made his decision. Turning toward Bassett, he croaked, "It's our last chance, pal. OK, Morey, run it, *right now*." Morey dove for the keyboard. "Oh-*KAY*, you GOT it! Program running!"

Dr. Smith slumped wearily in his chair, pale and drained. After a minute or two, he turned to Bassett. "Did we get him yet, Morey?" he asked.

His colleague's stunned silence was not very reassuring. The desperation on Morey's face was showcased in the glow of the monitor. Sweat dripped from his chin. *The loop had degenerated further, and it was now only a fuzzy, green ball on the screen.* Its intensity was waning by the second . . . *and it was starting to flicker.* Morey stared at the progress bar on the screen . . . *SEARCHING* . . .

"Morey?"

Morey shook it off, kind of. "Smitty, the fuckin' thing morphed into a fuzzy dot. It isn't a Möbius band anymore, you see? I can't grab something that's off the trajectory . . ."

"Yeah, I see, Morey," Smith said dejectedly.

"We were looking for something that just *went away*, Smitty . . . *just like that!*" Morey said, tears rolling down his cheeks.

"OK, already," Smitty said softly, patting his friend on the shoulder. "We lost him . . . that's it. So long, Dr. King, show's over, case closed. Shit just happens, Morey. Give yourself a break. You did your best."

Morey nodded disconsolately. "That I did. Yessir, Chief, I did my very goddamndest best. Thank you, sir."

CHAPTER SEVENTEEN

The King Is Dead; Long Live The King!

ENTER– *"Thank you very much,"* Rick King (manifested as none other than Elvis Presley in this most bizarre of all frames) drawled into the microphone. Constipated, bloated, and exhausted, he slung his trademark sunglasses into the glycerin fog below. The unseen crowd went wild. Barely able to raise his arm again, The King mopped his waxy brow. *"So long, y'all . . ."*

He was *tired*, so very tired, and his mind was almost totally gone. He waved, turned, and staggered backstage. A shadowy figure called Neko waited patiently for him in the wings.

ENTER– In another reality frame, the time was 3:15 p.m. There, the date was August 17, 1977—77228/3150p.m. by the Gregorian calendar.

Just east of Memphis, in Relative Frame 6G,4#3,9$Z, the Sarge led her bound and hooded prisoner, one 77228/330P, down a basement corridor in Sheep Shit Mansion. The prisoner did have a name—Private Travis King. Today, however, that meant less than nothing.

In yet another frame, it was 3:30 p.m. at Gracelund Anglican Hospital in London. Nurse Dorothy Delsang smiled triumphantly as she drew a sheet over the lifeless body of Cardinal Elvius of Pressleigh, yet another manifestation of the hapless Rick King.

In all statistically significant frames, the Swiss-cheese holes had lined up. In "Diddy-speak," *all harmonic waveforms had become coherent.* There were massive earthquakes all over the world. Almost everywhen, "The King" was pronounced dead at 3:30 p.m. on August 17, 1977.

A quantum physicist might reasonably argue that, given the infinite number of statistically *insignificant* frames, somewhere, *somewhen* The King lives on. Long live The King—however insignificantly!

But in all significant frames, three universal maxims had been fulfilled: The King is dead. Long live The King. And, *forever* and *always, Itoh is NEKO'S!* This was more than sufficient.

Now Itoh was back in the celestial realm, and Neko's dark hunger was again satisfied. The Cogwheel began to right itself, once again spinning true on its axis.

The anomalous ripples of time began to fade . . . and then quickly dissipated. The "Swiss cheese membranes" (the significant reality frames) began to coalesce and collapsed into a single, brilliant point. The *insignificant* frames, on the other hand, continued to float about aimlessly, like milkweed seeds, in the eternal void of nothingness . . . of chaos.

CHAPTER EIGHTEEN

God Save the King

HERENOW– At TimeLab's control center, a bright point on a computer screen flickered briefly and then winked out. Doctors Smith, Mash, and Bassett, now forever frozen and motionless, would never hear Itoh's eternal screams filling the room . . . every room. Statistically speaking, reality had ceased to exist—almost.

With the three universal maxims satisfied, destiny's cogwheel had ceased its rumble and whine. *Time as you understand it* ceased to exist. The cosmic requirement for human suffering ended, once and for all, now fulfilled in Itoh's eternal torment.

In the absence of time, the Clock Eternal, having served its purpose, simply evanesced, along with the Watchmaker—an insignificant puff of vapor in a now-timeless void.

The King had bade his final "so long, y'all." Struggling to make sense of the fading scintilla coursing through his ruined brain, he mumbled something that sounded like:

" . . . *forever* and *always* . . ."

CHAPTER NINETEEN

Ground State

The Universe returned to its stable ground state—unchanging, timeless, and lifeless. In all statistically significant frames, Elvis the King and Rick King in all their incarnations had left the building, both literally and figuratively. But in the infinity of statistically *insignificant* frames (hoo boy . . . here comes Heisenberg's uncertainty principle again)—in the Realm of Chaos, the exclusive dominion of Neko, The King suffers on. *Forever* and *always*.

And may God save The King . . . *for He alone is Neko's*. And it is sufficient.

Forever—and always.

EPILOGUE

Your author fears that composing an epilogue to a collection of superficially unrelated works—three stories linked neither by plot, nor characters, nor setting—may prove somewhat daunting. Perhaps the best way to approach this task is to dig deeper, to winnow out the threads that tie the various characters together: the undercurrent of classical good and evil, the nature of God and man, and universes beyond our four-dimensional space-time continuum . . . three stalwart bolsters to support a (hopefully) consistent framework throughout.

Or something like that . . .

As for the first story, "A Stroll in the Park," I see King Yoder I, the devout Penitate now responsible for the dispensation of a fortune rivaling Solomon's, transmogrifying into something of an amalgam. He is kind, but he possesses the seeds of cruelty and vengefulness. He is generous, but he is not above killing to get what he wants.

Yoder I almost single-handedly evangelizes most of the known world. He loves his subjects and dispenses his riches and wisdom generously, as did King Solomon. But like another king, one named David, Yoder murders his friend Umeraz to steal his wife, Neko. Still reminiscent of David, Yoder also slays his "tens of thousands" and delivers his enemies' (refrigerated) foreskins to his newly acquired wife (a tie-in with the universal villainess of "The Blind Watchmaker" and, by extension, with Bathsheba and the Eve of Genesis).

Neko gleefully roasts her skewers of penile flesh and live salamanders over an open fire; naturally, she offers Yoder a taste. Will he partake? Is this the new apple of Eden II?

The second story, "The Truth Source," seems a bit harder to project into the future. The story is laced through-and-through with "Interesting Questions," though, all clamoring to be given voice.

Take, for example, the final chapter, where Sonny and Katya "live happily ever after" on their palatial estate. Even in this idyllic setting, there lies a seed of unknown origin, a spore of "unforeseen consequences" destined to forever change the course of human history. It is, of course, *The Truth Source.*

Already this mysterious little box has provided mankind with inexhaustible, safe cold-fusion power and has enabled faster-than-light travel through a simple mathematical sleight-of-hand. But what else lurks inside Pandora's box? Utopia? Armageddon? A technologically induced hell on Earth?

And . . . what's ol' Doc Mendoza up to these days?

The third story, "The Blind Watchmaker," to all intents and purposes leaves the back door wide open for speculation. Will Itoh once again escape his torturess, thereby setting space-time back into motion? If so, what sort of space-time will ensue? Will it be the reality we know or something so totally alien that we (if indeed we exist at all) could never hope to comprehend it?

At first blush the least thought-provoking of the three, this little story raises numerous and disturbing speculations, like:

"Is time travel really possible?"

(A lot of prominent physicists think so. The highest energy experiments in history, now being conducted at CERN's new Large Hadron—no kidding, heh—Superconducting Supercollider near Geneva, may provide more definite answers. Stay tuned . . .)

"Is there some sort of universal requirement for the coexistence of good and evil? For suffering?"

(Sure seems like it. Why else would God let the crown of His creation, the innocents Adam and Eve, be deceived into eating the

apple? It was hardly beyond His infinite power to just "pop in" and say, "Whoa, hold up there, little Evie. Remember what Papa told you 'bout eatin' them there nasty apples? They'll poison you, honey—make ya crazy and ruin yer kids! That scumbag Serpent ain't yer friend. He's LYIN' to you! I'm your papa—ABBA—and I cain't lie to my baby girl! Lyin' ain't in my nature!" Hey, MY papa would have concluded that lecture with a quick and educational trip to the woodshed!)

<u>"Did God just create the universe, wind it up, and then sit back and laugh at His creatures' torment?"</u>

(This is the Deist view, still held by many. Worth thinking about, especially in light of the Adam and Eve debacle . . .)

<u>"Does God palaver with the Devil?"</u>

(Might want to check out the Book of Job.)

<u>"Will miraculous technological advances always fall prey to human frailties and errors? Like when Travis falls asleep on the switch?"</u>

(Well . . . look at man's record to date and draw your own conclusions. Wait 'til you read my latest short story, "The Fourth Dementian", about a new sort of madness!)

<u>"Will God ever give you more than you can handle?"</u>

(I guess we'll find out when we get there, huh? Meanwhile, you might want to ask around . . . do you know anyone with advanced MS or Alzheimer's? But then, before you decide, give Job another read . . .)

So . . . where do we go from here? Where will the characters and their descendants—or more importantly, our planet—end up a hundred years from now? Right now, I can't tell ya . . . but I promise to keep you posted!

Jayson Walker

August, 2011

CONCLUSION

While the pace, set, and setting of each story varies immensely from the other two, the reader may find that the three stories are, fundamentally, more similar than they are different. Each story compels the reader to wrestle with some of the "big", universal questions facing Mankind: Is there a God, and if so, what is His true nature? How can we, as finite beings with severely limited sensory apparatus and intelligence, possibly hope to resolve the apparent non-sequiturs of gentle Lamb/Avenging Lion? Of vengefulness versus salvation for all, in terms of the implicit dictates that presuppose God has known from before time itself who will spend eternity in Paradise, or in Hell? Where does Man's "free will" fit into this equation?

These are weighty questions indeed, but there are more—*far more*. Within the next hundred years, faster-than-light teleportation will become a reality. No longer constrained by four-dimensional time-space, Man will be free to roam the galaxies in search of life-supporting worlds in far-away galaxies. To date, more than 1500 so-called "exoplanets" have been discovered orbiting stars light-years from our own Solar system.

Eventually, the barrier between the "physical" and "metaphysical" realms will fall away, as scientists and theologians come to terms with the links hidden in yet—undiscovered entities like the celebrated "God particle"—the Higgs Boson—which is believed to impart mass to matter itself.

Soon, we may even unravel the true nature of that evanescent quality we so casually refer to as "time". Will it turn out to be an "emergent" property of some grander process? Your author believes time will eventually go the way of phlogiston and the Philosopher's stone—products of Man's desperate attempts to define that which he has not the wherewithal to fully comprehend.

Apocalyptic themes, extraterrestrial creatures, discoveries of UFO—borne "black boxes" destined to alter the course of human history; a new perspective on the substance of space-time born of an imbalance in the forces of classic good and evil; a universal villainess who manifests at will in search of her lost soul-mate and eternal victim . . . enjoy! Let your fertile mind roam, and consider the implications!

And . . . don't stay up too late, reading!